DIRTY SEXY
GAMES

Cover:
Laurelin Paige

Editing:
Erica Edits and Nancy at Evident Ink

Proofing:
Michele Ficht

Interior Design & Formatting:
Christine Borgford, Type A Formatting

DIRTY SEXY
GAMES

LAURELIN PAIGE

Chapter One

Elizabeth

"YOU'RE MARRIED!" EXCLAIMED my grandmother—Nana—embracing me, as I walked into the hotel foyer. She was happy and joyful, as was her daughter Becky, who was waiting behind her to hug me.

I was blinking rapidly, trying to stop the frustrated tears from rolling down my cheeks. I could probably pass off a few as sentimental, but the wave threatening was bigger than that. My family would certainly recognize it as more if it broke.

I had to swallow it back, had to rein it in somehow.

I focused on the sound of Nana's voice and the smell of her, warm and comforting and familiar, and tried to forget about the confusion and the war between me and my new husband.

It wasn't so easy when it was my mother in front of me. She could see right through the mask.

"What's wrong?" she whispered in my ear as she gave me the required mother/bride embrace.

I was saved from answering by LeeAnn Gregori, our wedding planner.

"Elizabeth!" she called, summoning me towards her. "We're waiting!"

I glanced over my mother's shoulder toward the *we* that LeeAnn referred to—the wedding photographer and my groom, Weston King. They were only thirty feet away from me, but it felt like a continent.

The ceremony that had concluded less than half an hour before made Weston and me closer than we ever had been, in theory. And yet, after the words he'd just said to me—*I can't go with you*—he might as well already be an ocean away.

I wiped at the stray tear and squeezed my mother. "Everything's fine," I lied. I should've been good at this by now, after five months of pretending, but right now it felt harder than ever. Perhaps because I didn't know anymore which parts I was faking and which I wasn't. The wedding was real. The feelings were real. For both of us, I'd learned.

The relationship, though?

Apparently that was still up for debate.

But if I wanted to convince my cousin this was all legitimate so he didn't challenge my claim to my inheritance, I had to pretend the relationship was solid as well.

I crossed the room with my head held high, a smile on my lips, making damn sure no one besides my mother could see the struggle inside.

"One in front of the Christmas tree would be absolutely spectacular," LeeAnn suggested, and the photographer agreed, posing Weston and me there. We did several variations of holding hands and embracing. I couldn't look directly into his eyes, had to force myself to look at his nose instead, or his eyebrows, knowing I'd be unable to handle what I would find if I looked at him for real.

He seemed to feel the same. Just as awkward around me.

"They're sort of stiff, aren't they?" I heard the photographer whisper to LeeAnn.

"They're very formal," LeeAnn said, making up an excuse for us on the spot. The poor lady probably didn't know *what* to think of us with all the bickering we'd done in her presence over the last few months.

Maybe Weston had heard him too, because all of a sudden he *did* loosen up, and in the next picture he pulled me to him and improvised a kiss. I wanted to push him away, because I was frustrated and angry at him for keeping me in the dark and confusing me and yanking me up and down like a yo-yo.

But even if it wasn't for the show we were putting on, I couldn't resist him. I'd never been able to resist him. I threw my arms around his neck and let him kiss away my worry. *He'll explain later*, I told myself while his lips were bruising mine. *He wants to be with me, just like I want to be with him. We'll make it work. Somehow.*

He pulled away and I searched for that same reassurance in his face that I'd felt in his kiss, but his eyes seemed to be trying to tell me something different than what I was asking.

"Weston? We can still figure—"

He shook his head. "Not now," he whispered harshly.

"Where do you want us?" a familiar voice came from behind the photographer.

I pried my gaze away from Weston and found my cousin Darrell had joined my mother and Nana and Weston's family, all gathering for the group pictures to be taken.

This whole charade had been for him. If I hadn't been afraid he'd contest the validity of my nuptials, I would have eloped with Weston at City Hall.

Which meant Weston may have just been performing again. He could have seen Darrell and thrown in the kiss to make the photo seem more authentic.

At least I could count on him for that.

As to whether or not he would tell me what was holding him in New York, what would keep him from having a relationship with me and moving to France, I could hope he would tell me later, but why would he, when he'd never opened up before? He'd never even bothered explaining his strained family dynamics to me.

It was probably safer not to hold my breath waiting for more.

The group pictures were easier to endure. Even though I still had Weston at my side, could still feel his heat in the press of his body against mine, there were others around me and their energy helped bring a genuine smile to my face.

Soon the pictures were finished. "Let's go!" LeeAnn said, in full drill sergeant mode. "The schedule has us back at the reception by now."

Weston followed after her, eager to be away from his clingy parents, but before I could escape, Darrell caught me by the elbow. The hair stood up at the nape of my neck. The last time he and I had been alone he hadn't been very nice to me, and I didn't expect that he'd be any kinder today.

He surprised me, though. "I must say, Elizabeth, I was very impressed with the sincerity of the ceremony. You and the King boy seem to have feelings for each other. It was hard to tell in the porno I watched from that nightclub footage of the two of you."

Turned out I was less in the mood for this than for his bullying. It made me feel more like a fraud than when he'd accused me of spreading my legs like a prostitute in the video he'd referred to as a porno. And when I'd grinded on Weston hoping to be caught on camera it *had been* pretend. So that was saying something.

But of everyone on the guest list for the day, Darrell was my number one priority. If I didn't fool him, there was no point in trying to fool anyone else.

With a sigh, I turned toward him. "What is it going to take for you to believe that I'm really happy and in love with Weston?" I certainly didn't sound like a bride who was happy and in love, but being harassed by my cousin on my wedding day certainly warranted some agitation on my part.

"I'm sure I won't be truly convinced until you're both settled in together and the transfer of ownership has gone smoothly," Darrell said. "But today was a good start."

My already empty stomach clenched like I was going to retch. Because from the last word Weston had given me, there was going to be no settling in together.

But it had never been the plan to actually settle in with him. Everything was on course, even if it felt like the train had run off the tracks and there were mass casualties, the only one hurting was me.

"Then you have nothing to worry about," I said with the fakest smile I'd ever given. I spun on my heel and went to find my groom so we could be announced to our guests as Mr. and Mrs. King.

Inside the ballroom, I forced myself to forget about what was on the line and the questions in my head. Weston and I separated, each of us to say hello and mingle with guests on our own, and while that hadn't been the plan, it turned out to be for the best. I could forget better when he wasn't standing next to me, forget that he'd declared feelings for me out of the blue during our ceremony. I could forget that he told me how he'd meant them as soon as we were alone together. I could forget that he then told me we couldn't have a life together and that none of it mattered.

I could forget, until I came to Jepson Arndt, an old friend of my father's and the current treasurer for Dyson Media, the company that I would soon be taking over.

"I'm eager to hear what your plans are for the company," he said, which sent me spiraling in a new round of dizzy nerves.

Was I ready for this kind of questioning? Was I ready for this company? Weston had been training me for the last several months, but there was still so much that I was ignorant about, so many areas where I was naïve. Jepson was a man well into his fifties with a whole career of experience behind him. I was less than half his age, my only experience in business gleaned from Weston's old textbooks and pop quizzes—and I would now be his boss. How did I ever think I could manage this?

Thankfully, he didn't continue the conversation in the direction that I thought he would.

But the new avenue he took was just as bad.

"I don't want to bog you down, though, with business details on your wedding day. We can leave that for another time. Perhaps we could meet privately some time soon. What are your living arrangements going to be? Will you be staying here? Or are you moving to France, like your father did?"

"I . . . we . . ." It was really stupid to not be prepared for this. I'd expected people to ask about our honeymoon, not about after. Weston and I hadn't planned an *after* together. We'd come back to New York, of course, and I would begin the process of taking over the company. At some point, I'd go on to France. Weston would stay in the States, and I would tell people he would come later.

And that would be a lie.

Instead of joining me, we'd get divorced.

Now I wasn't sure of any of it. Because if Weston wouldn't come with me to France . . . was there a chance I'd stay in New York for him?

"I'm putting my penthouse up for sale," I said, because that was one thing I was sure of. Even if I stayed in New York, Weston preferred living near his office.

Jesus, I couldn't believe I was even considering an alternate future, one where I gave up my dreams to be with him. But more than anything, I hated that I didn't know what came next.

"Then you're planning to come to France?" Jepson asked.

I turned my head to look for Weston, wondering again why he wouldn't come with me, wondering if I could change his mind.

When I found him in the crowd of people at our reception, I was hit in the stomach like a crash in stock prices.

He was dancing. We hadn't even had a first dance together—we hadn't put one on the agenda, but that wasn't the point—and he was dancing with Sabrina Lind, his ex-girlfriend and current employee.

Was that why Weston didn't want to come to France with me? Because he'd have to leave *her*?

My ribs felt as if they were suddenly squeezing together. I'd been jealous of her for months, and Weston had never given me any reason not to be. Donovan had brought Sabrina as his date, and I knew that Donovan was interested in her for himself, but that didn't say anything about Weston or Sabrina's feelings. I'd never had the impression other people's feelings were terribly important to Donovan Kincaid.

From this angle, I couldn't see Weston's face well, but it was impossible to miss the way Sabrina was clinging to my husband. She seemed almost desperate, like she needed him to stand.

Yeah, that was the way I felt about him too.

I was so frustrated. So confused. So unsettled. The tears that had threatened earlier pressed against the dam, hot and angry.

"Yes, I'll be moving to France," I said, because I needed the security of my plans. "Excuse me, Jepson, I need a moment please."

I didn't even care what it looked like, or what he thought of me, this giant in the empire that I was taking over. This moment felt so small and pale compared to the vast wilderness of betrayal and pain inside of me, a wilderness brought on by Weston King.

I had to get away.

And there was nowhere for brides to escape, I'd learned. All eyes had been on me from the minute the celebration had begun. Even trips to the restroom were nearly impossible with people swarming to compliment and praise and give their well wishes. But I needed someplace, a spot I could hide, if even for just a minute.

Desperately, I looked around and noticed the divider that had been set up to wall off the reception during the ceremony was nearby. It wasn't perfect, but it would do.

I slipped around the corner and finally, I was alone.

I made my way to the small stage that was now pushed all the way up against the wall, where Weston and I had so recently stood and made vows to each other. He'd looked me in the eyes and told me I'd changed his life for the better. He'd called me his home.

If I really was his home, why did it feel so much like I was spinning aimlessly?

With no one watching me, I could throw my head back and let the tears fall—not too many, just a few. I wasn't even sure what I was crying about, really. Everything. Nothing.

I was tired, that was it.

Tired of pretending my feelings for Weston weren't real. Tired of pretending my marriage was. Tired of guessing what was in his head. Tired of justifying what was in mine. Of not knowing if I could pull this off and tired of worrying about what happened next. Of wondering if my father would approve. Of being jealous of Sabrina. Of wearing these heels. Tired of men making me question my worth and my value and my place in the world.

I was a queen.

That was my place in the world.

With or without a king, I was a queen. I'd be a queen no matter how this ended. I had to remember that.

"Elizabeth?"

I startled, glancing at the source of the voice, simultaneously trying to hide my face while I frantically wiped the moisture off my cheeks. "Clarence," I said, my voice breaking. "I'm . . ."

He was at my side before I could figure out how to finish the statement. "You're crying. What's wrong?"

"I needed some air," I said pushing the emotions inside me, boxing them up. "It was so crowded in there." I couldn't look at him yet. Too frazzled. Too obviously lying.

"These aren't the *just-needed-space* kind of tears, Bitsy. Come on. I know you. Remember?"

I turned to look at him finally, to study him. He was just as attractive as he'd been in high school, with his broad shoulders and defined jawline. His slicked-back brunette hair and light brown eyes were maybe nothing special on their own, but the whole package came together quite nicely, tied with a Henry-Cavill-type bow.

But even though he still looked *good*, he didn't look the *same*. We weren't the same.

"You *don't* know me anymore. It's been years." Years since we'd been together. Seven, to be exact, and we'd barely seen each other since. I wasn't Bitsy anymore. The ways I had changed could be written in volumes.

"I think I still know you," he said sweetly rather than patronizingly. He reached his hand out to brush my face where tears had gathered along my jawline. "I really wish you'd tell me what's wrong."

And for half a second I considered it, considered telling him everything, not because I still had feelings for him or because I wanted him now, but because he was gentle and kind and there, and I really did want someone to talk to in the moment.

But the person I wanted wasn't Clarence Sheridan. And it wasn't just a shoulder to cry on. I wanted Weston King.

And confessing things to this old friend, practically a stranger now, would do nothing to get me the man I wanted.

"Really, it's silly. I was just sad that my father isn't here for my big day."

"Of course. What was I thinking? He died a little more than a year ago, didn't he? I heard about his passing. I'm so sorry." He rubbed his hand up and down my arm. He was trying to be comforting, but his fingers felt like sandpaper on my skin. Rough and wrong.

"Thank you. I didn't think I'd be so emotional about it." And now that I was already emotional and thinking about my father, I actually was sad about his absence too. "But, hey," I continued. "Let's not think about it anymore. I need to cheer up. Change the subject."

"Okay." He stood back and looked me over. "You're married! I can't believe it."

I almost wished I could take it back and keep talking about my father.

"Yep. I'm married." It would take a while before I got used to that. Probably just about the time my divorce was finalized.

"You're a beautiful bride. Stunning. I have to say Weston King is a really lucky guy."

Tell that to him, I thought. "Thank you."

Clarence sobered. "Are you sure there isn't anything else going on?"

I'd forgotten how persistent he had always been. "I'm positive. It's been a long day. I haven't eaten. I need to get back out there, though. Maybe we can catch up some other time?"

"Sure. But if there's anything you need, Elizabeth, you can tell me. You know that, right?"

I nodded. "Of course. I appreciate that."

"I mean it," he insisted. "Promise you'll tell me if you need me."

"I promise." I forced a smile, the seventy billionth of the day, and gestured to the ballroom behind the divider that was hiding us. "I've really got to get out there before they miss me."

"Right. I'll go with you."

Clarence put his arm out to escort me. I started to put my hand on his bicep but then hesitated when he started to walk. "Does my makeup . . . ?"

"Look up." He scrubbed at the corner of my eye with his thumb. "There. You're perfect."

No. I wasn't perfect. I was a mess.

I was married.

And I'd never felt so alone in all my life.

CHAPTER
TWO

Weston

S HE WAS THE most beautiful woman in the room.
She was the most beautiful woman in the world.
I couldn't take my eyes off of her for more than two minutes all night, which was how I noticed right away when she disappeared.

And then, ten minutes later, the most beautiful woman in the world—my *wife*—walked out from behind the partition arm in arm with her fucking ex-boyfriend. He was giving her the eyes of a lover, and suddenly I saw red.

The day was definitely not going how I'd imagined.

I'd been a nervous wreck in the beginning, reeling from the revelation that I had a son. But then, while I stood there at the end of the aisle waiting for Elizabeth to appear, it felt like the strings were finally coming together, knotting into a perfect bow instead of falling apart and unraveling like they had been for the past several weeks.

There she was, walking toward me with the simple strains of a cello accompanying her as she made her way. And it didn't matter anymore that I had less to offer than she had to give, that I was from a family of fuck-ups, that I could never be as selfless and noble as she was. She brought me up to her level just by allowing me to be in her presence. The name I was given at birth, King—it had always been a joke. Until Elizabeth Dyson stood beside me and finally made me royalty.

I was in love with her.

She was a beginning for me, and I never wanted her to end. If she did, if she walked away, if she didn't feel the same, I was pretty sure that I would end. During the ceremony though, with her hand held in mine, I wasn't worried about her leaving. And I wasn't just trying to clutch onto her because I felt like I needed her in order to be a father to Sebastian— this wedding, this fake wedding, had become the most real thing in my life. *Elizabeth* had become the most real thing in my life, and finding out about Sebastian had just kicked me into gear, made me understand I had to own what I was feeling.

So right there, in front of all our friends and family, I told her. And I meant it.

And I knew in my bones that she meant it when she said her vows to me, too.

When we walked back down that aisle together, as man and wife, I thought our lives were starting together.

How the fuck had I forgotten to factor in France?

It was my gut reaction to instantly say that I couldn't go with her, to say that moving out of the country was out of the question. The last words Callie had given me about our son were still so fresh in my mind—she'd offered me a place in his life, but only if I could be there. How could I possibly be there if I was halfway across the world?

I couldn't lose him. Not when I'd just found out about him.

And I couldn't lose her. I wouldn't have a home to give Sebastian without her. I couldn't be a man who could be a father without her.

Maybe it was something that could be sorted out without Elizabeth having to lose her dreams, without me having to lose a relationship with my child, but it wasn't something we could discuss in thirty seconds in a side room at our wedding. It would have to wait, even though it was a fucking tug of war between them inside me, and that perfect bow that my life had been tied up in? I was now desperately holding on to both strings as my arms were being torn in different directions.

The worst part was the look on Elizabeth's face, the plea in her voice. I hated not being able to give her an explanation yet, but I couldn't

drop the same bomb on her that Callie had dropped on me. Not today.
It all had to wait.

So I compartmentalized as much as I could, put Sebastian in one
corner of my heart and Elizabeth in another and focused on getting
through. Today the goal was to fool Darrell. We were so close to pulling
this off, we couldn't let him see the tension between us.

I'd thought I'd done a pretty good job of it too—we posed for pictures together, then mingled separately at the reception. I flirted with
the older women. I let my bachelor friends harass me. When Sabrina
mistakenly thought she'd seen someone that had scared her, and Donovan wasn't around to comfort her, I calmed her down by taking her for
a spin on the dance floor. She wasn't who I wanted to be dancing with,
but she'd become a good friend, and it was nice to have something else
to think about.

The trick was, I realized, to not be too near Elizabeth. She made
me impetuous and passionate, made me say too much. Distracted me
from the agenda because I wanted the point of the day to be *us*. I wanted
to take off her garter and cut the cake and have a first dance with her,
wanted all the wedding traditions we'd left out of the reception since
we weren't a *real* couple.

But now we *were* a real couple.

And it was harder to be next to her, worrying things might not work
out now that I actually cared.

But just because it was hard didn't mean I was going to stand by
and let Douchebag Sheridan make his moves on her. She was mine. End
of story.

I made my way over there so fast, Clarence was still with her when
I got there.

"Where have you been?" I asked, my eyes darting between the two
of them.

Her bright blues widened as though surprised that I'd caught her.
Did that mean she was guilty of something?

"I just . . . I needed . . . air," she answered, her cheeks pink.

"I saw her disappear and went to check on her. I noticed you were busy with other . . . guests," Douchebag said. Other guests. As though I should've been with Elizabeth instead. As though he knew anything about what was going on between us.

But maybe he did. I didn't know if they'd had contact with each other in the recent weeks since they'd reconnected. She had his phone number—I knew that because I'd given it to her myself. She might've even told him just now. Had she been gone long enough? How much time would it take to say none of this was real, that she'd thought it was, but Weston King had played her?

But I hadn't bailed on her. Not yet. Not ever, if I could help it. And I would help it.

I just couldn't fix it right now.

I put my arm around her waist, pulling her to me possessively. "Let's talk." I might not be able to fix it right now, but I had to be able to tell her enough to keep her, before she went running off to someone else.

She looked around, not just at Douchebag but at all of our guests. "We can't right now."

Okay, so there was no way we were getting across the ballroom with all these people. But I had an idea. "Come with me." I tugged her onto the dance floor, away from her past to a place we could be alone. Into my arms, where I'd wanted her all evening.

"Weston, I don't feel like dancing," she said through her teeth as she smiled at a passing couple.

"I don't fucking care if you feel like dancing. I need to hold you right now." That shut her up for a moment, and as I spun her on the floor to the slow song, she relaxed into my embrace.

I rested my head right next to her ear, intent on telling her . . . something. I just didn't know what would be the right thing to say. There was so much to share. So much to tell her. I still hadn't actually told her I loved her. And now I had to tell her I had a kid. Would she still want me now that I came with baggage? I didn't even know how she felt about the prospect of children. We hadn't even discussed what country we'd live in, much less what could happen down the road.

"I saw you dancing with Sabrina," she said before I had a chance to tell her anything.

I stiffened, because this was another drama of my own making. How long had I let her be jealous of my employee? There was nothing going on with her—hadn't been since Elizabeth had walked into Reach's lounge and into my life.

"I wanted to be dancing with you," I told her, feeling the weight of its inadequacy even as I said it. But I wasn't certain Sabrina's past was my story to tell.

"There was nothing stopping you," she hissed. "You could easily have asked me."

"You didn't want to do the first dance ritual."

"We said that months ago. Back when we said we were going to do scripted vows." She pulled her head back so she could look at me. "You have me on a roller coaster. One minute you care, the next you don't. How am I supposed to know what's real and what isn't?"

Her voice was thick with emotion and it slammed me with the want to make it better.

"I have you on a roller coaster so you turn to Clarence for consolation?" Well, maybe I *wanted* to make it better, but I was better at being an asshole. It came more naturally.

"You were dancing with Sabrina," she reminded me.

"In front of everyone. Not alone in a corner where no one could see us. Her cheeks weren't rosy when we were finished." The more I thought about this, the angrier I legitimately became. I didn't truly think Elizabeth would cheat on me, if for no other reason than she didn't like to break rules. But to run straight to him instead of coming to me was not okay.

"She was clinging to you the whole time. Is she the reason you won't leave New York?"

"I can't believe you even—" I cut off sharply as I noticed that there were eyes on us. Lots of eyes on us. The entire room was watching us, not necessarily because we looked like we were arguing—I was pretty sure we'd managed to cover that up. Most likely, they were just watching the wedding couple sharing a moment on the dance floor.

Elizabeth followed my gaze. "Oh, shit."

"Just keep dancing."

"We're continuing this discussion later," she warned quietly. She smiled again. She was so good at it, putting that fake dazzle on, but I was really getting good at telling the difference between the fraudulent and the authentic. Strangely, the real one was never quite as bright.

I would have given anything to have seen that dimmer smile right then.

IT SEEMED LIKE decades before LeeAnn was summoning us over to her. "You need to make a big exit," she said. "That means you need to leave before your guests do. It's time to say your goodbyes."

"Thank God," Elizabeth said, her relief evident in her sigh.

LeeAnn raised an eyebrow.

"My feet hurt," Elizabeth said, and though I was sure it was true, I was also sure it wasn't the reason she was glad this was almost over.

"Of course," LeeAnn said, like she should've known all along, though her own shoes were two inches taller than Elizabeth's. I had a feeling LeeAnn wasn't the type of woman who would complain about her feet hurting. It was the price you had to pay for looking good.

I preferred Elizabeth's honesty, as inappropriate as it may have been at the moment. I attempted to share a smile with her, but she missed it, and perhaps that was for the best. I was in a pissy mood from our fight, from Douchebag, from the frustration of being at an utter loss for how to solve these problems, and I wasn't sure my expression was even worth sharing.

Elizabeth headed over to her family to make her farewells. Most of my friends had already left—Donovan and Nate had both brought dates for the evening and had ducked out early. The last people on Earth I wanted to see at the moment were my own parents, but it was still a performance, and they were the ones I was most expected to say good night to.

"She really is a lovely woman," my mother said as I let her hug me. "I hope we get the chance to know her better."

I'd done so well keeping walls up all day, but at my mother's mention of a future with Elizabeth, my chest felt tight. "I do too," I said.

My mother's expression brightened, and too late I realized she thought that I meant that I would let Elizabeth into their lives, when what I really meant was I hoped that Elizabeth would be in *mine*. It wasn't something I could take back after the fact, either. Especially as my mother's eyes brimmed with tears, happy at the mere suggestion that I'd spend time with her.

"Oh, Weston. You can't imagine how much I've missed you." She pulled me into another hug. "One day, you'll have your own son, and before you know it he'll be grown up too, and you'll be saying goodbye to him on his own wedding day, and then you'll understand." She was blubbering now.

My throat got tight and I was afraid if I spoke I would blubber too. Because now I wasn't just thinking about Elizabeth and a future with her, but also how much I had missed my mother. And also the added knowledge that I now *did* have a son. Her grandson.

I hadn't even met him yet, and I felt like I'd missed so much. Two years of his life, I'd missed. It was going on seven years that things had been strained with my family. How many years was I going to let my mother lose?

There wasn't room for this inside of me. Not tonight.

"I love you, Mom," I whispered, not even sure she heard it.

I hugged my dad too, but nothing was amended when they walked away. There was still a massive chasm between us, but for just one moment, we'd both found a bridge and met in the middle.

My best man, Brett, a friend from college, announced our departure from the reception. There was a round of applause and cheers and it felt like the kind of standing ovation one got at the end of a performance. I took Elizabeth's hand in mine and waved to everyone as we walked into the hotel lobby toward the bank of elevators that would take us to the honeymoon suite.

As soon as the doors closed and we were alone in the car, she dropped my hand and folded her arms across her chest.

So that was how the evening was going to be.

I rolled my eyes and pushed the button to our floor. We rode up in silence, the tension growing thick and hot around us. I was used to the friction, the way it sparked and flashed between our eyes. I'd grown accustomed to the ticking time bomb. The space surrounding us had always been a warzone. Why should it be any different now?

I probably shouldn't have found that realization as comforting as I did. It probably shouldn't have turned me on so much.

As soon as we were in our suite, the bomb exploded, the bomb being Elizabeth. "We're alone now, so just tell me straight. You knew I was always going to France. If you wanted to be with me, you had to know it would involve living there. Is that not something you'll even consider? Is it Sabrina? Is it Reach? Is it Donovan? Because if it's fucking Donovan who's keeping you from—"

I grabbed her hands, which were flying in midair as she yelled, and pulled them behind her back at her waist as I cut her off with a searing kiss, my tongue plunging into her open mouth, robbing her of oxygen.

When she was thoroughly kissed, her lips pliable, her body sagging in my arms, I let her go.

"I'm tired, Elizabeth. I'm not discussing fucking anything tonight." I took off my tuxedo jacket and threw it on the desk. Then I began working on my cufflinks. "What I think we both need now is to release some tension."

Her spine straightened, her neck growing longer as she stared at me in shock. "You think we're going to have *sex* now?"

I loved how she made it sound disgusting, like she wasn't interested, even when I'd just been kissing her and had felt the lean in her body, had tasted the desire in her mouth.

Two could play the indifference game.

I shrugged. "I'm fucking someone tonight. If you want it to be you, you better take off your dress."

Her mouth slammed shut, and she only seemed to consider it for two seconds before she was fumbling with the zipper at her back. She struggled with it, but I didn't help her. It made me stiff to watch her frantically trying to strip down, just because I told her to. Just because she thought I might find a better offer if she didn't.

Like there was a better offer than her.

Like there was anyone but her.

I didn't take my eyes off her as I unbuttoned my vest and tossed it to the side with my jacket. I'd loosened my tie by the time she got her dress undone. It fell to the floor and she was left wearing a strapless corseted bra, one that had a low back so it couldn't be seen with her dress on, and matching lace panties—both in a white ivory so virginal and bridal it seemed dirty.

Jesus, she was a fucking wet dream.

And she was my *wife*.

I was so goddamned hard at that thought, my cock was a brick. I had to stroke myself through my pants, just to get some relief.

Elizabeth was watching me as closely as I was watching her. She saw what she did to me. She loved it, that little demon. That witch. That spiteful angel. Her lips quirked up the tiniest bit, taking pleasure in my misery, as she reached behind herself to undo the corset.

But I stopped her. "Leave it."

"Can I take off my shoes, at least?" she asked, her tone full of sass and sauce.

"Fuck no." So her feet were hurting, but that was part of the turn-on. That she was suffering. Suffering like I was inside.

I wanted to make her suffer more.

Suffer *and* feel good. The way she made me suffer and feel good and wish that I could only ever feel exactly that way all the time.

I unclipped my suspenders then undid the fly of my pants. My boxer briefs were damp from my dick leaking inside them, begging to be released, aching for Elizabeth's pussy. But I wasn't ready to bring it out yet. Not until she was aching for me too.

Scanning the room, I quickly found where I wanted to be.

"Follow me." I led her to the bench in front of the windows. She watched me, and I could feel her curiosity as I turned the lamp on and then opened the curtains all the way. With the light on, anyone who was looking in the building across from us should be able to see us pretty well.

"You and those damn floor-to-ceiling windows," Elizabeth said, her voice raspy and eager.

Yeah, she liked the windows too.

"You want me to close them?" I asked, but I was already rolling up my shirt sleeves, moving on to the next part of my preparation.

She shrugged with one shoulder. "Whatever turns you on."

"Lie down on the bench," I commanded.

She lay back, tentatively, as though she were concerned about getting it right, not as though she didn't want to do it.

"All the way, flat on your back," I instructed. "Then spread your legs, as far as you can."

I stepped back to look at her, imagining what someone would see from the other side—this beautiful redheaded bride, laid out on a table in front of her groom, a banquet feast just for him. The bench was the perfect size for her; it fit her from her head to the bottom of her ass, so when she spread her legs, her pussy was there at the other end, clothed in delicate lace.

I rubbed myself as I gazed upon her. "You're the most beautiful woman I know," I told her, massaging my crown through my briefs. She turned her head on the bench to look at me, her lips pouty, her eyelashes fluttering.

I continued. "You were so fucking sexy when you walked out into that aisle, I was almost pissed that anybody else got to look at you."

Her breathing quickened, but she parried me anyway, turning to look out the window. "That's a guy thing to say. You're so—"

"Stop talking unless you're screaming my name," I said tersely. "I'm already not in the mood to be good to you; I really don't think you want to push me."

Her head shifted back toward me quickly, her mouth opening with a slight gasp. "What are you going to—"

"I said no talking." Before she could say anything else or challenge me or make me want to throttle her, I moved to kneel in front of her pussy, hooked my arms around each of her thighs, and began licking at the lace barrier.

She responded with a series of moans and grunts. I kept it up, licking at her through the material, swiping up her slit, using the lace to create friction. I'd been sleeping with her long enough to know how to get her worked up now, how to read her signs. And every time she got a little bit close, every time her gasps got louder and her breathing more rapid, I pulled away, changed my tactic.

It wasn't too long before she was writhing, still dressed in her bridal underwear, wound up from my torturous tongue. So desperate, she started to beg, remembering my order that the only word she could speak was my name. "Weston, Weston," she pled.

She wasn't worked up enough. Wasn't destroyed yet. Wasn't torn apart inside like I was over her.

I pushed aside the panel at her crotch. My fingers found her wet and slippery as I slid inside her. She bucked up with her hips, urging me in deeper. But I continued my torture, fucking her shallowly with just my fingertips, licking in wide circles around her clit.

She was sweating, tears were trailing down her cheeks when she finally broke the rule I'd given her and spoke. "I don't know if you're trying to make me feel good or miserable," she said.

"That's the point," I said against her.

"Please, fuck me now."

I nodded, unable to take watching her squirm any longer. My balls already ached with the need to release inside her. "I'll close the curtains," I offered.

"No. I like them open."

God, she was divine. I pushed my pants down with my briefs just as far as necessary, and pulled her panties from her gorgeous legs. Then I was climbing on top of her, fucking into her hard, harder, so hard. She wrapped her legs around me at my waist, hooking us together, and when I looked in the window I could see our reflection there, could see what the neighbors saw, and it spurred me on more, drove me to pound into her faster and deeper and harder, harder.

It was the final dirty encore to our earlier performance.

We came together, both of us tortured and miserable and in desperate need of the release.

When I was calm enough, I pulled out of her and gathered her in my arms, carried her to her bed where I held her and made love to her the rest of the night. We didn't talk about the mountains between us.

We were married now. We had the rest of our lives for talking.

Or, at least we had tomorrow.

CHAPTER THREE

Elizabeth

WESTON WAS STILL asleep when I woke up the next morning. I spent several minutes tracing the dips and curves of his bare torso with my eyes, his abs so toned that six-pack didn't even cover it. My mouth watered as I gazed lower at the V-lines that peeked out from under the sheet—two short roads leading to pleasureland. But it was the sweet gentle rise and fall of his chest that had me hypnotized. I thought about how easy it would be to roll into his arms and fall back asleep, or wake him up with a kiss and urge him to make love to me again.

But there was a giant wall between us, invisible, yet I believed it was surmountable, and that had to be dealt with before I could truly be as close to him as I wanted to be.

I forced myself out of bed and into the bathroom. One look in the mirror said that the beautiful bride from the day before had gone, leaving a faded beauty queen in the wreckage. I needed a shower and breakfast, needed to pull myself together, needed to make myself look like a decent human being—needed to feel like a decent human being before facing my groom.

My husband.

How long would I be able to keep calling him that?

The shower did wonders for my mood. I washed off the makeup

and the traces of the extraordinary day I'd had before. I felt melancholy as I washed away the sticky leftovers of sex between my legs, as though a little water and soap would take away the memory of Weston's mouth and cock. But those memories were forever seared into my mind, deep, like ink into flesh. Whatever I left this marriage with, at least I'd have that.

When I was clean and fresh, I turned off the water and wrapped a towel around my body and another around my hair. I brushed my teeth and put makeup on my face until I looked like someone whom I recognized again. When I walked back into the bedroom, I found the bed empty.

Sounds from the other room said Weston was up and moving around. Hopefully he'd ordered breakfast, or at least coffee. I found a robe in my suitcase and traded the towel for that, then padded out to the main room of our suite.

My spirits dropped at what I found. Weston was dressed. Seeing him with clothes on was always somewhat disappointing, but more disappointing was that he was dressed to go out. He had shoes on and his coat in hand.

"Are you going somewhere?" I hated how weak my voice sounded.

His eyes darted around the room, looking anywhere but at me. "Yeah. I have an appointment. It shouldn't take too long. I'm just looking for my wallet."

"You have an appointment? We're on our honeymoon." Technically we didn't leave for our trip until tomorrow, and of course when all this had been planned, our entire marriage was a farce. But then suddenly it wasn't. And we needed to be together if we had any shot at all of figuring this out.

"There it is," he said to himself, finding his wallet in his jacket from the night before. As though I hadn't said anything at all.

I didn't even care anymore what it looked like for him to be leaving his bride less than twenty-four hours after our nuptials. I didn't care about putting on a show anymore. I cared about *us*.

"Weston," I called as he headed toward the door.

He turned this time and looked at me, really looked at me. His expression, which had seemed distracted before, focused and softened.

He crossed the room and pulled me into his arms, cupping my cheek with his hand. "I promise I won't be gone very long." He kissed the side of my lips.

I clutched onto his jacket. "But we need to talk."

"We do. We will. We have two weeks and I'm all yours. But first I just have to do this one thing. Okay?" His thumb grazed along my chin, sending goosebumps down my arms.

"Okay," I said when it really wasn't okay at all, but what choice did I have but to trust him? He kissed me again, for real, the kind of kiss that made my knees weak and my toes curl.

"Don't be dressed when I get back," he said half teasing, half commanding.

I nodded, though for the kinds of things we needed to discuss, being dressed was probably the wisest decision. As he headed for the door again, it felt like he was leaving, leaving for real, and his name came out of my lips again involuntarily. "Weston!"

He stopped, the door half-open, and looked at me longingly. "Two weeks," he promised again. "I'm all yours." Then he shut the door and was gone.

It wasn't the two weeks I was worried about. It was the whole lifetime after.

I stood staring at the door for a long moment after he left, sorting through the banquet of emotions I was feeling inside. He'd meant to comfort me with his words and his kiss—and he had, momentarily.

But now that he was gone, and I was left alone in the bridal suite of the Park Hyatt with nothing but questions and a brand-new diamond-lined wedding band under my engagement ring, his well-meant intentions vanished and were replaced with a brewing storm.

Alone, his comfort felt like rejection.

Alone, his words sounded like empty promises.

Frustration swept through me like a gale wind and I reached for the nearest object I could find, an empty water glass on the desk, and threw it as hard as I could against the door. It smashed at once into pieces, unleashing a dam of tears inside me. What the hell had I gotten myself into? I cried as I hugged myself, asking myself the same question over and over. Why did it hurt so much? I didn't even know who to blame—myself, my father, Weston, or Donovan.

And maybe all of this was stupid and dramatic and there was nothing even to cry over. I would get my company. That was what I'd wanted, right? And maybe I would even get Weston, but if I had him, then why was he rushing off to secret places on a Sunday morning at 10:00 a.m.? Why did he leave me in the dark? Why would he never let me in?

I bent over in an attempt to control the sobs racking my body, when suddenly there was a knock on the door. My crying halted, my body froze.

It was probably housekeeping. We'd forgotten the stupid do not disturb sign.

The knock came again, and I knew I had to answer it or they would walk right in. I crossed to the door, careful not to step on the glass, and opened it just to say, "We don't—"

But it wasn't housekeeping.

"Clarence?" I wiped the tears from my cheeks with the whole of my hand. God, this was the second time in two days he'd seen me crying. "What are you doing here?"

"Can I come in?" he asked.

"Weston is . . ." I didn't necessarily want to tell him that my husband wasn't there, and it seemed just as odd to invite an ex-boyfriend into my bridal suite when I was alone.

"He just left," Clarence finished for me. "I saw him."

My brows furrowed. "Did you know he had an appointment today?"

Clarence shook his head. "I just got lucky."

I processed what he'd just said, understanding that he'd meant he wanted to see me alone.

I couldn't think of any reason to tell him to leave. Honestly, I wasn't thinking very well at all. "Be careful. There's glass by the door."

I opened the door farther so that Clarence could step in, then let the door go so it could slam shut on its own, and I wouldn't have to dance over the glass again. Clarence looked at the mess on the floor.

"Did something happen here, Elizabeth?" he asked anxiously.

"I just dropped a glass," I said, tightening my robe around myself, conscious that I was naked underneath. "It's really silly how upset I got about dropping the glass. You must think I'm really emotional these days." Such a lame excuse. I picked up the hotel magazine and headed for the door to start cleaning it up.

Clarence took the magazine from my hand. "Let me." He bent down and swept the broken pieces onto the magazine, glancing up at me furtively. "You just happened to drop a glass right in front of the door, huh? It really seems more like it was thrown."

I turned away from him to the Kleenex box and cleaned up my nose before turning back to him. "I really don't know what you're suggesting, but maybe you could tell me why you are here today."

"Not trying to upset you, Bitsy," he said using his old nickname for me again. He dumped the glass into the trash can under the desk, set the magazine down, and faced me head-on. "I came because I want to make sure you're okay. Yesterday I was worried that you weren't. And now that I see you today, I'm even more concerned that you're not doing well."

More tears leaked from the corners of my eyes. Because I *wasn't* okay, and because Clarence had been the first person to notice. "You know, weddings are just really hard," I said holding my arms across my chest. "And relationships are really hard. Being an adult is really hard."

He crossed to me and put his arms around me, hugging me. "Do you want to tell me about it? Because you can tell me anything. You always can." He ran his hand up and down my back, soothing me as I cried on his shoulder. It felt like I imagined a father would comfort his child. A normal father, anyway. Not mine.

"I had a crazy idea about you actually. Want to hear it?"

I nodded into his neck, unable to talk.

"After I saw you a couple months ago, at the restaurant with Weston, when you told me you were engaged, I kept thinking about you. My father's in the television business here in the States, you know, and I asked him about you. Asked about Dyson Media and what was going on with it after your father's death. I heard about the terms of your inheritance.

It got me wondering, and I might be crossing the line here. This is a total shot in the dark."

My heart sped up as I listened. I could see where this was heading.

"Well, I just wondered if you were getting married just so you could get control of your father's business."

I pushed out of Clarence's arms and swallowed hard. "That's really inappropriate for you to ask," I said, choking on my words.

"I know. It is. Truthfully, it's probably just wishful thinking."

I looked up at him quizzically. "Wishful thinking?"

"I still think about you, Bitsy. When I saw you again I realized I still have feelings for you. If you're happy with this King guy, then good for you. I'm ready to let you go. But if you're not . . ." He took a step toward me. "If this marriage is under false pretenses, then I really wish you would've told me."

"And what would you have done if I would have told you?" I asked, despite myself, knowing it was better to leave it alone. "I mean, if it were all under false pretenses, I mean."

"I would've offered to marry you instead."

CHAPTER
FOUR

Weston

I PAID THE cab driver and stepped onto the sidewalk outside the brownstone in Brooklyn. I didn't want to be here. I wanted to be back in bed with my wife, wanted to spend the day making love to her, planning our future.

But as much as I wanted to be there, I needed to be here.

There would be time to discuss everything later, once I knew more about the baby. I climbed the six steps up to the front door and walked inside to the tiny foyer, looking for the number I wanted to press. And I tried not to think about Elizabeth's lips, her warmth, the way she looked at me when I told her I was leaving today.

There it was—*Callie Tannen and Dana Steadman*, apartment four. I bristled for a moment at the additional name on the plate. Callie had said that Sebastian didn't have another father in his life. Was Dana a man or woman? Would he be a father to Sebastian if I chose not to be?

I pushed the button and waited for Callie's voice. It didn't come, but a moment later, a buzz indicated that the door was unlocked. I walked in and made my way to unit number four, an easy route because it was on the first floor. Units one and two, it turned out, were garden level units. First floor was good. Not too many stairs. A good apartment in which to raise a child.

I lifted my hand to knock on the door, but Callie opened it

immediately. She was dressed in yoga pants and a sweatshirt, her hair tied up in a ponytail. She seemed slightly out of breath, like she'd been rushing around, and from the look at the items in her hands—a stuffed puppy, a toy dinosaur, and the remote control—I guessed that she was doing some last-minute straightening.

"Come in," she said. "I'm just cleaning a bit. It's impossible to keep up."

I stepped in and shut the door behind me as she walked over to a basket in the corner and dropped the toys inside, then she took the remote and set it on the coffee table before turning her attention to me. "Can I take your coat?"

I nodded as I began to take it off, my attention on examining every detail of the room. It was nothing like the minimalistic design of my apartment or the highbrow furnished penthouse that Elizabeth lived in. Callie's apartment was stuffed and cozy. Toy boxes and tables and toys to climb on were shoved in between every bit of furniture. The bookshelves had classics on the top shelves, but the bottom shelves were dedicated to kid-friendly objects and *The Very Hungry Caterpillar*. There was a miniature armchair next to the grown-up armchair, and as Callie took my coat for me I noticed there was also a potty training stool set up in front of the television.

This was a house where a kid lived.

This was a house where *my* kid lived.

"Is he here?" It was too quiet. I already knew the answer.

"Dana took him to the store."

"Dana's your . . . nanny?" I asked hopefully.

"She's my . . . friend. She lives here."

That was a relief then. Not a potential daddy substitute. And a relief that Callie had someone to help her, too. Someone who lived with her.

"I have some coffee brewed," she offered. "Would you like some?"

I nodded again, still not completely sure of myself.

She headed to the kitchen, which was connected to the living room in an open layout, and I followed her, finding my thoughts on the way. "Look, I'm still really pissed at you."

"Mmm." She poured the coffee into a mug and looked up at me. "How do you take it?"

"Cream, if you have some. I'm serious here. You stole two years from me."

She opened the fridge and grabbed the container of cream, the real stuff, like Elizabeth got, and poured it into my cup before handing it to me. Then she gestured that I should take a seat at the dining room table.

I sat. "Are you even listening to anything I say?"

She put her own coffee cup on the table, picked up a photo book off the counter, and put it on the table in front of me. She opened it to the front page and scooted it toward me. Then she sat down, too.

I looked at the first image in front of me, a picture of a newborn wearing one of those striped caps they put on babies at the hospital. His face was red and blotchy, but the rest of his skin was white and peeling. Next to the picture was a printout that read *Sebastian Maximilian King, weight: 8 lbs. 1 oz. length: 21 inches*.

Sebastian. My kid.

She'd given him my name. My ribs felt tight like they were pressed against my lungs. It was hard to breathe in. I couldn't stop staring.

A couple of other photos filled out the page, one where Callie held him to her bare chest, her expression one of exhaustion and joy. Another photo of him bundled up like a burrito laying in one of those plastic baby boxes hospitals put newborns in.

"I was climbing the stairs of the West Virginia state Capitol Building when I went into labor," Callie said, as I studied the pictures, memorizing every detail. "I was already four days past due, and it seemed nothing was going to get him out of me. There weren't any stairs in the duplex I was renting—I didn't live here yet. I'd already walked all over the mall, but it wasn't challenging enough. Politics were already in the family. So the Capitol it was."

I chuckled. I barely knew her, but from what I did know, her story was exactly what I'd expect. "Were you worried about making it to the hospital in time?"

"My sister was with me. She's a doctor. She drove the car and coached me through the whole birth." She leaned forward. "It took about twenty times up and down those stairs before I had any intense contractions. If I'd been living here already, I would have gone to the Empire. Or the Statue of Liberty. And then I might have been in trouble, because I had a fast delivery."

"I guess I'm glad you weren't here, then," I said, not sure if I meant it.

I turned the page, wondering if she saw my hand trembling when I did. Here were pictures of a newborn at home, various snapshots of the life of a woman raising a child on her own. Callie explained them all to me, narrating Sebastian's life. This was when he first rolled over. This was when he first smiled. This was when he first crawled. This was when he tried peas. This was when he tried cake. This was when he said his first word.

"What was it?" I asked, completely riveted by her stories.

"Mama."

She said it proudly and I hated myself for feeling jealous. Hated the bitter way the envy sat between my muscles and my bones, making it impossible to stay comfortably in one position for long.

I turned another page, unable to look at her.

"I know I can't give you those two years back, Weston. But they're in the past now, and there's nothing I can do about it. Except tell you his stories. Except share him with you now." She was sincere, and I could feel her genuine desire to connect with me, like the fingers of a fire reaching out to new kindling.

I was already burning for this kid. She didn't realize she didn't need to try that hard.

"What's this?" I asked, pointing at the doll that Sebastian held in many of the last pictures in the book.

"That's Bella. His baby. It's his favorite toy."

I looked up with surprise. "My son's favorite toy is a doll?"

"He chose it. He knows his mommy snuggles up with him and he likes the idea of being able to be like me. I hope you're not suggesting that he shouldn't play with a doll because of gender stereotypes or cultural standards, because—" she sat up straighter, ready for a fight.

"No, definitely not," I said, cutting her off. I really couldn't give a rat's ass about the gender bullshit. I'd liked cars as a kid. And superheroes. But I'd liked Barbie dolls too, mostly because they had boobs, but sometimes I dressed them up for fun.

I looked closer at the picture where Sebastian was hugging Bella like she was everything in the world. Had my father ever held me that way? "That's really sweet that he wants to love so young."

Callie relaxed. "Thank you," she said on a sigh.

I looked up at her, saw that her expression was more anxious than I'd realized.

"I really appreciate you not making judgments about this. About how I've done things with him."

"This is hard for you," I said, as I realized it.

She met my eyes and nodded, her eyes watery. I reached across the table and put my hand over hers.

It helped, because it was hard for me too.

"Want to see his room?" she asked, suddenly excited.

"Yeah, I do." I was equally excited, like it was Christmas day. I wanted to see everything of his, wanted to see his clothes, wanted to see his bed, wanted to see the food he ate and where he played. I was aching to fill myself up with him, like a starving man, only I didn't know how hungry I'd been until now. Each little piece of him I got only reminded me how much I didn't know.

"Who stays with him?" I asked as we stood from the table.

"I do. I don't work outside the home."

"Nice." The benefits of being a sorority princess, I supposed. Usually I rolled my eyes at my peers who lived off their trust funds, but this time it was a relief that she had that, because she had this option. I liked that she'd been the one caring for Sebastian. She'd kept my son from me, but not just to hand him to someone else.

She led me down a small hallway, past one bedroom that I assumed was hers to a second smaller room next to the bathroom. It was decorated in green and yellow, with a thick, plush, dark blue rug. There were toys everywhere along the walls, and in one corner a tiny bed. Another corner held a dresser. There was also a rocking chair and one of those LEGO tables with the big blocks, the non-swallowable precursor to the regular kind.

"I loved LEGOs," I told her, smiling at the memory of all the sets I used to build. Alone, and later with Donovan. How I'd shown those to my father when he'd come home at night.

"Sebastian adores those blocks, but he's not strong enough to pull them apart yet by himself. So he builds, and we tear down."

I nodded because I didn't know anything about child development and when they could do this or that. There was so much I needed to learn.

"And that's where he sleeps?" Would it be weird if I leaned down and sniffed the blankets?

"Naps only in here. I co-sleep." When I looked at her questioningly she went on. "That means he sleeps with me. It was easier when I was nursing and then he just got used to being next to me. Or I just got used to him being next to me."

"It's not dangerous? I'm not judging, I'm asking." Because I honestly didn't know.

"Like anything, there's mixed opinions."

So much I didn't know.

The weight suddenly felt too much to hold, like carrying rocks, and I sank down onto the floor, my back braced against his tiny bed.

Callie followed suit, sliding down along the wall opposite me so that we were face to face.

"Did you want him?" It suddenly felt like the most important question to ask. I had to know—as if knowing if he was wanted by her would change how I would feel about him. I hated to think of how alone she must have been. Knowing she was happy about his existence made it better.

"Oh, yes," she said and I had no doubt that she had. "Very much. Wait—are you asking did I try to get pregnant? With you?"

"No, but . . . ? We used condoms."

"We did. One broke."

"One broke," I said, remembering just as she said it. "Why hadn't I been concerned about that?"

"I was due to have my period any day. I told you it was the wrong time of the month for anything to happen."

That was right. She'd assured me it would be fine. I'd been tested for STDs since then, and I'd never heard from her again so I'd never thought about it again.

"And it should have been fine. I *wasn't* trying to get pregnant. And when I got back home, I waited for the period that didn't come and didn't come, and then I realized I was pregnant. I just *knew*. Without even taking a test I knew. Not because I had sore breasts or because I was feeling sick but because I've always been really regular and, I don't know, I just knew I felt different. Inside."

"And right away, you knew you wanted to keep him?"

She threw her head back against the wall. "I suppose I weighed my options. But I realized that I wanted to be a parent so I could give Sebastian a better life than the one that had been given to me," she said. And in that moment, I believed that she would, regardless of whether I was present in Sebastian's life or not.

"Yeah, I know exactly what you mean." God, this day was stirring so much inside me.

Callie tilted her head, studying me. "We're probably more alike than I realized, you and I. I'm sorry I didn't give you a chance earlier. Imagine what we could've found out about each other if we'd spent more time talking during that week we spent together." She smiled.

"Right? We might've even ended up friends." A thought occurred to me all of a sudden. "You know I'm not looking to make a family here. I like you and everything—what I know of you—but I am just not . . ."

She rolled her eyes at me. "I'm not flirting with you, you narcissist. Didn't you just get married?"

"I did. I did just get married." Thinking about Elizabeth was like the sun breaking through clouds on a stormy day. I wanted to be with her, wanted her light, wanted her warmth. I wanted the calm that I felt in her presence, inside her. "I need to get back to her."

"Of course."

I wrinkled my brow and tried to smooth it over with two fingers.

I still had decisions to make and questions to ask—but I didn't want any of my questions to take away any of my choices. "I can send money. I'll figure out what the right amount is for child support and make arrangements to start paying that, as well as back pay, as soon as I get back from my honeymoon."

"Weston, I don't need money. I didn't come after you for that."

"I know. But ignoring a financial responsibility is not something I'm going to do. As for the rest—being a father. It's not that easy. You say you want someone who's around, but my company is located all around the world. We have offices on three continents—so far. What if I had to move? Would leaving the country mean leaving all of this?" I gestured around the room.

She put a hand on her neck and circled her head as though her muscles were tense and bothering her.

"I don't know, Weston. I know I told you that I only wanted you in his life if you could be here. But logistically—legally—I can't really hold you to that." She sat forward, spreading her legs open in a V. "I want Sebastian to have a good relationship with you. I want him to know his father and not be disappointed and feel rejected. And whatever things keep you from him, even if they're legitimate things like work and life—they're going to have real consequences, and he's going to feel heartbroken. And I'm going to feel heartbroken because he does. But I can't force you to be anything that you are not willing or ready to be."

"Then you're willing to accept me as his father in his life, whatever I'm able to give?" It sounded terrible asking that, after what she just said. Because I didn't want to break her heart, and I didn't want to break this kid's heart either. Didn't want to destroy the foundation Callie had built for him out of love and stability.

Didn't want to recreate my own childhood in his.

But I had to know my options, had to know the choices before me.

"Yeah. He's a King." She didn't seem too happy with her answer though.

"Because you know that even if you don't tell him about me, if you let him grow up fatherless, he's going to notice that too. He's going to notice he doesn't have a dad like the other kids at school, whether he knows my name or not." I said that more for me than for her. Because it was time that I was responsible. Because I had to stop behaving like a child myself.

Because Elizabeth had made me want to be better.

"Do you wish I hadn't told you at all?" Callie asked.

I didn't answer because I was afraid of what I would say.

"I really have to go." I stood up, and she did as well, rushing to get my coat for me. At the door I turned to her again.

"I have a lot of things I want to say to you, but they are conflicting. Part of me is really angry at you, part of me really resents you, and I'm trying to come to grips with that. With all the things I've missed. I can't rewind time and be present for his first steps, first words. But another part of me is really grateful that you've done all this on your own, that you looked after our kid when I know it's probably been pretty hard, and with my reputation . . ." I trailed off. In her shoes, I likely wouldn't have told me, either.

She gave me a faint smile. "Maybe they can cancel each other out, and we can say we're even."

It didn't work that way, but I nodded, wishing that it did. "I have to go on my honeymoon. I have to tell my wife." Would Elizabeth even want to add a child to the mix? And would she want to do so badly enough to find a way to run her company remotely? My stomach sank again at the thought.

"I don't even know how she's going to react to all this."

"I understand. I'd like to meet her."

"I'd like to meet *him*," I countered.

"Okay. Next time."

My heart leapt at the idea.

And the only reason it was easy to walk away from this woman—practically a stranger—and her life, which was so foreign and unreal to me, was because I knew Elizabeth was waiting for me. And now more than ever, I needed her to give me roots.

CHAPTER
FIVE

Elizabeth

I TOLD CLARENCE everything.

He didn't pressure me to, and I didn't feel trapped or caught, like I had to confess, but I suddenly wanted to tell someone. Weston had Sabrina, and I didn't know how much he talked to her about our arrangement, but even if he didn't, he had Donovan. And Nate.

I had my mother, who smiled and patted me on the head and said things like "let's try a full-body cryotherapy treatment," and asked how good the sex was.

Clarence understood the arrangement for business reasons. He understood my motivations, why I wouldn't tell anyone, why I would choose someone like Weston King. And though I didn't talk to him about the gooey parts, or the naughty parts in much explicit detail, I could even tell him a little about that. That I'd fallen for Weston along the way.

That I was in love with Weston now.

"This marriage is real then?" he asked, when I'd finished telling him everything.

I tucked my feet underneath me and covered my knees with the robe. I was sitting on the couch, and Clarence had been a gentleman and sat far away on the armchair, careful to treat me like a friend and nothing more. Which was good, because I wouldn't have welcomed anything more. After falling for Weston, the thought of being hit on by another man left me cold.

"Yes," I said, because I was thinking positively. "I want this marriage to work. If it can—I don't even know if it's possible. We have obstacles between us that we haven't even explored because we never talked about us like a real thing."

"That's tough, I'm sure. But not impossible. Every relationship has obstacles. We did."

I peered over at him, jolted by the reminder of our past. What we had didn't compare to what Weston and I had. We'd been in high school. But come to think of it, the obstacles that broke us up hadn't been all that different from the situation I was in now. Clarence had been headed to college at Harvard and I had been going to Penn State, and though they weren't far from each other, we'd decided they were too far to make things work.

We'd been younger, of course. Inexperienced. Ready to move on and add more to our repertoire.

I hadn't really loved Clarence. Not in my bones and my toes and in the ends of my hair the way that I loved Weston.

But the similarities were still troublesome.

"I don't know if that makes me feel better or worse," I admitted.

"I'm sorry. I shouldn't have brought us into this." He leaned forward and put his palms on his thighs, staring at the back of his hands. "I guess I'm still wondering why you didn't ask *me* to marry you."

I took a deep breath in and let it out, thinking before I answered. "Honestly, Clarence, I thought it was too big of a favor to ask of anyone without having something to offer in exchange. I didn't think I had anything you would have been interested in bartering with."

He stared at me, pointedly. "You seriously thought you had nothing I'd want?"

My spine tingled as I realized he meant he would have been interested in me. It was sweet of him, and it surprised me to hear it, but I was over him. I'd grown out of him a long time ago.

"Too much time had passed," I said mindfully.

"Got it. That's fair." He chuckled to himself. "And it doesn't matter now because you found the right man for the job all around."

My entire body pulsed at the thought of Weston. "I hope so. But I mean, he's not even here right now."

"He's not," Clarence said standing up. "But if he wants to fight for you too—and Weston King's a smart man, he's going to want to fight for you—then he's not going to want to see me here when he gets back."

"I'm sure you're worrying over nothing." I started walking him to the door despite my words, just in case.

"I don't think so. I've seen the way he looks at you. Plus, I texted him about a month ago asking for your phone number, and he never replied. It all makes sense now." He buttoned up his coat, both of us standing by the door.

"You asked him for my number? And he didn't give it to you?" This was the first time I was hearing about it. "How does that make sense? It's not making sense to me."

"Obviously he didn't give it to me because he sees me as a threat. He wants you to be his alone, Bitsy."

I cringed at his use of the old nickname, and he corrected himself.

"Elizabeth. It suits you better anyway."

"I don't know if what you're saying is the only reason he wouldn't give you my number. Maybe he forgot. Maybe he's not good at answering texts." But I wanted to believe what he said. And I did believe Weston cared for me. "Anyway, thank you for telling me. And thank you for listening. And thank you for checking up on me."

"I'm glad I did. A little sorry you didn't choose me, but content to know you're happy." He smiled, and I knew he meant it. He was a good man.

"Next time I have to get married in order to get my inheritance, I'll definitely call you first," I teased.

I leaned in to hug him goodbye, and as I did I heard the digital beep of the lock, but before I could fully grasp what was happening, the door swung open.

And Weston was standing there, a deli bag under one arm and a tray with two coffee cups balanced in the opposite hand.

"Hi," I said, jumping away from Clarence. "You're back."

The door slammed shut behind Weston as his eyes carefully swung from one of us to the other. "I brought breakfast burritos and coffee. I hope you haven't eaten yet. I didn't realize we had a guest." His tone was flat and hard to decipher.

I took advantage of the fact that he didn't know that Clarence was in on the arrangement, and rushed to help, treating Weston like I would if we were keeping up our performance. It was a way to buffer the strange tension that had suddenly filled the air around all three of us.

"Let me help you. I'm starving. Thank God you brought food." I grabbed the bag and the coffees and set them on the desk while he attended to his coat.

"I was just in the area and decided to stop by. I didn't really get a chance to talk to Elizabeth at the wedding," Clarence said, trying to diffuse the friction.

"How thoughtful," Weston said coldly. He propped his coat on the back of the desk chair and turned to stare at my ex-boyfriend.

"I was on my way out," Clarence said. "Bye, Elizabeth."

I rushed to the door and opened it for him. I waved goodbye as he disappeared down the hall, then shut it again, but I didn't turn back to face my husband right away, worried he was, as Clarence had predicted, not happy about the circumstances he'd walked into. Honestly, if he *was* upset, I wanted to say fuck him. Because he'd left with no explanation today. And I was still pissed about that myself.

But I didn't want to fight anymore.

Taking a deep breath, I turned around, my back pressed to the hotel room door, and wrapped my arms around myself. "Thanks for getting food. I'm starving."

"You said that." He looked at me, a fist on his hips, examining my expression.

"Weston," I asked tentatively, still unable to get a read on him. "Are you mad?"

He tilted his head, his jaw working as he thought about it. "Mad? No. I'm not mad." He took four steps, even and bold until he was standing just in front of me, then placed his palms on the wood of the door next to my head, caging me in. "What I am is curious."

I swallowed, my pulse picking up. This close, I could see that his pupils were dilated, could see the flick of his gaze to my lips.

"What is it you're curious about?" I splayed my palms on the door beside me, as if that could hold me up. No other man could turn me on instantly like this. No other man could make me wet with just his presence. Make my body vibrate and hum and stir.

He brought one hand down and reached into the divide of my robe, sliding it up the front of my thigh.

"Are you mine?" he asked, his voice steady, and waited, as though everything that mattered between us rested upon the answer to this one question.

I couldn't answer fast enough, and yet the word came out choked, strangled by emotion. "Yes. I'm yours."

The strain in his face seemed to ease the slightest bit as his fingers found their way to the space between my legs. "Is this pussy mine?"

I nodded, spreading my legs farther apart to give him better access.

"Not good enough. I need to hear the words."

"This pussy is yours. It's only yours."

His fingers massaged my clit until I was gasping, then went down farther to where I was wet and aching. "This is mine? All this? Is it for me?"

As if I could have been wet from Clarence Sheridan.

"Every drop," I moaned, and he pushed two fingers deep inside me, twisting them so that I bucked against his hand.

He moved his free hand then to anchor me at my neck, and reached up to my lips with his thumb, rubbing roughly against them. "What about this mouth? This mouth is mine?"

"This is your mouth."

He leaned forward to tease my lips with his, brushing against me, sharing space and breath. It was hot. Hotter than actually kissing, somehow. With the way he was still finger fucking me below, claiming and taking ownership of me, I was going to come any minute.

Except this was only one-sided. I had my own stakes to claim.

I reached for him with my hand, fumbling until I found the thick bulge in his jeans. I covered it with my palm. "Is this . . . mine?"

He leaned his head back just slightly so he could look at my eyes, could gauge whether I was sincere or taunting him.

I might've been taunting him, only a few weeks ago I would have been. But now, I was so sincere.

"It's yours."

It was more of a relief than I realized it would be to hear him admit it. "Say it again," I whispered.

"It's only yours. I'm only hard for you. Only ever fucking hard for you."

I undid his jeans and stuck my hand under the band of his briefs. His cock felt solid and powerful in my hand. Like a staff. Like a scepter.

"Mine," I said, stroking him up and down.

His breaths grew thicker. "Whose ring's on your finger?"

"Yours," I answered, growing more confident in the game now. "Whose body am I touching?"

"Yours."

I pushed down his pants and briefs, freeing his cock, telling him what I wanted from him without words.

He moved both of his hands under my ass, and I threw my arms around his neck so he could lift me up, lining himself up at my hole. "Who are you?" he asked again, just before he thrust in.

"I'm Mrs. King. I'm your wife. I'm your home. I'm yours."

He drove into me, slowly enough that I felt every inch of him, but with full power, so that I was sure he was there, really there. With his eyes locked on mine he pulled out again, almost to the tip before pushing in again. And again. Each thrust purposeful and distinct. Each one defining his place inside me.

As he fucked me, he laid down the law.

"You're mine. I'm yours. I won't share you. And I don't expect you to share me. As long as this works, as long as you wear my ring, we are an *us*. We are a *we*. If that doesn't work for you, then you need to get off my cock right now because I'm not playing the pretend game with you anymore." He pushed my thighs up higher so that he hit me deeper, and the angle was just right, getting me in a spot that would have me exploding any second. "You got it?"

I couldn't speak, could only make a sort of mewling sound, high-pitched and breathy, which I knew he wouldn't accept, and he didn't.

"You got it?" he asked again, meaner, more intense.

"I got it. No games. We're together, and it's real."

"You better never doubt *this* is real," he said, glancing down at where we were joined. He slowed for a moment to watch as he worked himself in and out of me, then brought his gaze back to mine and increased his pace, driving me, riding me, urging me to release.

I fell over the other side like I'd been pushed. Tumbled into the bliss of my orgasm, growling out his name and digging my fingernails into his shoulders while he continued to stab into me at a frenetic pace. And in the bliss, the warmth, it wasn't just the explosion of endorphins. It was the words he'd said, the relief he'd settled in me. They didn't solve any of the problems between us, but they let me know where he stood. He wanted to fight for us too. He wanted us to be together, and if we both wanted that, then it was a good start.

There was hope.

I could feel him as he got close, as he slowed and stuttered, then suddenly he set me down and pulled out, and began stroking himself in front of me. With his free hand, he untied my robe and spread it open so my torso was bare in front of him. I watched, eyes wide, the same way that I had the night I'd spied on him in the living room. This time it was so much more fascinating because I was up close, so much harder because he was right in front of me, so much more arousing because I knew what he was about to do.

I felt another orgasm building in me, at the very idea, and reached down between my legs to touch myself, massaging my clit rapidly so that I could get there with him.

"Good girl," he praised. "Touch that pussy of mine. Come with me."

He got there first, freezing and then shooting strings of cum over my tits and belly. The sight was so hot. So fucking hot, I came immediately afterward.

Weston stood back, watching proudly as I shuddered through my second orgasm.

When I was finished, he pulled me into his arms, not seeming to care that I was sticky and covered with his cum. He kissed me slowly, languidly.

"Let's get you in the shower and clean you up," he said when he broke away.

I nodded and let him lead me to the bathroom, let him undress me and wash me and take care of me, because I was his. And even though he was mine, too, even though I was still a queen on my own—Weston King was the one who ruled me.

CHAPTER
SIX

Weston

I TOOK MY time washing Elizabeth. I thoroughly shampooed her hair, rinsing it out then washing it again just so I could have the luxury of listening to her moans while I massaged her scalp. I liked the freedom to keep touching her too, without any questions or explanations.

I'd have to give them soon enough, and I wasn't ready.

When I'd shown up at our room, brunch in hand, I'd been carrying the baggage of the morning. I was still thinking of Sebastian, and my primary focus was on how to make my life fit into his.

But when I walked in the door and saw Clarence holding my wife, everything changed.

It was a sharp reminder that I needed to think about things the other way around. My life with Elizabeth came first. My life with Elizabeth was the foundation. Before I could figure out how my kid fit into that, how to build him room and space, I had to be sure she and I were solid.

Were we?

How did I begin to find out?

It wasn't as simple as figuring out where we'd live or choosing whether to follow her to France. Even if I didn't have a son to think about, could I say that Elizabeth and I were ready for that? That was serious commitment, and while I was sure I knew enough about her to follow her anywhere, I wasn't sure she knew enough about me to just let me.

We had to draw up some plans. And I had to tell her things about me, show her everything before we laid down cement.

Except, we'd done it all backwards.

We'd already laid the cement. I'd already put a ring on her finger—twice.

And I didn't know where to go from here. Did we tear it all down? Start over from the ground up? Did we redesign and build on, like an addition? Did we piece floorboards and walls on top of what we'd already laid out and hope it was strong enough to bear whatever we put on top?

They were questions with hard answers, and it was easier to listen to Elizabeth's quiet murmurs as I gently took a washcloth to her most private areas than to confront the obstacles in our way.

But eventually the water got cold, and Elizabeth got clean. I turned off the shower and pulled her into the bathroom where I continued to dote on her, rubbing her down with a thick, plush towel.

She was dry and warm when she placed a hand over mine. "What now?" she asked, her eyes catching mine.

"We can heat up the burritos in the microwave. And the coffee. We should get some food in you."

"That's not what I meant," she said, her impatience showing in her tone.

"I know." I reluctantly let go of her so I could wrap a towel around my hips. "But let's eat. You're less cranky with food in you."

She scowled, but she couldn't argue because I wasn't wrong, and I had to fight the urge to pull her into the bedroom for another round of lovemaking because her pouty face was so adorable.

But as good as it would feel to be inside of her, I forced myself to look at the bigger picture. If I wanted to have the right to her body forever—and I did—sex was definitely not the answer.

Holy shit, I was a grown-up.

A grown-up with a kid. That thought never failed to punch me in the gut.

Since I was an adult now, apparently, I had to start acting it. I pulled my jeans back on and threw on a T-shirt, and as much as I wanted her to stay naked, I encouraged her to change into something non-accessible while I heated up our food. After we ate, I had things to tell her, hard things, and I didn't need to be distracted.

Ten minutes later, we were sitting on the couch in our suite, Elizabeth's legs thrown over mine while we ate our burritos.

"These are spicy," she said midway through her second bite. "Tasty, but spicy."

I raised an eyebrow. "Spicy? They have like zero kick. You're such a gringo."

"Weston!" she exclaimed. "You can't say things like that! It's not P.C.! Besides, you're almost as white as I am. Why isn't it bothering you?" She downed some coffee, chasing away the spice from her tongue.

"I don't know," I shrugged, taking another bite. I thought about it while I chewed. "It might be from all the chili peppers that Donovan had me eat as a pre-teen. He used to dare me, and I can never turn down a dare."

She laughed. "I didn't know that about you." She seemed to store that information away for later. "Do you like spicy foods a lot?"

"Yes, actually. The spicier the better. Why do you think I like you so much?" I cupped her neck with my free hand and ran my thumb along her jaw.

This was easy—touching and talking. This light banter was the way I'd always communicated with women, skirting any real issues, wading in shallow waters. It tended to get boring after a while, but whenever a girl beckoned me in deeper, I took off for another pond.

I didn't want to do that with Elizabeth. I wanted the courage to swim in her ocean, even if it meant getting all the way wet. Even if it meant I might drown.

She leaned into my palm, closing her eyes and savoring the contact. When she opened her eyes, she asked, "What's going on between us, Weston?"

Her voice was soft, her expression vulnerable, and I realized that she didn't get that I was already in deeper with her than I'd been with anyone ever before. She didn't know me, not like I wanted her to know me. And I didn't know her. I needed to learn her before I could trust her enough to walk blindly into the crashing waves. She needed to learn me. We needed time.

Fortunately, we had two weeks.

"Let's find out," I said, an idea forming.

She tilted her head, her gaze questioning.

This was good though. We couldn't really start again, but maybe we kind of could.

I dropped my hand from her neck and shifted to face her. "I meant everything I said to you, Elizabeth. In front of all those people, when I put that ring on your finger, I meant it. You changed my life, you changed who I am, and I want to be that man. For you. I want you to be my home. You are my home. But the truth of the matter is that while I was falling for you, I was trying my damnedest not to. And that meant that I was holding parts of me back, pieces of me that I never wanted you to see. Pieces of who I am that I never thought you would have to see because we weren't real."

I reached out to caress her cheek again. "We're real now. I don't want to lose that. But before we can move forward, I have to step back and show you things that we skipped. I've been trying to figure out the best way to do that, and I think maybe the best way is really the simplest. We just find out."

She took a deep breath in. "I really loved about ninety-nine percent of what you said there until the part where I didn't understand it. What do you mean by let's find out?"

"I mean," I dropped my hand from her face and leaned forward, excited by the idea. "Let's go on a honeymoon and take these two weeks to learn each other. Without the world around us to interfere. Without the mask of pretending. Without work. Without the internet. Without Darrell. Without having to put on the show. Without Donovan. Without Clarence."

"Without Sabrina," she interjected.

I grinned. "Without *any* of the things that distract us here in the real world." I couldn't help thinking that included Sebastian. And Mr.

and Mrs. Clemmons and the money I paid out in retribution for my father. "By the time the two weeks are over, I promise you will know everything about me. Hopefully by then we'll have all the information we need about each other to figure out what happens next."

She bit her lip in that funny way that she did sometimes and didn't say anything for a minute.

Which made me suddenly doubt everything I'd suggested. "Did that all sound stupid?"

"No, I think it sounds actually really nice. I like the idea of it very much."

I leaned into her and kissed her once, twice. Then longer, because I liked her taste and because she was mine and I could.

It felt too good, though. Too much of a relief, like I was getting away with something by not telling her everything up front. And that wasn't what I wanted. I wanted to take our time getting to know each other for real, but I had to tell her about Sebastian now.

Except when I tried to break away, she pulled me back to her. "We still get to have lots of sex too, right?" she asked, her mouth hovering near mine.

"That's definitely a given. Definitely, definitely a given." *She* kissed *me* this time. "We could start that right now, actually."

"Good, because I'm not hungry anymore for food."

Then I'd tell her about Sebastian tomorrow. Waiting one more day wouldn't hurt anything.

THE NEXT DAY started early. We had to be at the airport by seven, and I didn't get coffee until we were seated in the plane, which meant I wasn't fully caffeinated when I noticed the price on our tickets.

I'd come to terms with Elizabeth paying for the wedding. It was her farce, but also, her family was traditional and the bride's side took care of that expense.

I hadn't thought about the price of the honeymoon. That was usually the groom's responsibility, wasn't it? Elizabeth had made all the arrangements months ago. She'd been the one with the time while I was working, and the one with the money. Back then, when the whole thing had been fake, I hadn't had any qualms with her putting out for a honeymoon that was only meant to fool her cousin. Now I felt differently.

"It's our money," she said, rolling her eyes when I apologized for not contributing.

For some reason, that ruffled my feathers even more. "It's not *our* money. It's *your* money. You are the one with lots and lots of it."

"Right. So much that this plane flight is nothing. In fact, I would've booked a private jet except that I wanted our names on the roster so it would be easy for Darrell to track us down and know we went together." She fluffed her pillow and set it behind her back before fastening her seatbelt.

"That doesn't make me feel better."

My wife had a lot of money.

Fuck.

My wife had a shit-ton of money.

She turned her head to study my profile. "Is this going to be a problem for you? This was always who I was, you know. What's the difference now?"

I thought about it for a minute. Did it make me an inferior man because she had more dollars to her name than I did? Did it make me any less attracted to her? What did it really change?

"I guess the difference now is that I want to give you the world, but you can already buy it for yourself. So what do you need me for?"

She smiled in a way that made me feel like I was both charming and ridiculous. "Oh, Weston. I need you because the world you give me can't be bought."

She laced her hand in mine. It was the one with her rings sparkling proudly on her fourth finger. I thought about "my world," the world that I gave her. I loved the sentiment, but she didn't know everything about my world. She didn't realize there was an embarassing financial scandal and a secret child.

Maybe she'd want that world too, but in case she didn't, I wanted to keep her smiling at me the way she was now. That meant putting off telling her my secrets until the end of the honeymoon. She'd promised me she would stay offline and not worry about Dyson for two weeks. This was the same thing, wasn't it? It would let us enjoy each other without anything else pressing in on us. Let us get to know each other without the baggage.

I would tell her—I'd said that I would, and I meant it. Just not right away.

The flight was long. And boring. And did I mention long? Eleven hours. Even in first class it was too much time to spend in a plane. Particularly one we couldn't join the Mile-High Club in. The only benefits to the flight were that I could catch up on my sleep—something I'd been lacking the last two nights since I'd wed the beautiful lady sitting next to me, and it gave me enough time to properly explain the difference between the Marvel and DC universes, something Elizabeth was clearly confused about.

When we landed in Honolulu, we still had another short flight to Kauai, then finally we'd arrived. It was early evening by the time we rolled into the five-star resort Elizabeth had booked. We checked in and were told we had been given the honeymoon suite, and shown where to find the private bungalow on the beach. Our bed was covered with rose petals, and a bottle of champagne and chocolate-covered strawberries awaited us. Everything was top-notch and first rate. Truly, she'd planned a romantic and decadent honeymoon.

"This is amazing," I said to my bride, awed. I glanced down at the sheet of activities that she had reserved for us already: island hike, massage, windsailing.

Actually, this was a really, really *romantic* honeymoon.

My brow wrinkled. "Elizabeth, you booked this before we even started sleeping together. What exactly did you think would happen between us on this trip?"

"What do you mean?" she asked not meeting my eyes.

"I mean, these activities are incredibly romantic. A lover's trip to the waterfalls? A spa day for two?"

"It's basically just stuff for parties of two. A pretty hike. A massage. I thought we could both enjoy having the tension rubbed away. I don't understand what you're getting at."

"It's a *couples* massage. We're going to be naked in the same room together. I'm not sure that would have helped the tension." I stared at her, a shit-eating grin on my face.

"Just say what you're saying, Weston. Stop beating around the bush." She sighed at her own use of the word *bush*, knowing exactly where my mind would go.

I gave her a break about the bush remark, and instead attacked the real matter at hand. "Were you planning to make a move on me during this two-week trip?" Her cheeks reddened. "You were! You were planning to come on to me, Elizabeth Dyson!"

"I said no such thing. I admit nothing. Just . . . we were both going to be here, and all the pretend stuff was going to be over and if whatever happened happened, and you let loose, and I let loose, I don't know!"

She was turning adorably red, and I tossed down the activity sheet so I could grab both her hands, and pulled her close to me. With my mouth pressed near her temple, I told her the honest truth. "If I had somehow made it through those five months without jumping you, there is no way I would've made it one night in this room, sleeping in the bed next to you without having to fuck the living daylights out of you."

She hid her head in the crook of my neck. "You're just saying that."

"Swear to God. I would've jumped you so hard. You wouldn't have been able to walk when you got back to the mainland."

She looked up at me, her eyes blue and liquid like the ocean. "I worried about it sometimes. When I was still just *wanting* you all the time, and not sure what to do with it. I worried we would get here, and you would find some woman at the bar, that you would disappear for two weeks into someone else's bed."

I could feel her anxiety about it, how it once had plagued her, and I wished more than anything I could find a way to go back in time and let her know back then how much I'd wanted her too.

"And then sometimes," she continued, "I'd imagine I was the girl at the bar. I wondered what that would feel like, to be picked up by Weston King."

I leaned in to brush my nose against hers. I'd planned for us to order dinner to our room so that we could be alone, start getting to truly know each other, but suddenly I liked the idea of playing this game with her instead. It could be a much sexier way to accomplish the same thing. "Want to find out? Want to go be a girl at the bar, and I'll be Weston King?"

She perked up suddenly, leaning back, her eyes wide. "Can we do that? Oh, let's do that!"

She dropped my hands and started scurrying around the room, opening our suitcases, looking for things.

"You get ready first, and then go out to the main bar and order drinks and be you, and I'll get ready and then come down whenever. You be Weston and I'll be Elizabeth, and we'll meet each other for the first time. As though we never had this arrangement. As though there was never an inheritance on the line. We'll meet here in Hawaii, and we can learn all about each other and fall for each other. We can treat this whole trip like a do-over. Or not. You know. Whatever. What do you think?"

I tilted my head in amazement. It was like she'd read my mind, putting our real lives on hold while we dedicated this time to just us. In a way, this game gave me permission to put off the truth.

Was that an excuse?

Maybe. But she looked so excited and happy about the game, I was eager to cling to it, excuse or not.

So when she asked, "What is it?" I answered with a questioning lift of my brow.

"I still get to bang you, right?"

She giggled. "Everything is unscripted, but I'll tell you now that I am definitely going to put out."

"Then yeah. I like this plan a lot. I'll get changed and then game on."

"Oh!" She lifted her hand and wiggled her ring finger. "And I'm not taking this off. Everyone else gets to know I'm unavailable. You keep yours on too," she added sternly.

"Mine stays," I said, agreeing, wiggling my own wedding-banded finger. As far as I was concerned, I would be happy to never take it off.

Hopefully this honeymoon made her feel the same, and when I told her about my kid, she'd decide she wanted both of us.

CHAPTER
SEVEN

Elizabeth

I DISAPPEARED INTO the bathroom to get ready. I left my hair down, working with the humidity, letting it fall into its natural waves. I left my makeup soft and natural.

When I came back out, Weston had already left, so I could get into my dress without him seeing me. I chose a patterned maxi dress in mostly blues and browns with a halter top, two long slits up the sides, and a price tag that would make Weston flinch. A final look in the mirror told me I looked good, but casual. Perfect for an island resort. I finished the look with strappy beige sandals with a chunky heel, transferred everything to a small clutch purse, and made my way toward the center bar.

The weather was nice, the breeze perfect. It was fantastic to be outside without a coat after the cold winter months back in New York. Normally I would feel awkward walking alone at a place like this, but knowing I was going to meet someone made me walk with an assurance and confidence that I normally only felt in familiar circles. I caught a couple of men looking at me as I walked by, and normally their gazes would send me spiraling into awkwardness, but tonight they just lifted my head higher.

When I got to the entrance, though, I paused. I'd never been a woman who hung out in bars just waiting for a man to pick her up. I'd barely even gone with a girlfriend to this sort of venue. I felt much more comfortable in lounges and places that served only wine.

I scanned the crowd from afar and quickly spotted Weston alone at a high top. He already had a drink, some island concoction in a fun glass that was a specialty of the resort's bar, and was sipping it while glancing around, probably looking for me. He looked breathtaking as always, even wearing khakis and an untucked white button-down shirt. Part of me wanted to forget this entire ruse and just walk up to him directly, stick my hands up under his shirt and find the warm skin beneath.

He hadn't shaved since the wedding, and his face had gotten scruffy the last couple of days. He looked different this way. The rugged look somehow made me feel wild with him. As though I could be wild and rugged like that just by proxy. As though this wasn't a game at all, but a real chance at meeting the man of my dreams.

I knew what to do, what my mother would do, what all my friends would do. But I was still nervous. It was so out of character for me to go in there, beelining for the gorgeous, scruffy man alone in the bar. To stand next to him, take a sip of his island drink, and wait for him to offer to buy me one. This was how *he* picked up dates, not me.

Even though it was my idea, I hesitated.

He caught my eye from across the room, held it like a stranger who had just seen someone interesting. It was my cue to follow through, walk in, and introduce myself.

But just then drums began playing, and an overhead announcement said that the luau was now open for dinner.

I turned my head to the left where visitors were lining up to attend the feast. A bar wasn't my scene, but a luau was something that Elizabeth Dyson could get behind. And if Weston and I were here to meet each other on real terms, with our real characters—no more pretending, no more acting, no more playing a part—then I would never have walked into the bar where he was seated.

I looked back to him where he was now watching me with a curious expression, then I headed over to the luau and got in line.

Other people got in line behind me, and I knew it would take a while before Weston caught up—he had to pay for his drink and make his way over, so I entertained myself by playing a game of Candy Crush on my phone. I didn't look up again until I was at the cash register.

"One please," I told the hostess, a dark-skinned woman dressed in a Hawaiian print dress.

"What a coincidence," came a voice from behind me. "I'm by myself as well. I'll pay for both of us."

I lowered my phone as Weston handed over his credit card. Somehow he'd managed to sneak his way up through the line.

I looked him over from head to toe, taking him in as though I'd never seen him before. I remembered that even the first time I'd seen him he'd sent my pulse racing, and was surprised he could still do it with no more than a glimpse of those blue eyes. "Thank you," I said, hesitantly. "That's truly not necessary—"

"It's not necessary, but it's done." He flashed his dimple as he took back his credit card and put it in his wallet, then stuffed it in his back pocket. "It's my good deed for the day."

"Well, I can't argue with that."

Another hostess led us through an arbor where luau employees were waiting with fresh leis. A stout island man placed one around the neck of the woman in front of us, then turned to grab another one and looked in my direction.

"Let me," Weston said, reaching to take it from the man's hands. He then came around in front of me and dropped the fresh chain of flowers around my neck. "You've been lei-d," he said, waggling his eyebrows.

I couldn't help but grin. He really was charming. If I'd met him just like this, I would've been mesmerized.

I *was* mesmerized.

"Allow me the same honor." I grabbed another one from the man, who smiled at us, and placed it around Weston's neck. "You look good freshly lei-d."

"I can't possibly look as good as you. Getting lei-d suits you."

I rolled my eyes, but I was still smiling.

Next we were ushered in front of a beautiful tropical floral spot where a photographer was waiting to take our picture.

"Oh, we're not together," I said, because we weren't playing a part anymore, but in some way, we *were*. An alternate timeline part. As though we'd met here instead of months ago, and our matching rings were mere coincidence.

"The ticket was purchased together," the photographer's assistant said, confused.

I couldn't help the laugh that escaped me at how silly we were being, but Weston kept it up, looking at me and shrugging. "What's the point of a picture alone? Seems rather boring to me. I don't mind if you don't."

"I suppose if you put it that way."

He stood next to me and put his hand on my waist in a way that could have been considered overly friendly from someone I'd just met, or casual for someone I'd just married. The photographer said he would give us a countdown. On three I turned to glance at Weston and found him already looking at me, his eyes blue and clear, as though no secrets hid behind them.

The lightbulb flashed, and without having seen the proof, Weston said, "I'll buy two."

He arranged for the pictures to be sent to our room before leading us down a path to yet another host who offered to seat us.

"Two?" the gentleman asked.

I turned to Weston. "You know, just because you paid for me tonight doesn't mean that I feel obligated to be your date."

"I can respect that," he said, a smile playing on his lips.

"But you lei-d me. And I take that seriously. So now I think you're kind of stuck with me for the evening."

The host tried not to laugh.

Weston's smirk bloomed into a full dimpled grin. "As a gentleman, I feel as though you're my responsibility now. I am not the kind of guy to lei and run. I definitely have to have dinner with the girl afterwards."

I turned back to our host. "Yes. Two."

We followed him side by side past several long banquet tables already filled with people crammed in and chatting, getting to know those around them. My hand brushed against Weston's, and I felt the urge to lace my fingers through his. I wondered if he felt the same pull, that magnetic tug drawing us to always face the same way, forcing us together.

I liked this. I'd missed this—the part of a budding new relationship where you wanted to touch but didn't know if it was too forward. From the very first minute that I'd wanted him, I'd been forced to touch him, whether he wanted it or not. Whether he'd wanted *me* or not. I got what he meant about having skipped so many things. We'd skipped the uncertainty part.

It was erotic, the wonder. When would he touch me? When would our fingers finally meet? Would our whole bodies feel shock from the spark of electricity?

The hostess sat us together at the end of a long bench. I scooted in first, with Weston on the end, and I caught him checking out my bare thigh as my skirt rode up when I sat down. Normally I'd appreciate my husband checking me out like that, but in this game we were playing, I pretended to be a little shocked.

"You can keep your eyes above the table," I scolded him. "Thank you very much."

"I could. Maybe I'll even try." He scooted in next to me and we made stupid small talk about the blue-tinted rolls, childish banter that edged toward sexual innuendo and nearly sent me into a fit of giggles when he asked me to butter his blue ball of bread.

When there was a lull, the couple across from us asked how long we'd been together.

"We're not," Weston said, taking my cue from what I'd told the host earlier.

The woman frowned, her brows meeting above her nose. "But you're both wearing wedding rings. Aren't you . . . ?"

"Are we? I'm married, obviously. But we just met tonight. Are you married?" I asked Weston, improvising. Not caring what other people thought about us wasn't necessarily an Elizabeth thing, but I was having too much fun to break the scene.

"I guess I am," he said looking down at his ring finger. "Hey, that's another thing we have in common."

"This really is turning into kismet, meeting you here this way."

The woman across from me looked to her date, then back at us, even more confused than she'd been just a moment before. "I don't understand. Where's your husband?"

I sat forward, leaning across the table and whispered conspiratorially. "I'd rather not discuss it, if you don't mind. I came here to specifically *not* think about my husband, if you get my drift."

"Me too!" Weston exclaimed. "Or not think about my wife, I mean. I don't have a husband. It's definitely a wife."

"So much in common." I nodded winking at my husband/not husband.

"But," the woman started to say again, "the waiter mentioned when he brought your drinks that he was billing them to the honeymoon suite."

"Honey," her date said, "leave them alone. You don't want to pry into those open-relationship things. This generation does things much differently than ours."

I had to stuff a blue ball of bread into my mouth so I didn't dissolve into another fit of laughter.

For the rest of the dinner, Weston and I kept our conversation light, mostly joking about superficial things—commentary on the entertainment and the people sitting around us. The show broke for us to fill our plates with various island recipes—shellfish, salads, pork from the pig that had slow-roasted all day in a pit in the ground, poke, and the juiciest fruits I'd ever tasted.

Here we began to really talk, began to learn new details about each other.

"You have to try the lobster, it's so fresh it doesn't even need butter." Weston held out a piece of the meat he'd broken from a claw on his own plate.

I backed away. "I can't. I'm sure it's delicious, but I'm allergic."

"You are? That is the saddest thing I've ever heard."

"To all shellfish. I break out in the wickedest rash all over."

His mouth actually gaped. "How did I not know—?" he caught himself with a shake of his head. "How do you go on living?"

"Since I haven't had any shellfish for years and don't remember how it tastes, I thought I was living just fine. But maybe I need to reevaluate my misery levels."

"It's not fair. Not fair, I'm telling you." He shook his head again, then swallowed the piece of lobster himself. He wore an expression that said the taste was divine, but he kindly said, "It's so disgusting. You're not missing anything at all. Worst thing ever."

"I'm sure it tastes better than the poi."

"Burnt tapioca tastes better than the poi. Old caviar tastes better than the poi. Soy yogurt tastes better than the poi." Then he had to let me feed him the poi, the way the true Islanders did it, from their fingers, because he was very smugly making fun of my own soy yogurt habit.

He licked the mushy substance from each of my fingers until there wasn't a trace left, and I could feel each swipe of his tongue along my skin as though he were licking the full of my pussy, each heated trace notching up my desire.

"I take it back," he said when my fingers were clean, his hand still wrapped around mine. "Poi tastes pretty damn good."

Midway through dinner, I spotted Weston looking around the crowd.

"Are you checking out other women while you're on a sort-of date with me?"

"No," he laughed. "I was making a work observation. I'm off the clock, but it gets in your blood. Becomes a habit."

I set down my fork and patted at my mouth with my napkin. "Now I must hear this. What was the observation, and how does it get into your blood?" In all the months that Weston had taught me about business, he'd rarely put the spotlight on his own work. I knew he knew his job inside and out, but I'd never seen him in action.

"I was observing that nearly everyone at the luau is an adult. Likely because this is an adult-friendly resort. But the dinner still didn't sell out, so I was thinking that if they marketed this as adults only, or couples only, they might get better bang for their buck. It would seem more attractive, more exclusive. Might even be able to raise their prices a little, charge extra for the frou-frou drinks. Right now it's just a luau, same as everywhere else on the island. It wouldn't really change their clientele, but it would seem cooler."

"Oh. I see. That's a very astute observation." I rubbed my lips together as I considered everything that I knew about Weston and everything that I could glean from him just during tonight's interaction. "So you are an idea man?"

"I wouldn't say that. I'm all about the magic tricks. I like the sleight of hand." He took the plastic flower that was on the center of the table as decoration and held it in the air with his left hand. Then after a bit of flash and choreography, suddenly it had disappeared. Then—presto! He was pulling it from behind my ear.

"How the fuck did you do that? Do not tell me that that gets you girls?" Though I knew for certain it got him girls. Because it was totally dorky, but he was also totally hot. "Do it again."

"I'm not going to do it again. You're just trying to find out how I did it. And yes, it has totally gotten me girls." He stuck the flower behind my ear for real this time, perching it against my hair. "It looks nice there."

I held his gaze then flicked my eyes to his lips, wanting to kiss him, knowing it was too early, not wanting to break the spell. "You think of marketing like magic?"

"Yeah. It's telling people one thing while you're doing something else. It's just showing them what you want them to see." I nodded, encouraging him to go on.

"When Donovan—my good friend—came to me with the idea of starting an advertising company, he wanted me to be the salesman, the one who pitched to clients, sold the campaigns and the creative. He always teased me, said I had the face for it. The personality. But I wasn't really interested in that. I liked the idea of advertising, but I wanted to be the magic. The guy behind the scenes, planning the tricks. Scheming. So I agreed to come on, but only if we found another face."

I knew that there were five people in total running Reach, Inc., but I wasn't quite clear on everyone's roles within it. I used the opportunity to play dumb and hear the story of the company's formation. "Then you found another face?"

"Yeah. Donovan had another friend, Nate Sinclair. He was an art dealer, so he knew creative. A very good salesman. We didn't quite have the capital to go into it as large as we wanted to—as large as *Donovan* wanted to, so we got a couple of other guys. Even then, Donovan and I came with the most cash." Weston took a breath, then corrected himself. "Donovan came with the most cash. He loaned me a significant portion to come in as his partner fifty-fifty; the other three have smaller shares in the company."

And that was something I hadn't known. Something that didn't fully make sense, considering what I'd learned about Weston King and the amount he should be worth. "You borrowed money from Donovan to invest in Reach?"

He looked down at his plate and nodded. He swallowed—I could see the bob of his Adam's apple, even though he hadn't taken a bite of anything. It bothered him, this transaction that he had made with his friend. It bothered him to tell me.

"I think it's awesome that you have someone you feel comfortable enough with to have an arrangement like that," I said, and it was true. I'd never had to borrow money from anyone in my life, but there had been several times that I'd wanted to help out friends, and no one had ever been comfortable enough to ask me. It's a strange dynamic being the one with the money, maybe as strange as being the one without.

"That's a great way to look at it," Weston said, finally looking at me. "He knew I was good for it, anyway. I do have a trust fund I haven't touched that could more than pay him back if I ever wanted to dig into it."

I sat quietly, in case he wanted to tell me more, but when he didn't, I let it go, knowing he would tell me when he was ready. This was only day one in our tropical paradise, day one of getting to know each other, and he'd already confessed something that was obviously difficult for him.

We already had one less wall between us. We were already so much closer.

The second round of entertainment began then, and talk gave way to singing along to "Tiny Bubbles" and learning familiar Hawaiian phrases. When the emcee asked for a volunteer to come up to learn how to hula, I joked about taking the stage.

"You wouldn't do it. You're too classy for that."

I wasn't sure if he was challenging me or if he really thought that I was too much of a prude, too serious to have any fun.

Either way, it pushed me to raise my hand.

"The redhead in the back," the emcee said, calling on me. I really had given him no choice since I was practically standing and waving my arm like I was on a sinking ship trying to hail a lifeboat.

"No way," Weston said with a smile as I smugly took to the stage.

A couple of assistant dancers led me behind the backdrop while the main singer sang another traditional Hawaiian song. I was dressed in a coconut bra over my maxi dress, and a hula skirt—a genuine one, not one of those plastic things that came from a costume store—was put on over my head and pulled down to my waist. When the song was over, I was led back on stage and in front of everyone, I was taught the simple movements of a basic hula love story.

It was easy enough to catch on to, for me anyway. I'd taken ballet for so long that I was good at picking up new choreography. Isolating my hip muscles was a bit of a challenge, but when I looked into the audience and saw the expression on Weston's face, saw him hypnotized and practically drooling, I was more determined to get it right. For him.

Afterward I was congratulated with applause and praised by the artists. I was given both the coconut bra and the skirt to keep as a prize for volunteering.

Weston met me at the side of the stage with my purse. He took the bag that contained my hula outfit for me and gestured to a pathway that led away from the dinner crowd.

"Do you mind? I don't think any of the entertainment can top what I've just seen."

That damn dimple again. Made my stomach do the flip-flop. Even if I had just met him tonight, yeah, I would let this stranger lead me away. Stupid, maybe. Crazy, definitely.

"I don't mind," I said.

We started walking, our hands dangling near each other again, sometimes brushing so slightly I wondered if it was just the breeze.

"You looked good up there," he said, his face tilted toward me.

"No I didn't. It was silly."

"You did. You, really did. Your hips can really move."

We followed the path around the garden toward the sound of the ocean waves. Just around some larger bushes was a hidden nook where a group of palm trees were surrounded by thick green bushes with bright tropical flowers.

"Years of ballet had you fooled."

"You took ballet?"

"All my life."

"That explains so much," he mumbled to himself. More loudly, he said, "You seem flexible."

He'd been thinking about some of the ways he'd fucked me, I could see it on his face. We had done some rather advanced positions in terms of bending and twisting.

I stopped and turned to face him. "I've kept my body up through yoga. But I felt off, doing the hula. I was distracted. They tied the bra so loose, I kept worrying it was going to fall down. Did you notice I kept pulling on the strap?" I leaned back on the tree behind me, gazing up at him.

"I didn't notice. I was too busy wondering what was under your skirt." He put his hand on the tree behind me, dropped the bag on the ground at my feet, and took a step closer, erasing the space between us.

My breath sped up at his proximity. I squinted my eyes up at him. "Would you really say that to a girl you just met?"

"I just said it, didn't I?" His eyes flicked to my lips.

I glanced around, to be sure we were alone, then grabbed the hem of my skirt and pulled it up toward my waist. "Go ahead and find out."

"Would you really say that to someone you just met?" he teased.

"Do you care?"

He lifted my skirt the last few inches to discover that I hadn't worn panties.

"What a pleasant surprise." He rubbed two fingers along the bare skin of my pussy. "I can't believe you went out alone like this. So brave. To think that this treasure could have gone un-worshipped."

"I guess it's a really good thing, then, that we met."

"I'm not going to argue with that." He removed his hand from my pussy and brought it to my lips. "Open." I opened. "Suck." He slipped two fingers inside. "You have a really pretty mouth. Big, full, gorgeous lips," he said, his voice low and raspy, as I sucked on him until his fingers felt as wet as I did down below.

He returned his hand to the space between my thighs, parting me with his fingers. "You're beautiful here too. I can tell just by touching. Soft and wet and plump." He squeezed my clit with an expert amount of pressure, and I closed my eyes, surrendering to him.

His head lowered, and I could feel his mouth next to my ear, hear his breathing get heavier as my own breaths became more rapid. I clutched onto him as the tension within me began to build. He slid one finger lower, inside my eager body.

"You're so wet. And snug." He pulled out and thrust back in. Added another finger. My body bowed, begging for more. "Do you hear the rush of the ocean?" He paused, waiting for an answer. "Do you?"

I had to concentrate really hard to be aware of anything outside of Weston and my body and what he was currently doing to me, but somewhere nearby behind us, the ocean roared. "Yes. I hear it."

"The way the waves come in fast and sudden and overpowering, crashing on the sand, then pull out, taking everything in their wake with them? That's how it's going to be when I fuck you."

Holy shit.

I moaned, my hips bucking into his hand, greedy for more of his words and this feeling. Not sure how much I could take.

"Shh. It's okay. Keep listening. Surrender to that sound." He put his free hand around my waist to hold me up. "I'm going to fuck you fast like that ocean. Big like those waves. I'm going to overpower you. I'm going to make you come, make you crash. I'm going to take everything you give me and steal it away with me."

My pussy rippled around his fingers, which were stroking in and out of me, his dirty promises driving me crazy, partly because I knew he was good for them. Partly because I truly believed he *would* talk to me like this if we were indeed strangers, and that was so deliriously sexy.

But his words stoked something deeper, something I believed was probably also true. He really did want to win me over, really wanted to take everything I had to give. Really did want to steal it away with him.

Forever?

God, I hoped so.

"You know it, don't you?" he asked. "You can feel how it's going to be between us."

"Yes, yes. Please." I needed to release. I was so close, so desperate.

"Look at me when you come." He massaged my clit in small, tight circles with the pad of his thumb while he pushed his fingers in and out in a steady, unhurried rhythm.

I locked my eyes onto his, and everything tightened in my core. I let out a jagged cry as the wave crashed through me, my hips pumping onto his hand, mindless about our location and the possibility that someone could come upon us at any moment. His own gaze was feral and fiercely triumphant, and if I hadn't already been panting and breathless, that look alone would have stolen the air from my lungs.

I wanted to say something, when I could find the words, when I could speak again, but before either of those things happened, Weston fell to his knees and threw one of my legs over his shoulder so quickly I had to grab onto the tree for balance.

"Oh my God, I can't," I said as his tongue lapped at my clit. I was too sensitive. Too raw.

But I was also wrong. The need was already winding again, faster and tighter than before. He circled my rim with his finger as he sucked greedily at my tender, swollen nub, teasing me. Taunting me. When he licked down my slit and speared me with his tongue, I was lost. I came a second time, gasping and weeping, my orgasm tearing through me violently as he fucked me like this—with his mouth and his fingers and his tongue.

I was weak and boneless as he lowered my leg from his shoulder back to the ground. He kissed my upper thigh and then my belly, then tugged my dress free from where it was gathered between my back and the tree trunk. When he stood again, his face was flushed, his eyes dark. He pressed in close, but not so close that I could feel the erection that he surely had by now or felt obligated to kiss him.

He was a gentlemanly player, then. A decent guy. It was nice to learn that about him.

I dug into my purse and pulled out my room key and handed it to him, even though he had one of his own. "You're an overachiever. One orgasm would have earned you this."

"Maybe I want more than just the key to your room."

A warm rush of pleasure shot through me almost like an aftershock from my orgasms, just at the idea of this man trying to win my heart—a heart he already owned.

I wrapped my fingers in his shirt and held on, suddenly afraid he wasn't really real, that he'd disappear if I didn't touch him. "Should I be worried about how good you are at this?" I wasn't sure if I was asking as a woman he'd just met or as a woman he'd just married.

With a sigh, he settled his hands on my hips and leaned his forehead on mine. "I used to worry about that sometimes," he confessed. "But what's the story of Cinderella and the prince? Didn't he put the slipper on every woman's foot in the kingdom before he found the one who fit the shoe?"

I burst into laughter. "Are you using a children's fairy tale to explain your expertise at oral sex?"

He smiled—that full-dimple, little boy mischievous grin. "If you buy it, I am."

I laughed again. "I'm not buying it."

"Okay, okay. How about this—I'm good at giving this. Giving sex. Giving my body. I'm not so good at giving my time or my thoughts or my energy. My heart. I've given my body to a lot of women, but I want to give you more than that. If you'll take it. But you have to take my body, too—it's part of the package."

I sobered. He'd definitely answered the question for the woman he'd married, and it was exactly what I needed to hear.

And now I wanted to get back to the game.

"Take me to my room?" I asked.

He nodded then slipped his hand into mine and led me on the path toward our bungalow.

"Oh, by the way, I'm Weston," he said. "Weston King."

Oh yeah. We hadn't ever introduced ourselves formally.

"Nice to meet you, Weston. I'm Elizabeth."

CHAPTER EIGHT

Weston

I SAT IN the wicker chair next to the bed watching her sleep, imagining her reaction when I finally told her about Sebastian. Would she be angry? Would she be thrilled? Would she be as excited and curious about this little person as I was?

I still worried about telling her, but after our first night on the island, when I'd opened up to her about Donovan and the money he loaned me to start Reach, I felt less concerned about it. She'd accepted that confession with no judgment, and it had been freeing to share that baggage with her.

I was starting to get excited with the idea of telling her about my son. I needed someone to talk to about this incredible new discovery in my life and she was the only person I wanted to tell.

But we were playing our game. It was only our second day in Hawaii, the sun was just peeking out over the ocean horizon, and our agenda included nothing but hiking through the tropical island wilderness. We were still practically strangers in this version of us. It wasn't time to bring in other players yet.

A knock startled me, even though I was expecting our breakfast order. I threw on last night's pants and hurried to the door, signing for the meal and taking over the cart in just a few short minutes.

"Thank God, you ordered breakfast," Elizabeth said as I wheeled the cart toward the bed. She sat up, stretching, the sheet falling to her waist as she covered her mouth to yawn.

I freely ogled her bare breasts as I pulled the cart's leaf out and extended it over her. Her nipples perked from my attention. "Island fruit and yogurt," I said lifting the cover off her dish.

"Exactly what I would've ordered." She looked pleased that I knew her tastes, and I resisted the urge to point out that she'd infiltrated my every waking thought, that knowing what she'd want to eat had become as natural to me as knowing what I wanted.

I grabbed my plate of eggs and bacon and moved around the other side of the bed, hopping back in and scooting up next to her. Before I dug into my food, I set my plate on my lap and turned to her, wrapping my hand around her neck to pull her mouth toward mine. When I kissed her, she tasted like the pineapple she'd already snuck into her mouth, sweet and tangy. I kissed her again. "How did you sleep?"

"Really well. I think I sleep better with a body next to me. It's a good thing I met you last night." She grinned.

"I had a lot of fun," I admitted.

"If I were really a stranger, would I still be here?" she asked, her eyes narrowing suspiciously.

I let go of her neck and sat back against the wall. "You are here, aren't you?" I said, teasing.

She took a sip of her coffee then planted her eyes on me. "We're still playing, right? I like this—this just-meeting-you game. But I really do want to know if it's plausible that a girl would still be in your bed the next morning."

"Sure, I'm up for it. And yes, many women have been here the next morning. Which is usually when I say goodbye. I would not have said goodbye to you."

"What would you have done with me? Tried to convince me to stay in this bed all day?" She fluttered her eyelashes as though getting into the character she thought I wanted her to be.

"Well, yes. Probably. And if you insisted that we climb up to Hanaka-pi'ai Valley to see the falls instead, I'd be right behind you, but I would try to convince you not to wear any panties for the adventure."

"Then this is a legitimate scenario. Right on."

"Does that mean *you're* planning to go without panties?" God, this woman was perfect.

She didn't answer, but she grinned before turning back to her meal. I was glad she did, that she removed her focus from me, because I was feeling things for her at that moment, deep fuzzy feelings that likely showed on my face. And this level of adoration was definitely too soon if we were playing strangers.

But by the last day of our trip, there wouldn't be any games left to hide behind. And I could only hope we were still looking at each other with adoration then.

AN HOUR LATER, we were on the bus headed to Ke'e Beach, backpacks on our laps stuffed with towels, a change of clothes, and plenty of water and snacks for the hike.

"We're taking the shuttle instead of driving," she explained as she rummaged through her own backpack, "because parking is tremendously hard to find. Even at this time of morning." She pulled out a bottle of sunscreen and handed it to me. SPF 60. "Would you mind?"

She unbuttoned her denim shirt so that I could apply the lotion generously to her skin. She had a bikini top underneath, but the shirt was long-sleeved and her hair was knotted up high on her head to fit under a wide-brimmed sun hat. I put some sunscreen in my hand and then began working it into her creamy white skin, and it occurred to me she wasn't really cut out for the tropical sun.

"Tell me something. Why did you choose a vacation in the tropics? I'm guessing you burn easily." I *knew* she burned easily from the one time she'd forgotten sunscreen when we'd ended up at a Labor Day event earlier in the summer. But we were playing that game, the game where we didn't know things about each other, and I really *didn't* know why she'd chosen Hawaii. "Why not a vacation somewhere in Europe?"

"Well, it's December, and I knew I'd be tired of the cold when I planned it." She was facing the window but I could see her skin pinking up at her neck and collarbone as though she was embarrassed.

That meant there was more to the story. "But there are probably other warm places that don't require putting your skin at risk." I moved my hands down her torso, enjoying the goosebumps that sprouted at my touch.

She shrugged with one shoulder. "I was hoping to meet someone," she said cautiously. "There are only so many romantics spots. Paris was out of the question." She turned and looked at me, daring me to ask her why she wouldn't go to France—I wasn't touching that with a ten-foot pole. I wasn't ready to talk about the future, how she was planning to live there. When I didn't say anything, she went on. "And I figured resorts where I could show a lot of skin were my best bet. You know. In attracting a member of the opposite sex."

Her words registered. "This was about seducing me again," I said with a laugh. "You thought showing more skin, flaunting yourself in a bikini was the way to seduce me?" God, if she'd only known how turned on I'd been even when she was fully covered in those pantsuits.

She turned her head toward mine, her face fully red now. "Shut up," she giggled. "You're breaking character."

I kissed her, sweeping my tongue into her mouth with luscious deep strokes. I would've told her I loved her, it was on the tip of my tongue, natural the way that it wanted to spill out, but after she'd just admonished me for not playing by the rules, I felt I had to keep it inside. I hoped my kiss said it instead, told her all the ways I wanted her, eased every one of those anxieties about winning my heart.

It was hers.

Somehow, after a fair amount of making out, I managed to cover her with enough sunscreen to satisfy her by the time we arrived at the end of the road, quite literally. When we climbed off the bus, I saw that the road didn't go any farther from this point on the north side of the island, and as Elizabeth had warned, the sides of the road were full of parked cars, even at this time of morning. It wasn't even eight o'clock yet.

"See why we took the bus?" she asked. "Come on. The trail's this way." I followed her—as well as the entire crowd from the bus—to the trailhead, swinging my backpack onto my shoulders as I walked. I was looking out at the ocean, at the blue mixing with the pink in the sky, admiring the swirl of colors when she shrieked in front of me.

"What's going on?" I asked as she jumped into my arms.

"It's attacking me!"

I looked down to where she pointed. There was a brightly colored rooster on the path in front of us, crowing proudly as though guarding the way. I tried, and failed, to swallow a roar of laughter. "It's a chicken. You're scared of the chicken?"

"It's feral! It's coming right for me!" She clutched onto me tighter.

"It's actually just . . . standing there. But don't worry, I'll save you." I put a hand out in front of me, as though I meant to ward it off. Then, with her still clutching my side, I made a generous sidestep around it. "That was close," I teased.

Without letting go of my arm, she craned her head to watch the bird behind us. "He's still looking at me."

"He has an eye on each side of his head. He's looking at everything." I shook my head as I pulled her along the trail. "Brave, fearless woman wants to tackle Dyson Media. Afraid of a little chicken."

She pushed me, letting go. We were far enough away from the bird for her to seem less wary, even though she kept looking back after him. "You didn't see him when I did," she said defensively. "He attacked me."

"Whatever you say." I kept smiling, following after her cute ass, tight and curvy in her jean shorts. It was an easy target, something I wanted to follow, and I had to remind myself to look out at the stunning views every now and then along the two-mile walk to Hanakapi'ai Beach. We didn't talk much on this part of the route, walking single file, mostly because there were so many other people headed up with us. So much for getting a chance to talk to her alone.

Once when we stopped to take a break and drink some water, she seemed to notice my fretting as I watched a group of Boy Scouts pass us by.

"What's wrong?" she asked, passing the water bottle.

I took a swallow before I answered. "Nothing. I just didn't expect there to be so many people up here."

"It's a really popular trail. There will be less people climbing all the way into the falls."

So I'd have time to talk to her then. I could wait.

We made it to the beach in about forty-five minutes. The climb hadn't been too strenuous as we'd walked along the cliff walls that bordered the ocean. Hanakapi'ai Beach, however, surprisingly didn't have any sand, though the inlet was breathtaking. Like an undiscovered cove, untouched by modern vehicles.

"There's sand in the summer months," Elizabeth explained. "In the winter the tides come in too far."

"You sure did a lot of research. I'm impressed."

"I like to learn about the adventures I'm tackling," she said confidently. I studied her, recognizing the student inside. She did thirst for knowledge, eagerly wanting to know everything about the ventures she meant to tackle. I'd discovered that as I'd taught her business over the last several months. She was a quick study too, and I wondered how much she actually knew about me that I didn't realize she knew. How many secrets I was holding that she'd already uncovered on her own, simply by spending time with me.

It didn't make me feel as uncomfortable as I thought it would to be known the way I suspected she might know me.

And that did freak me out.

"Ready to head to the falls?" she asked.

I wanted to tell her that I would follow her anywhere. But I still wasn't sure it was true. Wasn't sure I would follow her to France. Wasn't sure that I *could*. So I just said, "Lead the way."

Elizabeth had been right—there were fewer people on the trail inland to the falls. It was hard to even call it a trail in some places. The path was so grown over and untrodden that there were several times I wasn't even sure that we were actually on the designated trail. It was nice to be alone, but the difficulty of the hike made conversation impossible. It took all our concentration to figure out where we were going and worry about not sliding through mud. And even on the parts that were easy, we didn't talk. We were too busy taking in the sights. Beautiful, strange flora and fauna I'd never seen before surrounded us. Breathtaking scenery that was lush and green and so patently different from the environment in which I lived, it was hard to believe that these plants were from the same planet that I was, let alone the same country.

It was another two miles from the beach to the falls, and I sensed we were getting near, only to take another break. Elizabeth climbed on top of a big boulder just off the path. When I took off my backpack and set it at my feet and bent down to get the water bottle out of it, I had to look up to meet her eyes. So perfect and beautiful and stunning. She'd taken the denim shirt off and stuffed it into her backpack, and beads of sweat rolled down her pale décolletage, gathering at her cleavage. I wanted to climb up the rock and lick every drop of sweat off of her, peel off her jean shorts, and find out if she was wearing a bikini bottom. Wanted to take her and claim her in this jungle.

I stood and handed her the water bottle, just to get closer to her.

She took it, her fingers brushing mine. "There is another reason I chose Hawaii," she said.

"Tell me."

"I told you I'd never been. But that's not entirely true. I came once with my mother when I was thirteen years old. She'd been dating this guy for a while—Victor—and it was getting kind of serious. Like maybe Mom was going to make a go at another marriage. At least, it was serious enough to try to blend her little family with him. He suggested we all go on a trip together to get to know each other, and he took us to Kauai. It was supposed to be a month-long getaway for the summer. He had a condo here and came every year."

She handed the water bottle back to me and I took it, too intrigued by her story to take a sip for myself.

"I was really excited. My father had promised to take me to Hawaii, I don't know, seventy-billion times, and he never came through. That was my dad, though. Lots of broken promises. So when Victor suggested we go, it felt like maybe he was going to be a brand-new dad. Like, a chance to do it all over. I mean, I was excited about seeing the island too. I was really into the idea of waterfalls, and my mom used to like that Fantasy Island show. We watched it together all the time. I wanted to go to a luau. It was all so exotic and just really in my zone at the time."

I'd never been that into the tropical islands myself, but my sister had gone through a phase, so I could picture what she talked about. I took a swig from the bottle. "Go on."

"Anyway. We were here one night. And I'd come out looking for my mother wearing just my T-shirt and underwear. I don't know what exactly happened, but the next day my mother packed us up early in the morning and put us on a flight back to the mainland. She said that Victor had looked at me in a lewd way. She'd seen him staring at me in my underwear, and she'd recognized his lustful look. And she wasn't going to stand for it. She'd argued with him. I guess. I didn't hear this, she just told me about it later. He didn't deny anything. And Mom decided there was no coming back from that. Once a guy looked at your daughter lustfully, he was never going to get over that. She ended their whole relationship."

She brought her knees to her chest and hugged them in tight. "And the thing is—I was mad at her. I was mad because she took me away from Hawaii when I'd been looking forward to the trip. And I was really mad that she denied me a chance at having another father. For a long time I really resented her for it. It took me several years before I understood that she'd actually made a sacrifice for me. She'd given up a guy that she'd maybe really loved, because she loved me more."

"Well. Are you okay?" The thought of a guy even looking at Elizabeth the wrong way made my primal male brain react. I wanted to cut someone's throat. Wanted to string the guy up by his nuts.

"Like I said, he didn't touch me. I didn't even really notice. After the fact, it did seem a little creepy how he'd looked at me, but it wasn't traumatic. Which is why it took so long to realize what my mother had done for me. When I did finally understand? You know, that that's the way a parent *should* be. Not like my dad who made promise after promise, laying out dreams and visions of the world that he never really intended to give me. A good parent sacrificed. A good parent took away those dreams and promises because it was what was in my best interest. I spend a lot of time talking about how shitty my dad is. But I don't spend enough time saying how awesome my mom is." She smiled, a shaky smile. "That's why I wanted to go to Kauai. Because I was only here for a day. And I wanted a do-over."

I reached out my hand to her and pulled her down the rock until she was standing in front of me, then wrapped my arms around her. "I'm really glad I'm the one who gets to finally have this adventure with you," I said, and I just held her.

After a few minutes, I said, "You do have a really good mom." It made me think about how I wanted to be like that. How I wanted to be a good dad.

A rustling down the path stole our attention.

"Don't stop now. You're almost there!" an older man said, coming toward us returning from our destination. He was about my father's age, and the woman next to him seemed to be about my mother's age. "If you listen, you can hear the falls."

Elizabeth picked her head up. "I can hear them. Race you!" She was gathering her pack and bounding down the trail before I could stop her.

"Thanks for the encouragement," I said to the couple, then headed after the woman I was pretending wasn't my wife.

It was only a hundred feet or so later before we came upon the falls. They were majestic and gorgeous, the kind of thing you imagined in paradise but never actually saw for yourself. There were people swimming in the lagoon of water at the base of the falls, and Elizabeth was already stripping her clothes before I even had time to get my backpack off my shoulders. She dove in, fearless, shrieking as she hit the water.

I watched her splashing around, taking my time as I untied my shoes. How did she do that? How did she live so open and free, her feelings so exposed to all the world?

I envied her.

And I loved her.

And maybe it was selfish and self-centered to wish that we could live in this tiny paradise forever, just me and her, but right now that's what I wanted more than anything else. Even if it meant sacrificing everything waiting for me at home. In this moment, I loved her *that* much.

Not able to stand being apart from her a second longer, I finished undressing and jumped in the water. She swam up to me immediately, throwing her arms around my neck and wrapping her legs around my waist. We bobbed around in the water like this, holding onto each other and kissing. It didn't even matter that there were other people nearby. We kissed like we were alone, and soon my cock was hard, pushing against the seam of her pussy, outlined clearly through her thin bikini.

"I could be fucking you right now, and no one would know," I said quietly at her ear. It was hot thinking about it, about being inside her with all of these people nearby. And I needed it all of a sudden, needed it desperately. Needed to mold myself to her, prove how well we fit together.

"We can't," she said, her breath hitching. She met my eyes and hers were dark and dilated.

"We could. It would be so easy to slip inside you."

She rubbed her pussy against my cock, which was thickening at the thought of being nestled warm in her tight channel.

I let go of her so I could push my swim trunks down far enough to pull out my cock, all of it underneath the water where no one could see. I nudged along the outline of her pussy lips with my crown, showing her how easy it would be. "Let me," I said huskily.

She nodded, slightly, just the tiniest jerk of her head, but it was all the permission I needed. I pulled aside the crotch panel to her bikini bottoms and lined my tip at her entrance. "You're going to have to be quiet. You can't give us away."

She bit her lip and nodded again, more vigorously as though begging for it. I pushed into her, slow and evenly, exhaling at the sudden cloak of heat around my cock. I grabbed her hips and pressed her tighter against me, so that I was as deep as I could go, stretching into the most sacred parts of her.

I stayed like that, without moving, just locked inside her, feeling the flutter of her pussy around me, watching the shallowness of her breath as we tread water. Elizabeth peered at the people around us, showering under the falls and playing in the lagoon.

"No one knows," she whispered, wrapping her arms tighter around my neck. "That's so hot that no one knows."

My cock twitched inside her, that's how hot it was.

"This is probably against a million health recommendations," I said, hoping that if I expressed concern it would erase the sin of having absolutely no guilt.

"I'll take an antibiotic when we're back in the mainland—don't you dare pull out."

"I'm not going anywhere."

I was content to stay just like that, fastened together and nothing else, but she pivoted her hips, pulling off of me, then tilted them in sinking back on my shaft with a whimper.

"Oh, it feels good." Her eyes teared and her lips quivered.

I kissed her, kissed her and rocked with her, memorizing the taste of her mouth and the grip of her pussy and the feel of her arms and her legs wrapped around me like a pretzel. It wasn't even about climaxing or release—it was about holding on. It was about being as close to a person as possible and not letting go. It was about hoping she didn't notice that I still had walls up, and praying to God that the ones I'd knocked down were enough. It was about loving her with everything I was, without the baggage that came with me.

And I would tell her about Sebastian—of course I would. I had promised myself I would tell her everything before we left this island. But I was leaving that story for last, in case she wanted me to be the man her father wasn't. The kind of parent her mother was. The kind of person I kept telling myself I could be.

Truth was, I wasn't sure I was strong enough to be the guy a woman like her deserved.

CHAPTER
NINE

Elizabeth

WESTON EMERGED FROM the ocean, an Adonis shining in the sun. He traipsed across the sand, seemingly unaware of the women nearby ogling him. It was impossible not to. He'd bronzed during our nine days in the tropics, and wearing only his swim trunks, his finest assets were displayed. His washboard abs. His perfectly sculpted biceps. His sun-bleached hair. That wicked grin. Not to mention that dimple that practically caused ovulation just by looking at it.

And it was mine.

His body, anyway. He told me in every way he could. With words, with actions. He'd given himself to me physically, and more and more he'd revealed parts of the man inside the perfect casing.

But there was still so much more inside him that I hadn't yet seen. Who did *that* belong to?

I watched him from my safe spot in the shade on the hammock swing behind our bungalow as he rubbed the towel up and down his arms, walking toward me the whole time. When he reached me, he dropped the towel on the sand, and bent down to kiss me, his wet hair dripping onto me and making me shiver.

"You look so serious," he said, plopping down on the deck chair next to me. "What are you thinking about?"

I twisted my lip and caught it between my teeth. We'd continued playing the stranger game since the first night we'd arrived, and the baggage-free personas we'd brought to our island paradise had enjoyed getting to know each other. I'd learned everything about Weston's love of graphic novels and his secret adoration of the art of magic while horseback riding on the beach and kayaking together. I discovered his secret love for grunge music while driving up a canyon. I'd learned he was just the slightest bit afraid of heights when we took a helicopter tour of the island. I discovered his amazing massage technique at our couples spa treatment, when after our massage therapists had given us each a rubdown, they'd left us alone in the room with an edible sugar scrub.

Who knew sugar could be so erotic?

But now I felt that game was played out. That we were stuck and not moving forward. As much as I'd learned about this wonderful, amazing man—as much as I fell harder for him every day—I was nowhere nearer to resolution for the future. We'd shared our pasts, but nothing of our present.

It was time for some honesty.

I pushed my sunglasses on top of my head and angled myself so I could face him. "I was thinking that in five days we go home. And I'm not really sure where home is."

His jaw tensed ever so slightly, and I worried I'd jumped too fast without warning, but he surprised me with his response. "Does that mean you're considering that your home could be somewhere other than France?"

The hesitant note of hope in his voice gutted me. "Of course I am. Just like I hope you are considering that France could be yours."

"Yeah." He took a deep breath and repeated himself. "Yeah, I really am."

I wanted to grab onto his arm and pull it, pull him like a taut fishing line until he sprang up from the deep and displayed the treasure he was hiding under the surface. But when I'd agreed to the trip, he'd promised to show me all of his insides by the time we left. I wanted to trust that. So I wouldn't push him.

Yet.

I covered his hand with mine instead. "Okay."

That night we ate dinner at the five-star seafood restaurant at the resort. The meal was amazing. I'd never had fish that tasted so fresh and divine, melting in my mouth with such succulent briny sweetness.

But without the stranger game between us, there was a new tension that hummed quietly around Weston and me, butting in and spiking up whenever the conversation turned anywhere serious. We were polite—too polite—and gone were the simple discoveries and easy stories that had flowed between us over the previous week.

Still, there wasn't anywhere I'd rather be. Wasn't anyone I would rather be with.

A piece of bread hitting my shoulder alerted me to the table next to us, a young mother already apologizing for her toddler even as I turned around. Undeterred, the child threw another piece. I laughed out loud at the mischievous look on her little face.

"Do you like kids?" Weston asked, a tentative edge in his voice.

I glanced at him, surprised.

"I like some kids," I said. "I don't have a lot of experience around them, but from what I have gleaned, they are pretty much just like tiny people. Some are amazingly wonderful to know. Some are assholes."

He laughed, full and hearty. "I guess what I'm asking is . . . do you want kids?"

I peered over at him, studied the strange edge in his features. Maybe it was just the candlelight playing tricks on me. But it *was* strange we hadn't had this conversation, looking at our situation on paper, anyway. How could two people get married and not know the other's stance on procreation?

Of course, our marriage had been under false pretenses. And so we were only just getting to this now.

"Yeah, I do. I definitely want kids."

His shoulders seemed to ease, the shadows disappearing from his expression, and I felt that I had answered correctly.

"You?" I asked to be sure.

"I hadn't really thought about it until . . . recently. But I do."

Good. This was good. With that, I felt the last remaining tension flow out of my body. I hadn't realized how much I wanted to be on the same page with him on this.

"I mean," I qualified, "not right now. Not for another ten years."

"Ten years?"

"Right. I am only twenty-five now, so I have time. Thirty-five is not too late."

"And you're set on that?" The hardness from before was creeping back into his tone.

"Well, yeah. I really am. I want to focus on my business right now. Dyson Media is an important legacy and I'm determined to make something of it. You know that. My father spent so much of his life dedicated to the business, and I learned from him that it was a job too big to have with children. He didn't have enough time to give to me and his work. Which wasn't fair to me. I don't want to make that same mistake with my kids. So I want ten years devoted to my business, then I'll be able to step away. Probably won't ever be a stay-at-home type, but I will definitely be an involved mother. It was one of the reasons I wanted to get my hands on my company *now*, and not wait. Because I recognize my biological clock is ticking, and I really need these things to be separate."

"Just because your father couldn't manage both doesn't mean that *people* can't manage both. Maybe your father was just . . . not a good parent."

I considered. "Maybe. But part of being a good parent is making good choices about how you build your life. And before I have kids, I want to build my life so that I have time to devote to them." It wasn't something I would back down on. It was more important to me even than living in France.

Weston didn't seem to like my answer though. He crossed his arms over his chest and scowled. "But what if you got pregnant sooner? What if you had a baby right now?"

"Right now? If I had a baby right now, it would be yours. And I would want it *so* much." I stared into his eyes, willing him to see exactly how much I meant what I was saying. "I'd welcome it into my life with completely open arms. And I would change my priorities where Dyson Media was concerned. I'd probably let Darrell stay where he is. I wouldn't be so involved, I don't know. It's not how I want things to be, so I am making every effort to not have to be in that situation. Because I want the best circumstances when I have a baby—when I have *your* baby." It made me feel vulnerable to say that last part, to admit that I wanted kids with him, but it also felt freeing and right.

"So you're saying that you would have a kid now, if you *had* to, but it's not what you want, which means one day you might even grow to resent it. Or me. Because it kept you from doing and being the thing that you really wanted to be first." His words were sharp, his body language almost hostile.

"Are you mad at me?" I couldn't understand why he was so upset over a hypothetical situation. He himself had said he only recently decided he wanted kids. He couldn't have some dying need to have a baby now, could he?

"No. I'm not mad." He turned back to picking at the remainders of his food, definitely seeming like he was mad.

I could feel him slipping away from me. "Can you tell me what it is I need to say then? Because I feel like I've said the wrong thing, but I can't say the right thing if you won't tell me what it is."

He shook his head, his eyes now watching the young couple with the toddler as they packed up their table, getting ready to leave. "Never mind. It was a stupid conversation."

I placed a hand on his forearm, felt it tense beneath my fingers. He was close enough to touch, but somehow it felt like he had a wall around him, some barrier I couldn't reach through. "It's not stupid. It's important, and I wanted to talk about it."

He shot me a glance. "We talked about it. There's not much else to say."

I set my jaw, actively conscious of the string of wrong things I could say that were rolling through my mind, wishing I could find the one right thing to say.

Finally, with tears threatening at the corner of my eyes, I swallowed back the ball lodged in my throat, and tried one more time. "I want to be inside you, Weston. In all the ways you're inside me. But I feel like I'm up against a door that I can't open unless you give me the key." I paused to steady my voice. "Give me the key."

His eyes closed briefly, my words settling over him, before he turned again to face me. "You're so far inside me, Elizabeth, that I don't know where you end and I begin anymore."

He opened up his arms, and I was instantly in them, moving from my chair to his lap, kissing up his jaw, licking at his salty skin until his mouth found mine. He held me close and tight, his lips locked with mine, unmoving, clutching onto me with a fierceness I'd never seen in him before. Like he was keeping me in place. Like he was afraid I'd leave, or let go first, or not love him enough.

I let him grip onto me like that, wishing his words and his embrace were enough to make me feel sure of our future together.

But they weren't.

I was just as desperate and scared as his kiss told me *he* was. Because if I was truly inside him, like he said I was, he wouldn't be holding on like he was about to lose me.

CHAPTER
TEN

Weston

I QUIETLY SLID the back door to the bungalow shut, making sure not to wake Elizabeth, and stepped out into the muggy night air. A couple of footsteps and I was in the sand, cool against the bottom of my feet. I stood in the silent night, gazing off into the dark distance, my thoughts rolling and loud as the waves against the shore. The time on my phone read two thirty-eight. I hadn't slept a wink.

I was a giant asshole.

With a disconcerted sigh, I ran a frustrated hand through my hair and wandered over to the hammock swing. It was better to be out here sorting through the wreckage in my mind than tossing and turning next to the warm body in my bed. I couldn't help but think I'd made a mess of everything. That I would be far less burdened in this moment if I'd just been clear and honest with my wife from the day of our wedding.

But I hadn't been.

And now, before I'd finished laying my groundwork, before I'd gotten brave enough and secure enough to tell her I was a father, she'd told me she didn't want children of her own—not anytime soon, anyway—and I'd blown up at her. All I could think was, how is she possibly going to want me now? Now that I come with a plus one?

All I could think was, I'm going to lose her, and I freaked out.

Hours of staring into the darkness while I listened to the sweet rhythm of her breath as she slept made me realize I might be overreacting. Made me realize I was definitely being a prick, not giving her a chance to embrace my son. I'd given her a hypothetical situation and taken her hypothetical response—a response aimed at biological children of her own—and decided that it meant something that it didn't have to. *Callie* was raising Sebastian. Callie was Sebastian's mother. My paternal relationship with this little boy didn't mean Elizabeth had to lose her dreams. What kind of blockhead assumed it meant otherwise?

This blockhead, apparently.

I groaned as I leaned back into the hammock, pushing off with the balls of my feet into a gentle swing. I had to tell her. I had to tell her everything. Every last thing I'd been storing inside of me, not willing to expose, had to be shared with her now. There wasn't any more putting it off.

As though the universe were intent on making me commit, it was then that Elizabeth chose to open the sliding door and interrupt my solitude. She stepped down onto the beach wearing the button-down linen shirt I'd had on earlier, her hair tangled from when I'd bent her over the vanity in the bathroom and fucked her hard, mercilessly, watching us both in the mirror as we rode through our climaxes.

With her hair tousled and the moonlight hitting her, she looked like an angel, maybe even an angel of death. An angel who was about to put me out of my misery, if I'd let her.

She found me quickly and started over to me before I'd even fully gestured for her to come over. I was still caught up in my self-made hell, but not so distracted that I wasn't wondering if she was wearing nothing underneath the shirt. My cock was already twitching against the drawstring of the pajama pants that I'd pulled on before I came outside, and when she sat across my lap, her long creamy legs stretched over me, I definitely got stiff.

"What are you doing out here? It's late." She wrapped her arms around my neck and I nestled my face into the curve of her shoulder. I kissed the delicate strip of skin that was bared there, sending more blood down to my cock.

"Couldn't sleep." I trailed my tongue along the spot I'd just pressed my mouth to.

"You should've woken me up." Her sultry voice was an invitation and I was ready to RSVP. I wouldn't even have to have her straddle me. I was sure I could press into her at this angle and imagined how good and tight it would feel to bury into her soft, sweet pussy while she continued to sit on me sideways.

But that was a guilty temptation I was intent on not taking advantage of. Not right now—I wouldn't feel good about myself afterward. I'd been given a moment of clarity, followed by the opportunity to talk to her for a reason. I needed to be better than I had been. Needed to be the guy who didn't blow it.

With a heavy sigh, I sat back away from her.

She ran her fingers through my hair and studied my features. "What are you thinking about?"

The tone of her voice held that note of hopeful longing, a distinct giveaway that she wasn't sure I would tell her anything.

Which made me only feel like a bigger asshat.

But also made me a thousand times more committed to baring something meaningful to her. I took a second to answer, gathering my words and confidence. "I was thinking about how stupid it is that I can't just tell you everything that's inside me. Why is that? They're only words. They're only sentences. And yet each time I think about bringing them through me, they snag at the back of my throat."

She curled her knees up against my bare chest, and I could hear the slightest uptick in the speed of her breathing—an indication that this conversation thrilled her? Scared her? Possibly both, but for the most part she played it cool, continuing to lightly stroke my hair.

"Are you afraid of what I'll think about you?" she asked, raw honesty layered in her tone.

"Yes. I guess that's the biggest reason why it's hard to say these things."

"I want to tell you that there can't be anything that you would say that would change how I feel about you. Because I believe that's true.

You couldn't have even really cheated on me, and that's the worst I can think you could do, since we were never really—"

I turned my head to face her, cutting her off abruptly. "I haven't cheated on you. Nothing has been directly against you. I haven't betrayed you, not really. Or maybe I have by not sharing with you earlier, but I haven't cheated on you."

"That's vaguely clear. But I feel even more confident in saying that nothing you can tell me is going to change how I feel about you, Weston. I also understand that you can't know that until you tell me. And I also understand that whatever you're keeping from me is a big enough part of you to matter. That you have to tell me before we can move on in this relationship. So you're just going to have to try me to find out that I mean it when I say it's going to be okay. Try me, and let me prove it to you."

"I'm trying. I really am. I haven't done this before. Never talked to a woman about anything real. Never talked to anyone, really, about anything real. Donovan sometimes. But mostly that was because he just already seems to know everything." I could do this, though. Even sharing this—this fear, the anxiety surrounding opening up to her—that was a brave beginning, as far as I was concerned. I got points for that, didn't I?

Points or not, I was scrambling trying to figure out where to go next. What to *say* next. Telling her was going to happen, but how to do it was another matter entirely.

"Maybe you could make it like a game of sorts. Maybe that would make it better," Elizabeth suggested. "It was so easy to get to know each other when we first got here when we played strangers. Should we play that game again?"

I ran my hand along the outside of her thigh, loving the feel of her skin underneath my palm. "Some of these things I would never tell a stranger." But maybe there was another game we could play. "Truth or dare?"

"Are you sure you won't just pick dare every time?"

God, she knew me too well. "Fair. Another game then . . . ?" Part of me was trying to find a way to involve stripping when a real answer came. "Two truths and a lie."

"Two truths and a lie. That's an excellent game."

It was dangerous because I would be able to gauge her reaction to my truths beforehand, making it tempting to change my mind and tell her the wrong thing was a lie if I didn't like how she responded.

No. I couldn't do that. Mostly because she wouldn't react terribly, I was almost certain.

"Let's play then. You go first." Because I was still a dick, after all. "Make it about sex. It's always good when it's about sex." Because I was still a guy.

Because I was still scared.

She chuckled. "Okay. All right. Let me think a second."

I continued to rub my hand up and down her leg while she thought, not letting myself get too worked up about what my turn would be. I needed to stay here, in the moment. If I thought about it too much, I'd end up running.

"I got it. I got it," she said sitting up a little, twisting her tight little ass to get more comfortable as she did, sending jolts of electric pleasure straight to my groin.

"Careful, Lizzie."

She ignored me and went right into her turn. "I lost my virginity to Clarence Sheridan."

"Oh," I groaned. "Please let that be the lie."

"I've never watched porn with another person. Or the Lelo vibrator is my tool of choice when it comes to masturbation."

She tilted her chin up as though she was proud of herself.

The smug little look on her face, the very close proximity of her ass to my cock—I had to briefly pretend there were zombies about to come crawling out of the ocean before I could concentrate on her three statements and try to decide which one wasn't true.

"I really wish the first one was a lie," I said. "But I have a feeling, a deep dark feeling that it's not. You don't have a vibrator. I'd know about that by now, and there's no way you've watched porn with another person. You blush too easily. *I* haven't even watched porn with another person."

"*You* haven't watched porn with another person? How can you not have watched porn with someone?"

"Who needs to watch porn when you're making it, baby?"

Even in the darkness, I could see her roll her eyes. "Anyway, you're wrong."

My heart lifted suddenly. Maybe she had never slept with Clarence Sheridan.

"I've totally watched porn with people. Multiple times. It's amazing."

"So you *have* fucked Clarence."

"And watched porn with him!"

Gross. The guy probably needed it to get a woman turned on. I took that as comfort.

I turned my thoughts away from Clarence for a moment. "Does that mean you have a vibrator?" I hope I didn't sound too eager.

"I didn't bring it on my honeymoon." She leaned down to run her nose along my ear. "But we can play with it when we get home, if that's what you're suggesting."

So much for calming down my dick.

Though, thinking about our ambiguous future did make for a boner killer. What if we never had a chance to play with her vibrator together? What if we never got to watch porn? I couldn't stand the idea of Clarence Sheridan going down in history as her best lover.

I needed more details about him.

"Was Clarence good to you at least?" I paused a second. "Actually, tell me he was an amateur. That's what I want to hear. That he didn't know what he was doing, and he was a total loser. With a tiny dick."

She laughed, the side of her breast jiggling against my chest. "He had a normal dick. Whatever that is. And he was . . . sweet. It was his first time too."

Oh, fuck. That meant it was a big deal for both of them.

It also meant he was brainless when it happened. "So he didn't know what he was doing. At all. That's what you're saying."

"He didn't know what he was doing," she confirmed. "It was over within seconds."

"That's what I wanted to hear. Thank you, Mrs. King."

"I have to be totally forthcoming, though—"

"Do you?"

She continued. "And tell you he did get better. We both did."

"I think I could've lived without knowing that." To make matters worse, my boner wasn't gone. In fact, now my cock wanted to go prove itself. Like, remind my wife that I was the best she'd ever have.

As if sensing the turmoil I was going through, Elizabeth brushed her lips against my jaw. "I don't need to tell you how good of a lover you are, Weston. You already know you own the title of Best in Bed. Best against any hard surface, actually."

"I don't necessarily know that." I mean, I did. "And, even if I do. It is nice to hear every once in a while."

She chuckled again, her body curling tighter against me as she did.

"I think you're a pretty hot lover too," I said softly. "Feisty and kinky and loud and soft all wrapped into one."

"Please don't say that was the beginning of your turn. Because I would have to guess that that was your lie."

"It's not a lie." I tickled her until she squirmed and my cock felt miserable again.

"Your turn, your turn," she sang, poking her index finger into my chest.

Yeah. My turn. My fucking turn.

I was tempted to take this round as a warm-up, give her some bull-shit statements that didn't really mean anything, but I also needed to get this over with, get inside Elizabeth, get her inside me as soon as possible.

Three statements: *I'm a father. I'm going to do better than my father. My father fucked up big time.*

The lie was the middle one—I already wasn't sure I was going to do better than anyone. I worried I couldn't even do better than my father. And maybe that was the hang-up with me where Sebastian was concerned—I had daddy issues. Big time.

Where did I begin to get over the failures of Nash King?

By talking about it, I supposed.

The next sentence that came out of my mouth was thought as it was spoken. "My father encouraged unethical packaging and approval of housing loans even after the financial crisis."

There it was. Out there. My most embarrassing family secret told to another human being. Told to the most important human I knew.

And all I could do was go on. "Statement two: He let one of his employees—Daniel Clemmons—practically a family friend, take the fall and go to jail for him. And statement three: I don't care at all what you think about me after you hear this, that I'm not afraid you'll think I'm like him or that I condone this, or that I worry you'll be appalled when I tell you that I feel so guilty that I haven't touched my trust fund—money that was made by squandering other people's life savings—or that I've been giving money monthly to the Clemmons family to try to make up for . . . everything."

I swallowed. "Obviously the last one's the lie. I care very much what you think about me. I worry very much that you think I'm like him—like my dad. Maybe because *I'm* afraid that I'm like him."

She was still for a moment on my lap. Then she was moving, adjusting herself to straddle me so she could take my face in her hands and look at me directly, and I held onto her, clutching her with shaking hands.

"Weston," she began.

But I couldn't lift my eyes to meet hers. I could just go on, could just blunder through the whole tale of it until it was told. "I found out when I was working at my father's office one summer. I was still in college. It was about seven years ago. Before the allegations even came out publicly. And I was mad. I was really mad. And hurt, but mostly mad. Because why did he have to do something unethical? Weren't we already making enough? Donovan didn't see it so black and white. We didn't have to go into business with our parents, he said, and we could do things differently, but we didn't necessarily need to be so judgmental about how things had been done before us. It wasn't exactly illegal. Which, okay. Sure. Fine. Everyone was doing shitty business deals."

"Weston," she said again, patiently.

"But then the charges came out and it really became an issue, because that's when my dad had the opportunity to make things better.

And he didn't. I told him he needed to take the fall. He'd ruined people's lives. To build *our* life. That wasn't right, and I told him he needed to take responsibility. I think he might've even considered it, except my mother—my mother . . ." I lost myself in the vivid memory of that day, her usually perfect makeup smeared down her cheeks.

"She begged and cried and said she couldn't live without him and there was no way he could turn himself in. But what about the Clemmonses? What about *their* children and his family? Daniel Clemmons was only following orders. He shouldn't have had to pay the price for everyone else. I do everything I can, give them everything I can, and I just feel like it's not ever enough. It's never going to be enough—"

"Weston, look at me."

Her insistence was sharp. I lifted my eyes toward her face. Her beautiful, angelic face.

She ran her thumb gently across my cheekbone. "This is not your fault. Okay? I am so sorry this happened, and it has to hurt so bad. But I don't think a fraction of an inch less of you for this. I probably think a whole hell of a lot more of you, if that's even possible." She tilted her head slightly. "Are you hearing me?"

I nodded, a ball lodged in the back of my throat that I couldn't seem to swallow down.

"I mean it. Are you really hearing me? Because I'm going to tell you again—your father's sins are not your sins. Who your father is is not who you are. I'm sorry that he's hurt you. You never deserved that. But it's not your fault."

I nodded again, hearing her. Accepting it. Knowing it, because I did already know it somewhere inside of me, and yet I'd still sought so valiantly to undo the damage done by my father. How many years had I wasted trying to erase his errors? How much time and money and energy had I spent feeling guilty for things I hadn't done?

Too much. That's how much.

Besides being my life, the whole scenario sounded obvious and oddly familiar, like I'd been on the other side of it before. Like I'd stood outside and looked in. And of course I had, I'd been looking outside at the same scene ever since I'd met Elizabeth. I'd been where she was, watching her lament the things her father had done in his business, hearing her tear herself apart, wanting to make it better while she put all the weight on her own shoulders.

I brought my hands to her neck and stroked my thumbs along her jaw. "Your father's sins are not your sins," I repeated her words to her, wondering if she could hear them now the way I just heard them from her.

Her eyes glistened in the moonlight and her lips trembled as she nodded tightly. "I know. I'm trying to know that."

She kissed me, or I kissed her, fierce and reassuring. When she pulled away, she said, "Let's go inside." She was already climbing off my lap, already tugging at my hand.

"I'm not done. I have more rounds to go," I protested.

"No more games tonight. I need to feel you inside me." She let go of me and started toward the bungalow door, peering over her shoulder at me with a beckoning glance.

I followed after her, because I needed that too.

The rest of my confessions would have to wait.

CHAPTER
ELEVEN

Elizabeth

F UCKING FATHERS.

I could write a thesis paper on douchebag dads, and that was just based on the experience with my own. Now there was Weston's to add to the list. At least mine had never done anything criminal. Not that I knew of, anyway.

I'd been naïve and ignorant not to consider that Weston had good reasons to not get along with his parents. I'd looked at the family portrait, not realizing there was dust and cobwebs hanging on the frame. Not understanding the reason for the pointed pinpricks made from darts thrown at the perfect face of the patriarch. I owed my husband an apology for that. Later, when he was able to hear it.

I did know that all men weren't like this, that there were *good* men in the world—men who didn't prey on weaker people. Men who didn't put themselves above everyone else.

Men who wanted their children and loved them and attended to them. Were part of their lives.

I believed that Weston was a good man. Everything he'd shown me about himself, his character, led me to believe that he was decent through and through, even if he didn't see it about himself. I was sure he would even make a good father—a feeling so strong inside me that it made my ovaries squirm and plead to do their biological job. *Someday.*

Someday.

If we made it through this, and more and more I was thinking that we would, we would make it to that someday. We would settle together and eventually raise children. Raise a family. Prove to each other that we didn't have to follow in our parents' footsteps.

But we weren't ready for that yet. Especially with the walls still between us, walls I could feel crumbling down. I could sense the last of Weston's secrets coming out of him. Like a magician pulling a string of handkerchiefs from a hat, I wouldn't have been surprised if he had kept divulging round after round of secrets in our game the night before.

It had just already been so much. Not for me—for him. I wondered if he even knew how deep these scars ran through him, how badly the betrayal from his father had damaged him. I'd been coming to terms for a long time where my dad was concerned, and I still felt like I was barely getting a grip on it. Weston, the way he kept it all bottled inside, I wasn't sure he'd even scratched the surface of his pain.

So I'd cut him off. I'd put the confessions on pause and brought him inside where I could comfort him with my body. I'd held him while he stretched out over me, wrapping my legs around his hips, taking every bit of anguish that he gave me.

It had drained him, and this morning he'd slept past his normal waking time. He didn't even stir when the waiter brought breakfast. So I'd thrown on a robe and curled up in the wicker armchair next to my sleeping spouse with my iPad.

We had sort of had an unspoken rule for our entire honeymoon to not get on the internet. We were leaving the real world behind, after all. But alone and curious I looked up everything I could find about King-Kincaid and the scandals they'd been implicated in. There were quite a few articles about several different improprieties, but the major headlines pointed to a loan-bundling scheme not unlike the housing default crisis of the early part of the century. Though he repeatedly stated he was only following orders, the blame of this scandal was mostly placed on CFO Daniel Clemmons who had twin adult autistic children, both unable to function outside the home. His wife cared for them full-time.

No wonder Weston felt guilty about it. It was terrible.

I wondered if Weston also realized that Daniel had done what he'd done willingly. That he'd also known it was wrong. My gut said that Weston did understand that, and likely his need to support the Clemmons family while Daniel was in jail had a lot to do with Weston feeling like they were in the same boat—that they were all a sort of club of orphans who'd been destroyed by the bad business choices of their fathers. Perhaps his monthly contributions made him feel less alone in that betrayal.

God, it must have been such a heavy weight for him.

After I'd read everything I could find on the subject, and I wearied of the tight, heavy feeling in my chest, I did a casual check up on all things Dyson Media. There wasn't a lot that I wasn't already up to date on, but I did find a few interesting things.

"What's got your attention so riveted?" Weston asked.

I glanced over to find him sitting up against the headboard, his arms stretching up above his head, showing off his toned torso. It was distracting, but not so distracting that I'd forgotten what I'd been so intensely focused on.

"Did you know that France just changed the regulations regarding pricing structures for children's media?"

Weston rubbed a hand over his scruffy chin. "I feel slightly embarrassed to say that I didn't know that." He was mocking me.

I didn't care. I was too excited about this. "They did. And because they did, everyone's business structures are going to have to change if anyone's going to make any money. Do you think Darrell knew this? Do you think that's why he sold off the children's portion of Dyson Media? I'd chalked it up to him making a malicious decision, but maybe he was actually acting based on insight."

"I don't see that there's anyway you could really know without asking him."

"Mmm hmm. And remember the guy who was rumored to take over as chief programming director? Marc Laurent?"

"Vaguely," he said, his brows knit into a frown. "Wait, are you working? Because I thought this was our honeymoon."

"Just for a second. You were sleeping." I grabbed the iPad and jumped onto the bed, moving up next to him.

"Hell yes. This is what I like to see. Put some porn on that thing. We can watch it together. Be my first."

I felt my cheeks heat but didn't respond. "Word was that Marc Laurent was going to take over as the programming director. It was all but announced. Everywhere. I was totally behind that move. Actually looking forward to it. The guy had great recommendations. And his resume? It was insane. He was beyond well-qualified, he's like a god in the French business world."

"Right, right. Then Darrell hired some nobody instead. Right?"

I'd already fussed to Weston about that several times, as part of my ongoing rant about how my company was being run into the ground while lining my cousin's pockets. "Exactly. But look." I tilted the iPad so that he could see the screen to read the headline: *Famed Television Executive Caught Up in Child Pornography Scandal*.

"Holy shit. Marc Laurent is a pedophile?"

"Innocent until proven guilty, but he's at least embroiled in a pretty major uproar. You think Darrell might've found out about that early on? And didn't want to be tied to it when it went down? It would have caused our stock to tank, I'm sure."

"Again, I can't guess what the guy was thinking. But it's possible. It's possible he made two really good decisions. Or, he just got really lucky."

I put my back against the headboard next to Weston and dropped the tablet in my lap. "One time is coincidental. But twice?"

"Are you starting to change your mind about what you think of your cousin?"

That was going a bit too far. Darrell had iced me out and blocked me from the company on too many occasions for that. But, to be fair, he didn't really know much more about me than I knew about him. "I just wonder if there's more to him than meets the eye."

"There's more to me than meets the eye under this blanket," Weston teased. "If you'd put the work away."

"Your breakfast is waiting," I said. It was already cold, but I thought

I should at least mention it to the guy.

Before he could decide if he wanted to eat it now or let it get even colder, my phone rang. "Well, speak of the devil," I said. My phone's ID showed the number was French, and it was one I'd long since memorized—the day he took over my father's company, in fact.

"Darrell. I was just thinking about you," I answered.

"Likewise," he said. Well, that was never good. But in this case, I was hopeful that since my marriage, he was planning on looping me in more on the decisions he was making overseas. He was probably calling to break the Laurent news, so I could praise him on a job well done. Or just to lord it over me that he clearly had inside connections I was not yet privy to.

"If you'd like to set up a time to talk, I'd love to chat when I get back from my honeymoon." I winked at Weston. "But we're a little busy."

"Oh, I'd say so. *We* have been very busy indeed. And I'm not so sure you're going to want to wait on this chat. How much do you actually know about this so-called husband of yours, anyway?" More than Darrell knew, that was for sure.

"Look. I'm well aware of what went on at King-Kincaid. And I fail to see how that has any bearing on my future with Dyson Media." Annoyance made my voice sharp.

"Call me after you open the email I just sent you, and tell me then just exactly what your plans for the future are, won't you?" I rolled my eyes and navigated over to my inbox. A link popped up on the same business gossip site that was reporting Marc Laurent, only this one had a different headline: *Dyson Media Princess Fairy-tale Marriage Shattered By Double-Timing King*.

I only clicked on the headline out of curiosity. Both Weston and I were famous enough in our circles to have a gossip spread about us now and then. Most of it was easily dismissible. I was ready to scoff at this.

He'd promised he hadn't cheated, after all.

"Go on," Darrell said, the hint of a smile in his voice. "I'll wait."

The new page that loaded came with pictures of Weston walking into a brownstone somewhere in Brooklyn, from the looks of the neighborhood. There are several shots of him in different angles coming and going. Then a picture of a woman carrying a toddler walking out the same door. *"Less than two weeks after their nuptials, Weston King seems to be stepping out on his new bride, Elizabeth Dyson. Does he have a secret family no one's talking about?"*

I rolled my eyes, not interested in continuing on. There wasn't even any proof the woman came out of the same door that Weston did. There were probably a lot of apartments in the building. This was fake news. Clickbait. That was all.

Until Weston saw the page over my shoulder, and said, "I can explain."

I looked back at the screen. Studied the pictures more closely. It was the outfit that Weston had worn the day he'd left me in the hotel. And the toddler . . . it couldn't be. But those dimples were unmistakable.

I scanned the rest of the article. *" . . . a senator's daughter . . . love child with Weston King."*

My stomach dropped.

"Darrell, we can discuss this after my honeymoon. I have nothing to tell you or anyone else right now." It took every single ounce of determination I'd inherited from my father to say it in a crisp, professional voice. Because inside I was boiling and twisting in knots. Twisted, boiling knots.

When I hung up, I turned to my husband.

"It's true?" It couldn't be. But my heart was hammering, and my mouth suddenly felt like it had so much cotton in it that it could barely open.

"I was going to tell you."

I jumped off the bed, suddenly needing to be away from Weston. From the man I'd so arrogantly thought I knew only moments ago. "Tell me . . . what? That you have a secret life? You've had a super-secret wife and kid? A secret other family? You said you didn't betray me! You said you didn't cheat!"

"No!" He moved to his knees, and his adamant tone made me hopeful that I had this all wrong. "No, I didn't cheat! I don't have a secret wife. I don't have a secret other family. Just a secret kid."

"Just a kid!" I could feel my eyes widen, could feel my blood vessels opening as indignant adrenaline surged through my body. "You have *a kid?*"

"Yes. I do. A son. He's two."

"You have a two-year-old son and you didn't think that maybe I'd like to know?" My voice cracked. I was surprised, most of all. And outraged. And hurt.

"I was going to tell you," he said hitting the bed emphatically with his palm.

"When?"

"I . . ." He faltered, but went on. "I was going to tell you today. After last night, I was ready. Before we left—before we went home—you would have known. There was the game we were playing and, and . . . I just wasn't ready to—"

I cut him off. "You know what I wasn't ready for, Weston? I wasn't ready for the entire internet to know more about my husband than I do." He started to protest, but I put my hand up, stopping him from saying whatever it was he wanted to say. "Did it never even cross your mind that maybe I should have known this *before* we exchanged vows? We had plenty of time during our engagement for you to mention him, or were you too busy pining for Sabrina and arguing about not getting a maid?"

Sometimes I got mean when I got mad. It was a trait I'd inherited from both my parents.

"First of all, I never pined for Sabrina, and you know that." His stern glare dissolved quickly. "And I only found out I had a kid on the day of our wedding."

"You only found out you had a *two-year-old child* on the day of our wedding? I don't understand." I was pacing now, making long, wide arcs around the bed as I rubbed either side of my temple with my index fingers.

"Callie came to me in my dressing room."

"Callie is the senator's daughter?" My belly ached with the familiar way he said this stranger's name. "Are you sleeping with her now?"

"No." Then he said it again, louder. "No! I don't even know her. I hadn't seen her in almost three years, I'm telling you. She just showed up." He was talking fast and frantically, as though he thought I could disappear at any moment. He wasn't wrong. "I thought she was there for the wedding, and she dropped by my dressing room—"

"An ex drops by your dressing room on your wedding day," I muttered. "Only you would think that could be innocent."

Never mind that mine dropped by the honeymoon suite. *We* didn't have a child.

He scooted on his knees closer to me. "I was a wreck of nerves thinking about marrying you. All of my thoughts were tangled in *you.* All my feelings. Everything. Then half an hour before the wedding she shows up—Nate let her in, I think—and she dropped this bomb on me. I didn't have any time to react. Didn't have time to think. Didn't have time to do anything. I had no one to tell—"

I stopped abruptly, leaning forward. I placed both hands on the bed. "You should have told *me!*"

He reached for my wrist but I pulled away before he could grab it. "I know! I was going to. I wanted to. I did, I really did. You were the only person I wanted to tell and I've been dying not to share it. But then you dropped this new bomb about France. About *moving* to France, Elizabeth, and here's Callie who's just told me that I have a kid, and that the only way that I can be part of his life is to actually *be in* his life. A kid that I might love, and I probably do love so much, and I haven't even met him yet. And on the other hand there's you—this woman that I *already* love with everything that I am and couldn't imagine a minute of my life living without, and now I have to choose? I didn't know what to do, Lizzy. I didn't know what to do." There was torment and exasperation in his voice, in his body. In his movement, as he ran his hand through his already tousled hair.

My chest squeezed and pinched, my breath knocked so far out of my lungs it took a moment to speak. "You love me?"

His head tilted to the side, his expression ridiculously soft and warm. "Isn't it the most obvious thing in the world?"

"Maybe. I didn't know, though. You never said."

"I guess I didn't know how to tell you that either. I've never told a woman I love her before."

I could've guessed that about him. But hearing it confirmed made my heart skip and ache all at once. "Well, you picked a fine time to mention it. And by fine time I mean a really terrible time. I don't even know how to deal with those words right now. I'm still trying to deal with this other thing. And I'm mad at you, you asshole! You hurt me by not telling me this." I sniffled, tears close. "But for what it's worth, I love you too."

He smiled, just enough to let that amazing dimple show. "Yeah, that was definitely obvious."

Even now he could be such a fucking charmer. "Whatever. So I wear my heart on my sleeve. Not a bad thing."

"One of the things I love most about you, actually."

"Weston . . ." A sudden urge to cry crept up along my spine, but I tamped it down. Barely. Wondered if he could hear every bit of confusion and anguish inside me.

"Lizzy. I'm sorry. I'm sorry I hurt you. I never wanted that." He held a hand out in my direction then dropped it, his fist folding tightly. "I want to hold you right now. So bad."

It was tempting. I wanted that too. Wanted to crawl up into the bed and kiss him and let him apologize to me in earnest. Wanted to hear him tell me he loved me a million more times before it became real.

I shook my head. "Fuck. What about Darrell?" We'd worked so hard to make this marriage look believable. "He's aware of the situation already, clearly. What will happen to my claim on Dyson? This makes our marriage look as false as he always suspected it was."

"Tell him that you married a guy who has a kid from a previous relationship. There's nothing unusual about that in this day and age."

He was trying to reassure me, but I was spinning. "It's unusual when the bride doesn't know anything about it. It's going to look like I know nothing about *you*! I *feel* like I know nothing about you."

"You know everything. Everything there is to know about me. I swear. Everything inside me belongs to you now. What else do you want me to tell you?"

"Tell me again why you didn't think you could tell me this as soon as you found out. Because I still don't get that. Like you just said, people come to marriages with children all the time these days. Why did you think you would have to choose between me and your child?" It didn't make any sense. I wasn't going to keep him from his child. Why would he even think that?

"Because . . ." He sat back on his heels and took a deep breath. "I want to be with you, Elizabeth. I mean that. I want to follow you wherever you go. And you've made it clear that being with you means being in France. But now I have a kid—a kid who needs a father in his life not just on occasion. A kid who lives with his mother. In the United States."

Oh.

Now I saw it.

It was a big problem.

"I think I need to sit down." I made it over to the wicker chair and sank down into it. My father's biggest sin had been not being there. How much of his absence from my life had to do with the fact that he'd resided on a different continent? Maybe if he'd been a different man, it wouldn't have mattered where he'd lived, but it sure had to have been a big part of it.

I certainly wouldn't wish that parental separation on another kid.

Weston stood and wrapped the bedsheet around his waist, then he came and knelt in front of me. "Do you see why I couldn't tell you?" he asked.

I looked down into his blue eyes. "Because you didn't think I would understand this?"

"Because I know you, baby. And you would have told me to choose Sebastian."

Sebastian. The little boy had a name.

I could picture him—the photo from the article only showed him in profile—but even with just that I could see he had Weston's features. His eyes. That dimple.

My husband was right. I would have told him to choose his child. There wouldn't have been any room for discussion. I wouldn't have even bothered with this honeymoon. I'd have sent Weston in the direction of his son's door and told him not to look back.

And, yes, it would have hurt like hell. But parents are supposed to sacrifice for their kids. I'd learned that from my mother.

"I can't tell you to walk away from him," I said, confirming what he already knew.

Weston gathered my hands in his. "But I will. To be with you."

"No, you won't. Because if you were the kind of guy who would do that, you wouldn't be the kind of guy that I'd be in love with. And I am in love with you. Obvious and stupid as it is."

"I know, Lizzy. Me too."

I bit my lip hard, trying to trap the sob inside.

With the sweetest of sighs, Weston pulled me down to the ground and into his arms. "We'll figure something out. This isn't over. We're going to work it out."

I listened while he said, "We're going to figure something out." And then I got up, and I walked into the bathroom.

I listened, but I didn't let myself believe it. I'd learned long ago not to trust men's vague assurances.

I knew who to thank for that lesson.

Fucking fathers.

CHAPTER
TWELVE

Weston

"IT'S NOT A secret that I had a baby out of wedlock, but my father isn't really going to appreciate major press about it." Callie's clipped tone buzzed in my ear like an annoying fly.

I stretched my feet out and propped them on the bed and sank down further into the wicker chair. Just what I needed—two women mad at me. "It's not a major news site. It's a stupid little gossip pit. No one will see it. It's not going to grab network attention."

"It's obviously worrisome enough that you called me about it. And I never had to worry about any of this shit before you came into Sebastian's life."

I rubbed a hand over my face and willed myself not to throw the phone across the room. "It isn't a big deal. I only wanted to make sure that you weren't going to say anything until we had a chance to say something together. Just in case anyone came knocking on your door asking for more information." I could hear my voice getting tight with irritation. "And let's not forget that it was *you* who came into *my* life."

That last bit hadn't been fair, and the timing had been particularly bad since that was when Elizabeth had decided to finally come out of the bathroom. After she'd heard me out, even encouraged me a bit, she'd gotten suddenly cold and sullen and had retreated to the en-suite for a long bath. I'd heard the click of the lock before she got in, signaling that

I was not invited to interrupt.

It had probably been about two hours since that door had shut in my face, and now she approached fully made-up, her hair dried and styled in luscious waves that dripped down her shoulders and back. She was wearing a sundress or, a midi dress was what she'd called it when she'd unpacked, a long straight thing without sleeves that hugged around her curves and fell all the way to her ankles. It was crimson and low cut with a giant slit up the middle, and even though I'd been under her skirt many times now, it was the kind of dress that made me want to pull it up and look again.

But her lips were still turned into a frown, and I doubted she appreciated walking out and hearing me talk to my ex-lover. The mother of my child.

I stood up, striding away from my wife. "Look, Callie, like I said, it's not a big deal. Just don't talk to anyone. I'll contact you when I get back to the mainland. Cool?"

"Fine. I wouldn't talk to anyone anyway."

I wasn't really expecting anyone to reach out to her, but, just in case Darrell sent someone, I didn't want anything she said to be misconstrued or twisted in a way that would harm Elizabeth.

I paused now, wanting to say something else, not sure how to ask about someone that I'd never met before.

"Is there anything else?" Callie asked brusquely, and then I could hear it, the gentle sweet chatter of a toddler in the background.

"Is that . . . him?" It was so weird that my chest could feel both tighter and lighter all at the same time.

"Yeah, he's supposed to be asleep, the goofball." Callie's voice got softer as well, I noticed.

My eyes darted to Elizabeth, because she was the one I always wanted to share things with, which just came naturally. But though her head was tilted and she was obviously watching me, she wasn't glowing the way I felt like I was glowing. But she wasn't hearing what I was hearing either.

And it wasn't her kid.

Could Sebastian ever be part of her family?

The thought that he might never have a place in her life put a damper on the moment. "I'll let you go so you can get him to sleep. Good luck with that. And . . . him . . . Give him a hug for me."

"Okay, Weston. I will." She hung up, and again I looked to Elizabeth to see her reaction. This time she gave me a tight smile.

"That was good," she said. "You did good."

I let out a sigh of tension that I didn't realize had been knotting through my muscles. "I just don't have any idea what to do. I don't know how to be a dad. I need you, Elizabeth. I need you to—"

Her expression shadowed. "I can't talk about this right now, please. I need a break from it. I need to get out of this room."

"Oh. Sure. Whatever you need." I hoped I sounded supportive rather than punched in the gut. Which is how I felt. She was always so open and engaging. I didn't like seeing her like this, didn't know how to interact with her when she was closed off. And I definitely didn't want to let her out of my sight, even just for a few hours, but if that's what she needed, I would give it to her.

I would give her anything.

"We have tickets for the harbor cruise tonight. We can still make it if we leave now. You'll want to hurry up and change."

"You want me to go with you?" This time I definitely sounded too eager.

"I said I wanted to get away from *it*, not *you*. It's our honeymoon, you dork." She stepped over to the bed and sat on the edge so she could begin putting on her strappy sandals. "Plus, it would be kind of embarrassing to go on a romantic sunset cruise by myself. So hurry up."

She didn't have to ask again.

GETTING OUT OF the bungalow seemed to lighten the mood, but Elizabeth remained quiet and aloof for the rest of the evening. Neither of us had really eaten during the course of the day, and while I didn't have much of an appetite either, I forced us both to take a full plate of appetizers. The first glass of champagne was served as soon as we'd taken our seats, and with the gentle rocking of the boat and empty stomachs, alcohol didn't make a great addition. Elizabeth nibbled her food, getting down some cheese and pineapple before pushing her plate away.

"You're going to get seasick if you don't eat more than that," I prodded.

But she waved me away dismissively and kept her focus on the guy who was telling us stories about the island and the state of Hawaii in general.

As the sun set, and the night got cooler, Elizabeth wrapped her cardigan around herself. A couple of times I attempted to pull her into my arms under the guise of warming her up, but both times she only leaned on me momentarily before finding a reason to push away: to stretch her neck and peer at a splash in the distance, to reach down and tighten the buckle on her shoe.

I got the hint after that. I left my arm draped along the back of the seat behind her, accepting that she'd wanted me near, but she wasn't ready to let me in. I certainly was the last person to fault her for that.

She relaxed more as we made our way back toward the shore and the entertainment turned from the storyteller to a lone singer with a ukulele, his rich baritone singing the familiar songs of the Pacific islands. Her muscles relaxed as her thigh finally pressed against mine. Then her arm nudged against my rib cage, and I wondered how I'd ever lived without the heat of her body. How I could ever exist without hers close to mine.

Back at the dock, I climbed down from the boat first, then turned to give her my hand, helping escort her down the stairs. I'd used that as an excuse to hold her hand—since when did I need an excuse?—and then I wrapped my fingers through hers and didn't let go, holding on tightly as we walked back to the beach.

When she didn't pull away, I took it as a sign, and I plunged into the subject we'd been avoiding all evening, the one that had sat like a third person between us throughout the entire harbor outing. "I've never met him, you know," I said, sure without a doubt that she would understand who I was talking about. "It isn't like you, who lived with your father and then he suddenly went away. Sebastian has no idea about me. If he never meets me, it's not going to be the same sort of loss."

She stiffened, attempting to yank her arm away, but I held firm, dead set on keeping this little bit of contact.

Once she realized she was trapped, she sighed and looked out over the water. "He will still miss his father. Orphans, kids who were put up for adoption, children who were abandoned—all the research says they have abandonment issues because a parent has left them. It doesn't matter the circumstances. You would forever change the scope of his life."

I had probably heard that somewhere before. It wasn't the sort of thing I took note of. But I believed her, if she said that it was true.

"And, besides, Weston—I saw you. I saw your face when you just heard him on the phone. Your entire being lit up. You *want* him. Why would you deny yourself that?"

She was looking at me now, hard and deep. So hard and so deep that I thought she could probably see into my pores and capillaries. Behind my eyes and into the very lobes and neurons of my brain.

"Because I want you too," I said, sure that she could see that in all the things that she was looking at inside of me. Sure that it was as plain as the midnight blue sky above us. "I want you that much, too."

We'd reached the sand, and she stopped and faced me with her whole body. "I know that." She squeezed my hand, as though that simple gesture could amount to understanding all the feelings that I contained for her.

I would find a solution. I had to.

"Callie doesn't have a job," I said, suddenly remembering that. "Maybe she could come to France with us. Who doesn't want to live in Paris?"

"You can't just expect someone to pick up and move to another country!" She smiled at herself, hearing the words as they came out of her mouth. "You can't just expect someone who's *not* married to you, I mean. Someone who has no investment or commitment. And do you think that I really want that? My husband's ex-lover, moving across the ocean just because he said so? That's kind of creepy. I would always question why she would be willing to do that for you. It would just be icky all around."

"You sound jealous," I said with a grin that was completely

inappropriate for the moment. But jealousy meant she still cared, so I couldn't help myself.

While I was busy gloating, she tugged her hand away and started walking. I trotted right after her, about to apologize when she spoke first. "Hell, yes, I'm jealous. She has a part of you that I don't have. It's not fair."

"Oh, Lizzie." I wrapped my arm around her, even as she bristled. "You think I don't wish it were yours? I would give anything that my first child was with you." I kissed her shoulders and along her neck.

"Really? You want babies with me?" She was pouty and unsure. So vulnerable, and I realized that with all her confessions of when and how she wanted to have children I'd never confessed this to her.

I felt like a vulnerable teenager myself when I said it. "Yes. I want babies with you. I definitely want babies with you. I get this really strange fuzzy feeling all down my spine every time I think about it."

Her lower lip was still pushed out, but her body eased into mine. "Me too. I feel that way when I think about having babies with you too."

We walked quietly for a bit, just enjoying the sand and the beach and the beautiful island night. After a bit, she asked, "How did you know her?"

I was glad she'd asked. Part of me felt guilty for not telling her all this already, but I hadn't known if she'd wanted to hear it. I didn't want to tell it, to be honest. It made me feel shallow and promiscuous. Probably because I *had* been shallow and promiscuous. And though it wasn't news to Elizabeth, I didn't love reliving the details.

Still, it was fair that she knew. I wanted her to know.

"I met her at a rich kid's party in Aspen. She was on a ski trip, but she sprained her ankle their first day in town. I occupied her time while her friends hit the slopes." I paused, considering how best to say the next part. "We didn't leave my hotel room much."

"Got it." She was quiet and I could practically hear the wheels turning in her head. "I . . . thought you always used condoms."

Ah. "I do. I did. There was a . . . condom malfunction."

Elizabeth nodded. "I suppose that was bound to happen with your lifestyle."

With that tone, she obviously meant it to be a dig—I could feel the barbs piercing and twisting as the words settled on me.

But I probably owed her at least that one. So I took it, and swallowed the urge to respond.

"Why did she wait until now to tell you? Did she say?"

"She didn't know me. She made an assumption about how I'd react, and didn't even try to tell me. Also, she has issues with dads. I guess that's the 'in' thing these days."

She half-smiled. "And now she's changed her mind just out of the blue?"

I shrugged. "Maybe seeing I was getting married made her think I might actually be family material. I don't really know. I didn't ask. I was pretty overwhelmed with everything going on that day."

"That makes sense." She kicked at a branch of seaweed in our path. "What do you think you would've done if she'd told you before? If you had found out when she was pregnant?"

God, I hated to even think about it. My stomach soured with the acidic honesty. "I think she was smart not to give me the chance to find out. I wasn't ready to be a father until you came along. You're the person who made me finally think about having a home. Finally made me think that I could maybe be good for that. That maybe I *wanted* to be part of one."

"Of course you're good for being part of a home, you silly." She turned her head and placed an open mouth kiss on my neck.

She was right—I was good for being part of a home—but my home was with her. I wasn't anything but scraps of a shallow, promiscuous man without her, and I couldn't be good for anyone—let alone be a good father—in that condition. If I had a future with my son, it simply had to be with her at my side.

"I'll fly back and forth. It will work," I said, determined to figure out the solution to the twenty-ton dilemma weighing down on us.

"That's not going to work," she said immediately. "My father said the same thing. It lasted about three months."

"Elizabeth, I'm not your father."

"I didn't mean to imply that you were. I'm sorry. And I know that you would do better than him." She came up along the steps to the lifeguard station and paused against the railing. "But realistically, Weston. How can you manage a company and spend so much time in the air? Those are long flights. And if you're going to manage the advertising division in France, they're going to need you there."

I stuffed my hands in my pockets. "So I won't manage. I'll take a lower position. I can take a pay cut. Haven't you heard? My wife is, like, a billionaire, and apparently what's hers is mine." Jesus, that felt terrible to say, even in jest.

I immediately regretted it, though I knew Elizabeth would agree to it without batting an eye if I genuinely asked her to.

She furrowed her brows disapprovingly. "Do you really want to give up control of your company? I thought you loved what you do."

"I do. But a beautiful woman told me about making sacrifices, so . . ."

"I think that's very noble of you. But even with less work, I don't think you understand what you're committing to, going back and forth like that. It's going to get real old, real fast." She hesitated, and before I plunged in with a new argument, she continued. "No. This is not the best option for us. I don't want to be away from you that long. It's not the best way to start a marriage, either."

"You're not helping me here, honey. You keep shooting down everything I suggest."

"I'm sorry. I don't mean to seem so impossible." She swung around the railing to the steps and sat down on the fourth one up. "I've just already thought everything through myself. I've been thinking about every option, all day long—why do you think I spent so many hours in the bath? It's the only thing that's run through my mind since I found out, and it all comes down to the same thing. There's really only one good solution—"

"Do not say that it's splitting up."

"It is an option." Her gaze crashed into mine, holding it with earnest. "At least, for a while. Until you've established a relationship with Sebastian, and I get a better handle on things at Dyson headquarters, it could be—"

"No," I said, adamant. "Not even for a little while. Not an option."

She chuckled. "Just throwing it out there. Anyway, it wasn't what I was going to say. I was going to say that the best option would be for me to get a different CEO to run Dyson. My place is up for sale, but we still have your apartment. We can live there. I don't need to be hands-on with the corporation. It's gone this long without me. I can let the board run it. Maybe Darrell can even stay in charge? If he's doing it under my authority, maybe he'll stop padding his accounts at my expense and pad both of ours."

God, I loved her. I loved her so much. It felt like a living thing inside me, this love, the way that it would stretch and poke at me, the way that it would kick and squirm.

I squatted on the stair below her until I was at her eye level. "There is no possible way to tell you how much it means to me that you would offer that for me. There's also no way that I'm going to let you do it."

"It's not really giving up anything," she protested.

"Elizabeth, everything that you have done since I've met you, everything that you have been working for and toward has been to one day get you to the top of that company. There is no way in fucking hell that I am letting you give that up, especially for a child that isn't even biologically yours."

"It doesn't matter that he isn't from my womb." She reached her hand out and cupped my cheek, the spark of her touch sending a jolt through my nervous system. "He's part of you. That means he's part of me too. That means I want to be there for him. If you let me."

Heat spread through my body, like the sun was out and shining on me instead of the moon. "You undo me, Elizabeth Dyson." It took me a minute before I could say more. "I'm really very moved by that. I didn't know it was possible to love you more, but that right there. That would've done it. But it doesn't change the fact that I can't let you do that. I can't let you leave your dreams behind. You'd get resentful. I don't want to give you a future you resent. That is not what I'm bringing to this marriage."

"You don't know that. I might be perfectly happy. We could have a family of our own, now, too. Instead of waiting, I could get pregnant right away. Maybe this is the universe's way of saying we should start earlier."

I leaned forward and kissed her quick, because having a baby with her was an amazing and beautiful concept, but the timing was so wrong. And I didn't know how many kisses were left before she realized it, too.

"As eager as I am to knock you up, Lizzie, I'm not keeping you from France. We are picking another option. End of story." To further prove that I was done discussing this particular solution, I stood up and scooted past her up the stairs.

This lifeguard stand had the typical lookout chair at the top, but there was a larger enclosure all around it, with a roof and walls that came up mid-torso. I went to the farthest one and looked out at the island behind. A group of people were seated around a firepit about one hundred feet away, laughing and enjoying their evening. Other than that, the beach was quiet and empty.

Elizabeth came up behind me, and placed one hand on my arm as she nestled up to my side.

"It's beautiful tonight," she said.

I turned to look at her profile, studied the way her hair was tossed by the gentle breeze, zeroed in on the spot underneath her ear that I loved to suck on. It was a spot that always made her limp and boneless in my arms.

I was half hard just staring at this gorgeous woman.

Who was I kidding? I was fully hard. A heavy lead bar pressed against the linen of my pants. I was busy working out how I could convince her that we were alone enough to fool around when she grabbed my shirt into her fists and pulled me closer.

"Kiss me," she said, her voice thick and raspy, the way it got when she was aroused.

Fuck, yeah. This was exactly what I wanted to be talking about.

I turned her so that her back was against the wall and trapped her with my hands on either side of her. "Kiss you? Where do you want me to kiss you? Do you want me to kiss you here?"

I bent down to press my lips along her jaw, and she tilted her head back, granting me access to her neck.

"Or do you want me to kiss you here?" I bent lower, sucking at the delicate hollow at the bottom of her throat.

She let out a soft whimper, and my hips pressed against her, my aching cock searching for relief. When the rigid center of my itch rubbed her lower belly, her breath cut sharply.

Jesus, that only made me harder.

I reached up and undid the one button on her cardigan and slipped it off her shoulders, leaving it loose on her lower arms. Then I unbuttoned the top few buttons of her dress, peeling down the red fabric until her breasts stood up white and perky in the dim moonlight. Her nipples were furled knots, sharp and steepled. So tight and aroused, and I could imagine her clit plump and swollen, a perfect companion to the two peaks in front of me.

I leaned in and took one nipple into my mouth, licking my tongue along the tip before sucking the whole of it. "Is that where you want me to kiss you?"

"Mmm," she said, barely a response, as if the words were too much effort.

"Where? Here?" I gave the other nipple the same attention, following it up with a few extra flicks of my tongue against the tender tip. Her knees buckled, and my arms slid around her waist to hold her up.

"Should I get on my knees to kiss you?" I started trailing kisses down her belly, but she tugged at my collar, pulling me up.

"I want to kiss you here," she said, just before her mouth lifted up and closed over mine.

We kissed. With long, luscious strokes, I licked into her mouth as I palmed her breasts, savoring the gasps of pleasure that formed in the back of her throat. I could taste them. Who knew that sound had a taste? This sound did. A taste of hunger and vulnerability and pure fucking lust mixed with straight-up Elizabeth. That's what her gasps tasted like.

Her hands found the bulge imprisoned in my pants. Frantically, she began working at my buckle, magically undoing the belt and the zipper without ever looking down.

That amazing girl, that goddamn brilliant girl, got my pants undone and my cock free before I'd even lifted her skirt, the skirt I'd been dying to get underneath ever since I first saw her wearing it.

"You're in such a hurry," I said, wanting to slow her down, wanting to hold this moment.

"I need to. Need this. Hurry." She massaged my cock in her hand, and there wasn't a way I could argue with her. What Elizabeth wanted, Elizabeth got.

Hurrying my pace, I gathered up the bottom of her dress and flung it over the sides of the wall behind her, and found her pussy bare and glistening. "You've been so good to me, baby. Leaving your panties off. Just like I like it."

She'd done that so often on our honeymoon trip. She was such a good, perfect wife.

"Want to make you happy," she said, tugging mercilessly at my cock with one hand while pulling me nearer with her other at my shoulder.

"Put your elbows on the wall behind you," I told her, wanting to gain control.

With her lips in a slight pout, she did as I ordered. I stepped closer, looking down at her beautiful pussy. Even in the darkness, I could see how wet she was. I took my cock in my hand, and rubbed my crown up and down her folds, splitting her opening so I could see the pink, shining and greedy as it clenched around my tip.

Fuck, she was a goddamn erotic sight. Her tits plump and primed, her dress pulled down just enough to put them on display, her shoulders back, pushing them forward even more. Her skirt thrown up around her waist and over the wall left everything below her midriff naked and exposed to me. My erection was angry and throbbing now, sliding up and down through the wet arousal of her seams.

And she was mine. Forever mine.

It was the first time that I really believed that. The first time I really felt that we were sure. The first time that I was fucking her and feeling like it wasn't about trying to hold onto her, but about knowing we were going to last. Somehow the vision of a future with this sensual, breathtaking creature made me want to not rush through it, but also made me feel spun up with need I could barely contain.

I dragged the head of my cock up to her clit once more and circled it, pressing on her nub until I could see her muscles tense. "You have such a good pussy, Lizzie. This pretty, pretty pussy? One day, I'm going to put a baby in here. Would you like that? If I put a baby inside your pretty pussy?"

"Weston," she begged, her lids heavy. "Please."

Her entire body quivered, and I couldn't take it anymore. I had to be inside her.

Once more, I drew my head back down along her lips until I found her hole, waiting and hot. "Here? Here, Lizzie? This is where I'll put a baby. Would you like that?"

"Yes, please. Do it now. Put it in me now."

It was sex talk. She was on birth control, and she wanted me inside of her—not the baby, not now—but the idea of it, the knowledge that one day I would . . . It was overwhelming and intense and so incredibly hot.

I thrust inside her. Hard. Again. And again.

"Like that? Right there? Is that where you want me to put the baby?"

She clenched around me immediately, erupting into an orgasm that appeared fierce and mind-blowing, all the while stuttering over and over again, "Yes, yes, yes, yes."

"I'm going to. I will. Right there. Your belly will be so round with my kid. Your pussy will be spoiled with my seed." I told her all this, thrusting into her madly, defining our future, how I would make babies with her, and fuck her, and love her, day after day, night after night. Over and over and over, again and again.

I came with an explosion, white hot and terrifying. It shot through my body, stiffening every muscle, and I grunted as I ground into her, desperate to spill every last drop of myself into her.

When I was done, I held her and kissed her and promised her again that everything would be okay. That I would find a way to keep her and the child that I'd made.

This time, thank God, she didn't push away.

CHAPTER
THIRTEEN

Elizabeth

I'D JUST GOTTEN off the phone with the movers who were packing up my apartment when there was a knock at the door. Thankful that I'd pulled on yoga pants and a sweatshirt, I headed to the peephole and peered out. I saw who was waiting on the other side of Weston's door, frowned, then undid the deadbolt and opened the door.

"Mom," I said, accepting her hug as her constant companion, Marie, brushed past me, her arms full of takeout. "What are you doing here?"

"You canceled lunch. So we brought lunch to you." She shut the door behind her and opened the door to the powder room then closed it, searching for the coat closet.

"I canceled because I have so much to do." I opened the correct door for her and held it as she took off her coat.

"You still need to eat." She hung up her Donna Karan wool wraparound and turned back to me. "I miss you. You've been gone for two weeks."

Begrudgingly, I let her hug me again. "What are you going to do when I'm living in another country?"

Her embrace tightened. "Visit. A lot." When she pulled away she took my hand in hers and pulled me with her toward the kitchen table. "Come eat. You haven't had lunch yet, have you?"

"I haven't even had breakfast. I just woke up." Weston and I had only gotten home the night before, and I was still jet-lagged and on Hawaiian time. Somehow, he had dragged himself out of bed and gone to work. I'd had every intention of going to my apartment to direct the movers through packing, but after pushing snooze a good dozen times, I resorted to a phone call.

What I needed wasn't food—it was caffeine.

As if reading my mind, Marie called from the kitchen. "I just put on a pot of coffee. Want some water in the meantime?"

"No. Thanks. This is great." I dug into the bags on the table and pulled out a container of fried rice and another that ended up being cashew chicken.

Marie continued to make herself at home in Weston's apartment—our apartment?—opening cupboards until she found plates, and delivered them to the table. She set one in front of me and my mother and another one in the third place for herself, then went back to the kitchen for napkins.

"You got some color," my mother said, grabbing a pair of chopsticks out of the bag and tossing another pair toward me. "You must have made it out of the bedroom. Tell us about the honeymoon."

"Is Hawaii as beautiful as it was ten years ago when I went?" Marie asked.

My mother pounced on the pause before I could answer. "Who cares about the island? I want to know about the sex."

"Mom! I'm not going to tell you about that." I tossed the chopsticks down and stood, darting to the kitchen to grab a fork. "We were having sex before we got married, anyway."

"And I wanted to know about it then, but you wouldn't tell me. I thought maybe you'd be more divulging after you had a ring on it."

"No, Mom. Gross. Hey, how did you get past the doorman?" I wasn't just trying to change the subject. I actually was curious if I should be concerned about security.

"I have my ways," she said, waggling her brows as I took my seat again next to her. "But seriously. The honeymoon was good? The wedding was gorgeous. Everyone bought it as the real deal. It didn't seem fake at all."

"When that boy made his vows . . ." Marie paused from pouring the coffee to clutch her heart. "I swooned. I swear on my mother's grave. I actually swooned. I don't care if it was scripted. I don't want to know if it was. Because I swooned."

"He did a really good job," my mother concurred.

And it suddenly occurred to me that there was so much I needed to catch my mother up on.

I took a bite of chicken, deciding that I needed fuel before I tackled the debriefing. After I swallowed, I dabbed at my mouth with a napkin. "The wedding *was* good. I think it did what it needed to do. And the honeymoon was also really nice. Both of us had a really nice time."

"*Really nice time* is code for lots and lots of fucking, Marie," my mother said, exchanging a playful glance with her friend.

"Mom. Stop." I could feel my face heating as Marie set a steaming mug in front of me. "Thank you. You didn't have to do that. You didn't have to bring me lunch either." I offered the last statement to my mother since I knew she was behind it.

"I told you, honey. I missed you!" She smiled fondly at me, studying me too closely, the way mothers do. "You do look good. A little rosy in the cheeks, but otherwise you didn't get too burned, I see."

"I wore lots of sunscreen. And hats. And I stayed in the shade a bunch too."

"Good girl. No skin cancer for you."

"This is a fabulous apartment," Marie said from the kitchen where she was cleaning out the sink, likely washing up after Weston's breakfast.

"Marie! Don't do that!" I jumped up and swiped the bowl out of her hand.

"It was one dish. I was putting it in the washer for you."

I squinted at her, doubtful she was going to stop at one dish, as I loaded it into the dishwasher myself. "It is a nice place," I said with a sigh as I closed the dishwasher door afterward, looking out over the living room where the sun was shining through the giant windows. As much as I'd bitched about the place, I'd grown to love it. The layout was refreshing. The natural light, spectacular. The memories, irreplaceable. "It's too bad Weston might sell it when we go to France."

Weston's latest plan was to feel out Callie's interest in moving to another country, despite my hesitancy about wanting his ex anywhere near me, and if that didn't work, he was set on traveling back and forth, living a week every month in the States. In that scenario, he wanted an apartment in Brooklyn, closer to Sebastian.

Truthfully, I'd rather have his ex close to me all the time then have Weston alone with her on a regular basis.

But, really, none of it felt like a long-term solution. Nothing felt figured out. Nothing felt settled.

"Sell it?" my mother asked from the table, her mouth half-full of spring roll. She finished chewing before she went on. "Won't Weston want to move back here after the divorce?"

I wiped my hands on the dish towel and pivoted toward her. "There's actually probably not going to be a divorce."

"Heavens, it *was* real!" Marie exclaimed behind me.

"Elizabeth! Are you saying—?" my mother put her hands to her face, a frequent reaction when she was flustered or excited.

"I'm saying that Weston and I are in love." It still felt strange to say that. Strange and dizzying and bright. As though there was a secret light switch hidden somewhere inside me and when it was flicked on, it burst forth a megawatt ray of solar brilliance. And all it took to turn it on was to think of how much I loved Weston. To think of how much he loved me.

My mother squealed and jumped up from her seat so I took the few steps to meet her in yet another embrace.

"Oh my God, that's so wonderful! I'm so happy for you! You're happy, right?" She leaned back to look at me. "Yes, you're so happy. This is amazing. Marie, our baby is really married! I should have worn a better dress for the photos. Thank goodness you looked as spectacular as you did. My God, you really got married!" She swept me up in her arms. Again.

"Yes, Mother. We're happy. It's real. *I'm* happy."

I was also terribly confused. But wasn't that the way with love?

"So then you'll be settling down in France together seriously. You're really going to make a home there." When she let go of me this time, she put her hand to her chest and rubbed the spot right below her throat. "I'm going to have to consider moving overseas. I don't know if I can live so far away from you if you're actually putting down roots."

Though I appreciated that my happiness was a priority for my mother, it was more than mildly annoying that even she didn't consider my move as real without a husband attached. Sometimes she was just as much of a traditionalist as my father had been.

But that battle was pointless considering the thing I was going to say next.

"About putting down roots . . ." Though Weston had his ideas of what we should do, I still thought my idea was better. "What would you think if we didn't move to France? And we stayed here, instead."

"You know I'd love that, darling. But what about the company?" She tugged at my shirt, straightening it on my shoulders. "Why are you even thinking about this? Does Weston not want to move?"

"No, he's willing to move." I brushed past her and headed back to my seat at the table, wanting to be have space between us so I could talk without feeling so "mom'd." "Just. Imagine that. If we settled down here . . . we could start a family."

"Angela! Babies!" Marie exclaimed from behind me.

"Elizabeth, are you pregnant?" My mother didn't seem quite as excited as her friend.

"No!"

"You promise? You can tell me if you're in trouble. I don't even think they call it 'in trouble' anymore. But you know I'll understand." She came and sat down at the seat Marie had set for herself, directing her focus completely on me.

"I told you. I'm not pregnant. I'm just saying I could get pregnant. I could put someone else in charge of the company. I could be less hands-on and raise kids instead. I could be a full-time mom. Like you."

Her face scrunched up as much as her Botox and fillers allowed. "Oh, honey. I don't know about that."

That had not been the reaction I'd expected. "Why not? Don't you want grandkids? You were happy not working, raising me. Weren't you?" My heart thumped in my chest, afraid she'd say no and turn my whole image of my childhood upside down.

"Yes. I was," she said to my relief. "Very happy. But you are not me. You would be bored out of your mind. And you fought so hard for your company. You should go to France. You've said for years that you were planning to wait to have kids. I think you should stick with that plan, if you ask me. Is Weston pressuring you otherwise?"

"No. He's not. Sometimes plans change, though. With a new person in my life, I thought I should rethink everything."

"You shouldn't have to rethink your dreams if you've really found the right man. Don't rethink this. You will regret it. Go to France, do your thing, win big, or fail even, and then have your family. You have years for that."

"But, Angela! Babies!"

I glanced up to find Marie had paused from dusting the appliances in the kitchen to make her comment. "Stop cleaning!" I scolded, knowing it was hopeless.

"Babies can wait," my mom said. She smoothed her mostly drawn-in eyebrow with her pinky. "I'm not old enough to be a grandma yet anyway. Unless you're already pregnant. You're sure you're not?"

"I'm sure. Geez."

She narrowed her eyes. "Then what is it? There's something. I can tell. I know you, Elizabeth. What's going on?"

I threw my body back against the chair in a frustrated huff. My mother always managed to bring out teenage behavior from me. "Fine. There's something else. It's Weston. Sort of. He . . ." There was a part of me that wanted to really throw him under the bus, wanted to make him the bad guy for keeping the secret that he'd kept.

But a bigger part of me realized that if we were going to make our marriage work, I had to treat us like a team.

So I stuck to what was relevant. "He just found out that he has a two-year-old son that he was unaware of until now."

"Oh my God," Marie said, dropping the duster and stepping closer for the gossip.

"I know. It's been complicated, to say the least. He found out on our wedding day."

"Oh my God." From my mother this time.

"Right?" I filled them both in on Callie and her surprise visit, on the bomb she dropped and the dilemma about Weston wanting to be part of Sebastian's life yet also wanting to be with me in France.

When I'd finished, they were both sitting at the table on either side of me, staring at me with wide eyes.

"Are you going to say anything?" I asked, looking at my mother. I hadn't intended to ask her for advice, but now that I'd spilled everything, I realized I wanted it. Especially since she'd shot down the only solution I'd thought was viable.

"I'm not sure," my mom said glancing to Marie, as though seeking some support before saying something difficult.

I tensed. My mother didn't usually give hard words. I gave her hard words more than she delivered them to me.

"Spit it out, Mom. What are you thinking? Are you thinking it's never going to work? Daddy couldn't handle seeing me and being part of my life so how the hell is Weston going to make it work?"

"I don't think that's fair to say," my mother said, surprising me. "Your father would probably have been a lousy father even if he was on the same continent. He was simply more invested in his business than he was in a family. It's just the sort of man he was. If Weston intends to be a father who is devoted to his son, I'm sure he could work it out."

Again, I felt relief.

But . . ."Then why are you so hesitant? You seem hesitant. What am I missing?" The way she was cautiously staring at me, I felt like I was missing a whole lot.

She answered with a question, which I hated. "What are the terms of the inheritance again? How long do you have to be married?"

"They're vague. It just says I have to get married. I wanted a solid marriage so that Darrell had nothing to stand on if he chose to fight it in court. What are you thinking?"

"That Weston's secret love child gives you a good reason to want a divorce."

"Mom!" I scooted away from her. "Why would you even say that?"

"Because I know you were worried the marriage might not look real if you got divorced too soon, and I'm seeing this as a way out of that worry. It's actually kind of a lucky break."

"It's not a lucky break if I'm not intending to get divorced anymore. Did you forget that part? Where I said I loved him? And he loved me?" It was my turn to steal a glance with Marie, as I checked to see if she thought my mother was being as insensitive as I currently thought she was.

But Marie looked as though she thought my mother's idea wasn't so bad. "Maybe you should hear your mother out," she said, nodding toward the woman who'd raised me.

"Then tell me already. Quit dragging this out. What is it I'm not thinking of?"

My mother tapped her pink-painted nails on the table, seeming reluctant or unsure of how to proceed.

Then she shifted in her chair and dove right in. "I'm going to just be real honest with you, honey. Marriage is hard. Whoever you are. Whatever circumstances you are in. Especially the first year of marriage. And here you are trying to add a really big job on top of that new marriage. And on top of that, you're adding the additional stressor of moving to a completely new country, which isn't too big of a deal for you because you've spent so much of your life in France, but what about Weston? Then again, on top of all of that, Weston is trying to form a new relationship with a son he just found out about? You will have to build a relationship with that child too, you know. Plus you're adding the stressor of being apart so much. That's a whole hell of a lot of stressors. I'm pretty sure that any good marriage counselor would tell you it's *too many* stressors. How can any marriage work under those circumstances?"

"That is an awful lot of stressors," Marie said, nodding.

I hadn't thought of it exactly like that. Some of it, but not all of it. Not in quite those terms.

I didn't like those terms.

"That's why I suggested living here. It would take out half of the things you just said." My throat was tight though, because I'd already heard her opinion on me living in the U.S., and because I really didn't want to give up being a major part of Dyson Media. And that only left one real option.

"I see," my mother said, patting my hand. She tilted her head and nodded understandingly. "You know that's not going to make you happy, though. You know you're going to be miserable like that."

"But I love him, Mom," my voice cracked and a stupid tear surprised me by rolling down the side of my cheek. "And Weston has never loved a woman until me. It's like we're meant to be. Like we're supposed to have found each other. Supposed to have taught each other how to love. What's it all for if we don't end up together?"

"That's amazingly beautiful. And so very special. Even if it ends, it doesn't mean it won't have been special. Remember that Hollywood movie that came out a couple of years ago? It won the Academy Award. Where the two artists were really in love and they split up because they knew they had to go follow their dream and that they couldn't be together while they did that. They didn't end up together, but in the end they were both really happy because they lived for their dream, and they found other love and it all worked out in the end."

"I hated that movie," I said, my lip trembling.

"It is a really heartbreaking movie, Angela," Marie agreed.

"The point is," my mother said, raising her voice to drown out Marie, "you may very well have been meant to find each other. You may very well have been meant to teach each other how to love. But you might not have been meant to live together forever. I was meant to find your father, and I was meant to have you. But I was not meant to live with that man forever."

"No one was meant to live with that man forever," I said, wiping at my nose.

"You know, honey. If you and Weston have something real, something that's really meant to last, then he'll still be here when you're ready. Go off and run your business for five years or so. Come back and then see if he's waiting. If he is, then you'll know. And if he isn't, then you'll know that too. Real life isn't like a romance novel. You don't always have to end up with the guy."

"I don't think I like real life anymore." I was definitely wishing my real life didn't include a know-it-all mother.

That wasn't true—I was grateful for my mom and glad she'd stopped by. I needed to hear what she had to say, even if I didn't decide to listen to her.

Was I actually thinking of taking her advice?

Nothing she'd said had been wrong. In fact, she'd been very right. About everything. That was the worst part. I wouldn't—couldn't—accept that her plan was the only way forward.

"I need Weston," I said, refusing to give him up so easily. "I need him to help me run the business. He's taught me a lot, but I'm not ready to do this on my own. I need him by my side!"

"Pfft." She waved her hand, dismissing the notion. "You'll hire advisors. You were planning to run the company before you fell in love with him, so why not now? Do you really think Weston's going to have time to give you the kind of attention you think you need when he's focused on being a new dad? Besides, I bet you know more than you think you do. All you need is little confidence."

I rolled my eyes. Confidence would fix everything. Right. She was talking like I was preparing to give a lecture, not run a multibillion-dollar corporation.

She had a point about Weston, though—could I really rely on him to be my pillar of strength, my backbone, and my right hand when he was going to have his hands full figuring out this fatherhood thing? It wasn't fair to him to even expect that. And it wasn't fair to me to not have someone to rely on.

"I don't know what to do," I said, my voice tight with emotion.

"This is a lot, I know," Mom said. "Think about it. Think about all of it. One thing your father was good at was making plans. He looked at every angle, thoroughly researched every option before putting any plan in motion. Follow his lead and do the same."

"It just feels so . . . cold," I said. "I don't like following his lead."

"Honey, it's your *heart*. Making plans to keep it safe is the opposite of cold. Besides, your dad isn't here to threaten Weston into safeguarding it. Which he certainly would have. I know this inheritance thing feels archaic, but I can tell you—when he put it into place, it was because he assumed you'd be more like me. He thought you'd fall in love and want to spend your time on that. And you have. So now it's time to channel him and make a logical decision about that love, whatever it is."

"Thank you, Momma." I sat with her words for a minute, then added, "I like it when you say nice things about Daddy. I really didn't know him that well, and I forget that he was a good person too, until you remind me. I appreciate that you remind me."

It made it a lot easier to deal with the fact that I was my father's daughter, knowing that he wasn't all bad after all. Knowing that if I made that choice, the choice my mother had suggested, it would make me like my father, but that wouldn't be the worst thing in the world.

AFTER MY MOTHER and Marie left, leaving me with lots to think about, I decided to take at least part of her advice and research all my options thoroughly. I picked up my phone, feeling the weight of the call that I knew I needed to make to Darrell, having promised I would get in touch with him when I was back on the mainland. I still hadn't cleared up Weston's double family. As soon as I did, it took away the option of using Sebastian as a reason for a divorce.

I couldn't do that.

Could I?

I didn't know yet. Maybe. I needed more time to sort out all my alternatives.

So it wasn't Darrell that I called.

"Elizabeth, what a surprise." Clarence sounded genuinely happy to hear from me. "To what do I owe this pleasure?"

"Well, I was wondering something. Did you mean it before, when you offered to help me in any way I needed?" My stomach curled as the words came out of my mouth, feeling as though I were committing some sort of betrayal just by having the conversation.

"Yeah. I definitely did. What do you need?"

"I'm not sure yet."

CHAPTER
FOURTEEN

Weston

I PICKED AT a piece of tape on the package sitting on my lap for the fiftieth time then smoothed it back down before pulling out my phone and looking at the clock on the screen. "We're going to be early," I said.

Elizabeth didn't answer, seemingly lost in her own thoughts as she stared out the window of the cab driving over the Brooklyn Bridge.

I understood. This was a lot. A lot to ask of her when she already had so much on her plate. But that was marriage—sharing everything. Sharing the little and the lot, even when the "lot" wasn't bargained for.

It was Saturday. Three weeks since I'd married her. Three weeks since I'd found out I was a father to a little boy. And today, together, we were finally meeting him.

I couldn't decide if I was excited or nervous or was coming down with the flu. I definitely felt like I wanted to throw up.

My knee started bouncing and the present slid onto the seat next to me, bringing my attention to it once more. "Did we get the right gift? I should've gotten the construction set. It had three times the pieces."

I was met with silence. "Elizabeth?"

She turned her head toward me. "What? No. That set was made for a five-year-old. This is perfect. It's age-appropriate."

Age-appropriate. That was a term used at the ad office. Not in my actual life. Not before now, anyway.

Elizabeth covered her hand with mine. "He's going to love it."

I laced my fingers through hers and held on. It was soothing to touch her. And shocking, as though I hadn't touched her in a long time. Since we'd been back from the honeymoon, we hadn't been as connected as we had been before. She seemed more distant, more guarded, but I was sure she was just preoccupied with the overwhelming obligations to the outside world that we now had to face.

There was also much for me to catch up on at Reach, and I still hadn't broken the news to Donovan that I was leaving—mostly because I wanted to have my exact arrangements in place before I did, not because I was afraid of telling him. Not that at all. And Elizabeth was busy packing and arranging the transfer of business. She wanted to be in France before the New Year. Christmas was in two days. It was all happening so fast.

And I still wasn't sure how to be enough. Enough for Donovan. Enough for Sebastian. Enough for Elizabeth.

But I loved her. And I knew she loved me.

And I knew I loved this kid.

And somehow, *that* would be enough. I just hadn't yet figured out how.

I fiddled again with the gift. "Should we have asked for it not to be wrapped with a ribbon? Is that dangerous? Could he choke on it?"

Elizabeth twisted her lip. "I can't remember the exact age that strings stop being a concern. But it's not going to be a problem. We're going to throw away the wrapping as soon as he opens it. Stop worrying, honey. He's going to love the present and he's going to love you." Her phone buzzed, and she looked down at the cell, her face falling at whatever she read on the screen.

"Is it him again?" I asked, grateful for the distraction of something else toward which to aim my anxiety.

"Yeah." She slid her fingers across the screen, declining the call, and tucked the phone away. "I told him I'd get back to him when we were done with the honeymoon, and I still haven't."

She was talking about her cousin, Darrell. He'd called a few times since he dropped the news about the gossip site that had outed me as a dad, but she'd declined all the calls. "Why don't you just respond to him? Let him know it's not a concern."

She hesitated, taking a slow breath, then letting it out before she answered. "I don't know."

I could understand. How long had I waited to tell her things because it was easier not to deal with it? She already had so much on her mind, it made sense that she didn't want to have a confrontation with her cousin right now as well. "Give yourself a few days then. Talk to him after the holidays."

She opened her mouth, but the car was slowing, so she asked, "Are we here?"

"We are." I looked again at the time. "We're really early. Almost half an hour early." I must've been really anxious when we left.

"Well, we can't sit in here. And it's too cold to stand outside."

"I'll let her know we're here."

Elizabeth settled up the cab fare while I texted Callie. We climbed out of the car and stood on the sidewalk, waiting for her to respond. A tall, muscular woman with thick, straight, dirty blond hair brushed past us and headed up the steps of the brownstone, her arms full of groceries. She glanced back at us, her expression wary.

"You're right that we can't just hang out here. This is the kind of neighborhood where people call the cops on loiterers," I said. Luckily, just then Callie responded.

No problem. Come on in.

"Here we go, Mrs. King." I shifted the gift under my arm so I could take her hand again.

"Here we go. *Daddy*." Her smile was the confidence I needed. We walked up the steps together.

⌣⌒

"SORRY AGAIN THAT we're so early," I apologized as we walked across the threshold into Callie's apartment a few minutes later.

"It's fine. Really. Let me take that, then I can get your coats." She reached for the gift in my hand and set it on the coffee table.

I turned to help Elizabeth with her coat, covertly checking out the room for Sebastian. I didn't see him but saw the woman from outside, the one who'd been carrying the groceries. She was in the kitchen now, putting them away. She must be Dana—Callie's roommate.

I handed Elizabeth's coat over to our hostess, then began to work on taking off my own jacket as I continued to take in my surroundings. When I caught Callie's eye, she said, "He's not up from his nap yet. He should be awake any minute. I can go get him, but he might be cranky."

Maybe I hadn't been so sly in my search for him after all. "Let him sleep," I said, hard as it was to let even another second go by without meeting him. "It will give us time to get the introductions out of the way. Callie, this is my wife, Elizabeth." I put my hand on Elizabeth's lower back, where her waist cinched in just above her luscious ass, and displayed her proudly. I still wasn't used to her being *my wife*. Wasn't used to *having* a wife. I liked saying it as often as I could.

I noticed Elizabeth checking Callie out, her gaze moving up the length of my ex-lover's body before it hit her face. I was sure it was supposed to be as covert as my own examination of the room, and I hoped that Callie hadn't seen it, but my chest broadened and puffed at the obvious hint of jealousy.

"It's such a pleasure to meet you," Callie said, shifting the coats to her other arm so that she could shake Elizabeth's hand. "You must hate me. Showing up in your life the way I did."

"I don't hate you. I don't know you." Elizabeth's honest answer was somehow warm with honesty rather than snappy. "I hope that we can get to know each other, though."

"I'd like that." Callie smiled, then slipped inside the coat closet to hang up our things. When she turned back, she said, "I really hope I didn't ruin the honeymoon. I've had a lot of regret about the way that I approached Weston. I really didn't think I had another way of reaching him, but in hindsight, it was a crappy thing to do to you."

"I suppose . . ." Elizabeth glanced from Callie to me. "It did change the dynamic of the trip, in a way. But I didn't know about any of this until the internet article came up."

Callie's jaw dropped, and I could feel my neck heat with embarrassment. "Weston! You didn't tell her?" Her eyes cut back to my wife. "And you didn't murder him? Maybe my father is right—miracles do happen."

"I was a coward and an asshole. I didn't want to—" I broke off, realizing that Callie didn't need my excuses, and Elizabeth had already heard enough of them. "Let's just leave it at—cowardly asshole. Thank God, Elizabeth is the most amazing woman I know, and she's been very supportive about all of this." I tugged that amazing woman to my side, wrapping my arm around her waist, hoping she could feel just how much I loved her, how much I appreciated her in this moment.

"You *must* be an amazing woman to have tamed this notorious player," Callie said, agreeing.

The woman in the kitchen snorted, as if trying to hold back a laugh.

"Oh. That's Dana." She twisted her neck toward the kitchen. "Get out here and be friendly, will you?"

"Fine." Dana hung up her reusable grocery bag on a hook on the wall, and then headed over to us. "Nice to finally meet you," she said shaking my hand, eyeing me much the same way that Elizabeth had eyed Callie.

Callie had said she'd been a big help to her, and very supportive. Nannied a bit, if I was recalling correctly. It was nice to see that the mother of my child had someone on her side, so I tried not to take offense.

Elizabeth had a different reaction. "Oh," she said suddenly, as if understanding something that she didn't before. Then her lips pursed together tightly, as though hiding a smile, until it was her turn to shake Dana's hand.

"A real pleasure to meet you," she said to her, even more enthusiastically than she had to Callie. Maybe she was relaxing into the situation. I was too. Though my nerves hadn't calmed completely, the pleasant introductions combined with the scent of fresh coffee brewing made me feel better. It felt like one by one, the unknown factors were fading, and now there was really just the one left.

One big one.

But this was good. Really good, getting all the adult stuff out of the way before Sebastian woke up.

"You haven't had any trouble because of the article, have you?" I asked, since we'd recently been on the topic. "No one tried to bother you or ask more questions?"

"Only person I know who saw it was my father," Callie said. "He's left me two messages, which I haven't returned yet. *That's* the King who knocked you up?' I hadn't bothered giving him details before so he'd assumed you were no one he'd know of."

I cleared my throat, trying not to appear too concerned while simultaneously offering up a prayer that our fathers had never done business together. "It doesn't necessarily sound like he's happy now that he *does* know."

"Nah. He's probably glad the press is linking me to a father at all, for once. Especially a guy as reputable as you. It's like a Christmas present for him. Better than whatever no-name 'loser' everyone is assuming knocked me up and left me to do this alone. Or, just as bad in his eyes, getting pregnant from a sperm bank. "

Yikes. Her conservative senator father had more issues than *Forbes* magazine. That had to be tough to deal with for Callie in this day and age, where so many children came without a wedding first. Where women chose to become single mothers for no other reason than the fact that they wanted a child. The man really needed to loosen up.

"Can I get you something to drink?" Callie offered. "We have coffee, tea, eggnog—"

"Is it too early for hot toddies?" Dana asked, already heading back to the kitchen.

"It's two in the afternoon, so yes," Callie said.

"But it's the holidays. Anyone interested?"

A little alcohol sure did sound like a nice way to ease the rest of the knots in my shoulders, but I wanted to be a responsible parent.

"I'd like one," Elizabeth said, surprising me.

"Fine. I'll have one too," Callie conceded.

Well, if everyone else was doing it . . ."Me too."

Dana grinned triumphantly as she put the kettle on.

"Since you opened the door to the conversation," Elizabeth said, crossing one jeans-clad leg over the other as she sat on the couch, "might I ask why you decided to tell Weston at all? He's explained to me your reasons for not telling him in the beginning. What made you change your mind?"

I appreciated my wife for this question. I knew it had to be hard for her to understand Callie's decision. Elizabeth would have been eager to unite a father with his baby, and keeping her pregnancy away from me was not a choice she could easily relate to.

Callie tucked one leg underneath her on the loveseat as she sat down, then glanced at her roommate. "Actually, Dana convinced me."

Elizabeth and I both looked toward Dana, who beamed and said, "Guilty."

"She pointed out that I was being selfish by not giving you a chance," Callie continued. "She also reminded me that this was the age that Sebastian would start realizing that other kids have dads. The most helpful thing she said, probably, was when she pointed out that keeping Sebastian from his father wouldn't change any of the things that happened with me and *my* father. Which, I guess was when I realized I was thinking of myself. Not of Sebastian. And not about Weston. So I reached out." She smiled knowingly again at Dana before changing her focus back to me.

Me, with my own problem father. To think how close I was to never knowing . . .

"I'm really grateful that you changed your mind. And really grateful to you, Dana, for being such a positive influence, and I can tell you're very important in Callie and Sebastian's life. I'm very grateful to that. For what it's worth."

Next to me, Elizabeth made a little sound, but I didn't understand what she was trying to say, or what she might've been trying to warn me about, so I just took her hand again and squeezed it, guessing maybe she was just moved by the whole situation, much like I was.

"Then this means you're on board? That you're going to be part of Sebastian's life?" Dana was the one who asked, as she brought the first two mugs of hot honeyed bourbon over to us.

I let go of Elizabeth's hand to take my drink, then lifted it to my lips for a sip, delaying my answer. Of course, it was too hot, and I burned my mouth. I had to put it down on the coffee table right away to fan my tongue.

Also, since I'd been asked a question, all eyes were on me through the entire mishap. Dana stood with her arms crossed across her chest, biting back a laugh.

"When they say hot, they mean *hot*. Thank you. I'll let that cool." I watched as Elizabeth wisely set hers down right away. "And yes, I definitely want to do the dad thing." I still was not quite ready to talk about all the details. My dream was to ask Callie to come back to France with us, but I needed to feel out her situation first. As tight as she was with her friend Dana, it was starting to seem like maybe that wasn't the route to go. Besides, it wouldn't be very nice of me to take my son away from his favorite babysitter.

And that left the option of once a month, full-week visits. I wasn't sure how Callie was going to feel about that one either.

"I'd like to try to work out some arrangements before we leave today. But that doesn't necessarily have to be right this second." I looked around the room, at the faces of all the women, hoping someone would be able to steer the conversation in a different direction.

But nobody had anything to say. "Or we can do it now. First of all, though, I want to be able to reassure Elizabeth." My wife sat up straighter next to me, and it almost seemed as though she shook her head, but the movement was so slight I might've misread it. "We are newlyweds and all. I need her to realize that there isn't going to be anything between you and me, Callie. That you have no intentions of creating the family that the internet scandal says exists."

"Weston," Elizabeth said quietly.

I couldn't ignore that; she definitely was trying to get my attention.

"Honey, this is important. I want you to hear it from Callie. You don't mind reassuring her, do you?" Callie had told me to my face that I was a narcissistic asshole. All she had to do was repeat that for Elizabeth.

It even seemed she'd be happy to say it, considering the laugh she was stifling.

Dana was also stifling a laugh, not so successfully.

Elizabeth shook her head more noticeably now.

"What? What's going on?" I asked.

"Weston," Elizabeth said. "I'm not worried."

I smiled patiently. "You say that now. But you'll feel better if you hear it."

Elizabeth sighed. "I mean, Dana and Callie are together."

Right. Together. Good friends.

"*Together*, Weston."

Oh.

More than friends.

No way. "No way," I said. "You're a lesbian?"

Callie nodded.

That explained why there was only one other bedroom besides Sebastian's. "Or, I guess, bi. Because you slept with me." It was important to get the labels correct these days. And bi made me feel better, for some reason.

"Lesbian is really more accurate," Callie said.

"You were the last guy she was with," Dana said proudly. "And she's not going back."

"I—turned you lesbian?" No, no. This was not happening.

Elizabeth took one look at my face and started laughing so hard she was shaking.

"This is terrible. Really, really terrible." I'd never felt so much a champion for the disenfranchised minority as I did right then in a room full of women laughing at me and my sexuality.

"No, it's not," Elizabeth reassured me, through her mirth. "This is good."

"Yeah," Dana confirmed. "I guess I owe you too, Weston King." She pivoted on her boot heel and headed back to the kitchen to pour another two mugs of toddies.

Thankfully mine had cooled enough to drink because, goddammit, I needed it.

As I brought the mug to my lips, I realized what else Dana and Callie's "together" meant—Callie was tied to Dana in a way that was far stronger than friendship. And Dana was a lot more to Sebastian than his favorite babysitter. That meant that asking them to move to France for me was a lot harder. Impossible, probably.

Not that I was ready to give up the idea.

"Dana, so, do you . . . work?" It wasn't the best attempt at casual conversation, but it was what I had.

"Look at him; he's seeing if you're worthy of me," Callie said. "Better than my father who won't even acknowledge Dana's existence."

I felt a painful stab between my ribs of sympathy for her situation, for being so estranged from her family. I could definitely relate to that. At least they didn't see any ulterior motives in the question.

"Yes, I do." Dana returned with a mug for her partner then sat down next to her on the loveseat. "I work for the State Department. It's actually how we met." She looked at Callie the same way I was sure I looked at Elizabeth. "We were at a party hosted by the state for the senators and representatives and their families."

"Ironic, isn't it?" Callie said. "My father actually brought us together in a way. I'd probably cut off all ties if it wasn't for Sebastian. It's seemed really important to have my family around since he's been born, whether we all get along or not."

The pain in my ribs increased and twisted. My parents still didn't know about Sebastian. I had to tell them, too. Add that to the list of issues to deal with.

"I'm so sorry your family isn't understanding or supportive. My father was a misogynistic asshole," Elizabeth said, "if that helps. He wouldn't let me have my company until I was married."

The women exchanged appropriate sounds of horror and sympathy while I silently tucked away the idea of having *my* family all together in one country. The State Department was not the kind of job where you could just fill out some papers and transfer from one place to another. You went where they sent you. Besides, people who worked in politics generally liked their politics. It wasn't like Dana could find an easy replacement for that in France.

"Now that she's going to run the company though," I said, using the opportunity to drop the next bombshell, "we have to move to where Dyson Media is headquartered. Which is Paris." I paused a moment, letting that settle. "I know that throws a wrench in what you want in terms of me being available as a father. But I *do* still want to be involved in his life."

Callie stiffened, and next to her, so did Dana. "How do you intend to make this work from a different country?" Callie asked. "Skype? That's not really the kind of involvement I was thinking when I said I wanted you involved in his life, Weston."

"I know. I know," I rushed to calm her. "I've already thought about that and talked it over with Elizabeth. We've decided that I will travel back and forth frequently. I'm going to get an apartment in Brooklyn and spend a week here each month. I was hoping you would agree to let Sebastian be in my care for the full week. After he gets to know me better, of course."

Callie wrapped her arms around herself and bit her lip, glaring at Dana. "That's not really what I'm comfortable with."

"He'll be nearby," Dana said comfortingly. "If he has an apartment in Brooklyn. You will have him for three weeks every month. That's still the majority. And think of all the extra time we'll get to spend alone together!"

"I can't be away from him for more than a few *hours* at a time already. That's too long. It's too soon. He won't like it either; he needs me. I was thinking more like weekends. A couple days at a time." Callie was visibly rattled.

"Sure, I understand." I *did* understand. I was taking away her child, in a sense.

But he was my child, too.

"Then maybe we could at least agree to share him every day for a week? I could take him during the days and bring him back at night?" It wasn't exactly what I'd been planning or hoping for. Flying across the ocean every month, I really wanted to have as much time as I could with him.

But she'd made a good point about his preparedness. Having almost no experience with kids except that I once was one, I really didn't know what kind of emotional attachment was normal for a two-year-old.

"Yeah, maybe. Maybe that would work." She didn't have time to sit with the idea, because just then a burst of chattering sounded over the baby monitor. "Look who's up. I'll go get him. Be right back."

She rushed off, and I rolled my shoulders back, trying to loosen the sudden tension that had crept up from the conversation and the renewed anxiety about meeting my kid.

My kid.

What if he didn't like me? What if I didn't like *him*?

What if I saw him and couldn't let him go?

"We'll figure it out," Dana said, encouragingly. "Just give her some time. Remember, it's just been her and him. She needs to get used to the idea of sharing that."

I nodded, willing to believe her, but too focused on the terrifying moment approaching.

As Callie walked back into the room, I stood up, unable to sit any longer. My heart was beating so fast I could feel it in my throat. My hands felt clammy and my muscles jittered.

But as anxious as I was, my focus was locked on the little boy in her arms. From the second I caught sight of him, my vision tunneled, and he was the only thing I could see. Nothing anyone said or did could make me look away. The house could be burning down, and I would still be focused on this wonderful, amazing, beautiful little boy.

His hair was long, with curls at the end, similar to pictures I'd seen of myself as a child. So blond in some places it was almost white. His eyes were bright blue under the longest lashes. His lips were incredibly thick and pouty, his face angelic. His outfit looked like something a grown-up would wear—a plaid button-down shirt with khaki pants. One sock was half-falling off his foot.

Elizabeth stood and automatically reached to fix the sock. Sebastian looked down at the woman touching him.

"Sock," he exclaimed, pointing with a pudgy finger.

At the sound of his high, light, tiny voice, it felt like pieces of my chest broke off inside and scattered everywhere, spreading through me like no drug I'd ever known.

Elizabeth watched me with a curious smile on her face, stepping out of the way so that Callie could continue her path toward me to show me my son. "Yep. Sock. That's your sock. And this is your daddy. You see your daddy, Sebastian?"

Sebastian took a second to draw his eyes from his sock to his mother's pointed finger, and then finally to me. He met my eyes and smiled.

I tried to smile back, but my throat felt so tight all of a sudden, it was hard. Inside, my chest did that weird thing again, breaking and spreading throughout me. And my voice was shaking when I asked, "Can I?" I was already holding my arms out toward him.

"Of course," she said. "Want to go to Daddy?"

Sebastian was even smaller than I'd pictured, and I suddenly realized exactly why Callie was so protective. He was hardly more than a baby—I didn't expect him to welcome a strange man. But he surprised me, opening his arms and reaching for me the way I was reaching for him.

I held my breath as Callie let him go, and then I was holding him on my own. Holding my son. He was lighter than I'd thought he'd be. So very light. How could something so little and tiny be big enough to permanently change my life?

My eyes pricked.

He studied me as closely as I was studying him, and the quick rise and fall of his chest reminded me to take my own breath. I let air into my lungs, slowly, taking in every detail of the moment with my indrawn breath. Memorizing this first moment—the first of a lifetime—with my son.

Sebastian reached out with his pointer finger, all his fingers splayed, and touched my chin. "Chin," he said. Then reached higher to try to stick them in between my lips. "Mouf."

"Sebastian!" his mother scolded. "Don't stick your fingers in people's faces!"

I took his arm, pulling it gently away in accordance with his mother's words. "That's right. That's my mouth." I was practically trembling. My kid knew where my mouth was, and it rocked my world. Surely other two-year-olds weren't this smart. He was a genius. A miracle.

I swiveled so he could see Elizabeth. "Look here, Sebastian. This is . . . Lizzie," I said, quickly deciding that was the easiest thing for him to call her. "Can you say Lizzie?" I didn't know if he could repeat words at this stage in his development, and I didn't care. I was making conversation. *With my son.* We could speak complete nonsense, and I'd be happy.

"Izzie," Sebastian said, pointing to my wife as she stepped up next to him. "Izzie mouf."

Elizabeth let out a happy, tearful sound that made my skin tingle. "He said my name!"

"He did! I want him to say my name." I was greedy and content all at once.

"He'll say it, I bet. Ask him," Callie prompted.

Fuck, my knees were shaking. "Sebastian, can you say, Daddy? I'm Daddy."

The room was silent, all of us waiting and watching for him to perform—poor kid.

Sebastian looked back to his mother who nodded in reassurance. "Go on. Can you say Daddy?"

"Daddy," he said, looking back at me, the d's so light in the middle of the word they were barely there. And when everyone applauded and cheered, he said it again, stronger. "Daddy."

"That's right. I'm your daddy. That's me." I hugged him to me tight, pressing my mouth against his hair. He smelled like baby powder and wet wipes and baby shampoo and by God I was ready to declare the combination my favorite scent in the world.

Except then I looked over at my wife standing next to me, her eyes brimming, and I knew her tropical body wash/perfume scent so well now that I could almost pick it out on the air, and I remembered that *it* was my favorite scent in the world. Especially when it was mixed with the musk of her arousal or the after-smell of sex.

I guess now I had two favorite scents. Two favorite people. Two favorite worlds to build my own around.

Why the hell did loving them both have to be so complicated?

Today wasn't for the complicated parts, though. Today was for the good parts.

I brushed away the worry of the future and sat down on the ground with Sebastian in front of the coffee table. "I brought you something. A present. Do you want to open it?"

I reached over for the gift before he could answer and handed it to him.

His eyes lit up, big and bright. His mouth formed a perfect O shape. "P'esent!" he exclaimed in that toddler voice. He immediately started grabbing at the ribbon, and I looked to Callie to make sure it was okay.

She nodded reassuringly, and sat down on the ground near us.

There was no way he was getting that ribbon off without help, so I tugged it off for him, but then he only wanted to play with it.

"Give it to Mama," Callie said, calling to him.

Sebastian looked at the red ribbon in his hand, contemplating before he happily flung it over to his mother. Then she pointed him back toward me and the gift. I nudged a corner of the wrapping paper up so he could grab it and together we tore all of the paper off.

"Oh!" Sebastian said, pointing to the picture. He was so surprised and pleased, it was written all over his little face. I swelled with pride as he examined it. The box contained a big block LEGO train set.

"I hope he doesn't already have it," I said.

"Nope. He'll love it." Callie gathered the rest of the paper and Dana took it, along with the ribbon, to the kitchen to throw away.

"Tain! Daddy, tain!"

Every time he said *daddy*, my heart did that ricochet, shocking new parts of me to life that I didn't even know had been dead.

"You want to open it? Let's open it." I started to open the box, which turned out not to be as easy as it looked.

"Yeah, they make these things impossible," Callie said.

She was right. Once I got inside the box, it was even worse. All the pieces were fixed to the plastic backing with elastic ties. It was going to take forever to get all fifty-six pieces out of the box.

"Tain. I want tain," Sebastian said, tugging at the pieces unsuccessfully, as his little voice rose in volume.

I managed to get one piece out while Sebastian was grabbing at the others. "Give it to me," Callie said, "I'll work on the rest."

Elizabeth knelt down beside her. "I'll help."

I handed the box over Sebastian's head to his mother. He followed, trying to get at the other pieces while they were working on them.

"Sebastian," I called. "Over here. Look at this." I rolled the single train car back and forth along the coffee table. Somehow that only brought his attention to the bourbon that I'd left there, and his eyes once again widened in delight.

Thankfully Dana swept in and grabbed my mug as well as Elizabeth's, just before Sebastian stuck his hand in. "I'll take those," she said, sticking her tongue out at him.

"Sebastian," I said again. "Look." I ran the train piece again along the table and he watched, mildly interested, but also torn between wanting to find out more about what was going on with his mother and the other pieces. Before I lost his attention totally, I decided to do a little sleight of hand—taking the car, waving it around, and then I made it disappear. "Uh-oh! Where'd it go?"

Sebastian's look of surprise was comical. He grabbed my hand and turned it over, but there was nothing there. Then he grabbed my other hand and examined it with equal intensity. He walked around my entire body looking everywhere for the train car.

"It disappeared!" I said, wiggling my fingers to show that it was nowhere.

Immediately, he started to cry.

"No. No. Don't cry. It's right here." I grabbed it from between my legs where I'd dropped it. "It disappeared but now it's back. See?"

"Disappeared," Sebastian said, his lips still quivering. "Come back."

"Right. It disappeared, but it came back. I'll do it again." I did the trick again, waving my hands, distracting him so he didn't notice the drop. Once again, the tears started the minute the object was out of sight.

"I don't like dis'peared," Sebastian said.

This time, I brought it back quicker. "But it comes right back." He stopped fussing. The third time I did it there were no tears at all, only a big smile when I brought the object back into sight.

"Come back!" he said, taking the car from my hand. He ran the train along the table himself then. "You made come back."

"I did. I made it come back," I told him. Then I pulled him into my arms again, hugging him, tight. Tighter than a squirmy little toddler wanted to be held, because it felt like I had so many hugs to make up for, so much time that I'd missed. I hugged him and I held him, and I breathed him in. And I whispered in his ear, "I'm going to be a good dad, Sebastian. I promise you. Whatever it takes. Whatever you need. And sometimes, maybe I'm going to disappear. But I promise, I'll come back. I'll always come back."

He pulled away, rushing over to claim the new cars Callie and Elizabeth had freed, bringing them back to me. I showed him how they hooked together, feeling the pride swell again when he did it himself. He was so smart. So perfect. And I *made him*.

Yes, I would always come back.

I didn't know how everything was going to work out with all of us just yet, how we would survive the lengths we had to go to in order to all stay together, but I could promise him that at least, and mean it.

Couldn't I?

CHAPTER
FIFTEEN

Elizabeth

WESTON WAS A natural father.

I knew it even before I'd seen him play with my cousin's child back in Utah. And why wouldn't he be? He was a charmer, loved games, and had an easy smile. And a heart so big it was made for parenting.

I was jealous of him, in a way. I didn't know that I had that natural instinct in me—the desire to give and sacrifice for others, especially a creature that could barely communicate. I appreciated conversations with intelligent human beings. I didn't like messes. I liked things neat and orderly.

But how could I not fall in love with that child, that baby boy that looked exactly like the man that I loved so much? Was it just because Sebastian belonged to Weston? Or because he was such an amazing kid in his own right, which he certainly was? Or was it that I wanted a baby of my own, more than I realized?

I didn't know. But I really did want to be part of his life, part of Sebastian's life.

And the shitty thing, the terrible, rotten, incredibly certain thing that I knew after seeing Weston with Sebastian was that I *wouldn't* be a part of his life.

Weston needed to be with his child.

And since I couldn't keep them from each other, I would have to let them go.

It took everything I had not to let the heartbreak show on my face while I watched Weston's heart grow fuller.

We drove back to the city, my husband as talkative and excited as when we'd driven to Brooklyn. He relived every moment with Sebastian, commenting on every single thing the child had said and done, relating the entire afternoon to me as though I hadn't even been there. I understood, and I was happy for him, *so happy for him*, and his endless stream of narration made it easy for me to hide away the turbulent storm of emotion inside me.

Yes, it would have to be faced. Eventually. But I understood now more than ever why Weston had pushed away telling me about Sebastian in the first place, how he'd kept stretching the days of our honeymoon before disclosing the information that would change everything. My frustration over that had drained completely. Because now I was the one keeping my secret plans to myself.

It would wait another couple of days. Until after Christmas. I wasn't going to ruin that for him.

For us.

Before we left Callie and Dana's, we'd made arrangements to see Sebastian again. Dana, it turned out, didn't have any family living close by, her parents both long deceased. Callie's family celebrated the holiday on Christmas Eve. Weston and I had plans to spend the twenty-fourth with my mother and Marie, and we had a standing invitation to his parents' for Christmas Day, which we hadn't yet committed to.

Now we were going to get to spend the holiday with Sebastian, and, with that change in the agenda, Weston wanted to take him to meet his folks. Callie and Dana had agreed, even finding a restaurant in Larchmont that served Christmas dinner so they could drive up with us and have a nice meal out together while we were with the Kings, then we'd all return together. That way, Sebastian wouldn't be too uncomfortable during such a long day without his mother.

All of it had worked out perfectly, everyone agreeing easily, all the stars aligning as though it were meant to be, and with each piece that fell into place I felt more and more secure in the path I had set forth.

If only it didn't have to hurt so much.

But I'd been hurt before, and I would hurt again. At least this time the hurt came from a father who was doing the *right* thing.

It wasn't until we were back at our apartment, after we'd had dinner and Weston had opened a bottle of wine for the two of us that he noticed I was unusually quiet.

"You know, you haven't said much since we left Brooklyn," he said, stretching out on the sofa in the living room. "What's going on in that head of yours, Lizzie?"

I flipped on the lights to the artificial tree, the one Christmas decoration we'd had time to put up. It didn't even have ornaments on it, just a string of white lights, but it set the mood nicely with all the overheads dimmed. Then I turned to face my husband.

"I don't know. Today was a lot, you know? In a good way. I guess I'm just tired now."

"Come be tired on my lap." He set his wine glass down so he could tug off his pullover sweater and toss it to the ground. Now he was just wearing his button-down long-sleeved shirt. Plaid, not unlike the one that Sebastian had worn in miniature form.

Jesus, one day that kid would grow up and look like him. It was almost unfathomable. To imagine those tiny limbs growing and forming into long, muscular, strong, toned arms and legs. Hands that were soft and sweet now, but would become large and capable.

I took him all in once more before wandering over, then I curled up onto his lap, tucking my head under his neck and bending my knees up against us.

Automatically his arms came around me, wrapping me up tight. "That's better," he said.

Weston started kissing along my neck and I leaned my head against my shoulder to give him better access, wondering how many more times I would feel his lips on my skin, how many times I had left where simple kisses would give way to abandoned clothes and tangled bodies.

However many times it was, it wouldn't be enough.

I had to *make* it be enough.

"Tell me something," I asked, as a shiver rolled through my body from his light nip on my earlobe.

"Right now?" His tongue traced along the shell of my ear, sending me into a dizzy wave of euphoria.

"Yeah." I was breathless. But determined. "Tell me what it's going to be like."

He paused to look at me, trying to read my mind by studying my eyes. "What *what's* going to be like, baby?" He slipped his hand under my sweater, the warmth of his fingers against my skin shocking me into a moan. "What it's going to be like when I fuck you? Don't you think it will be better if I show you?"

He bent to kiss me, but I put my finger up to stop him.

"What it's going to be like in the future. Like . . . this day next year. When our routine is all settled in. When Sebastian knows you and Callie's comfortable with your arrangement and I know what I'm doing with my company and your trips back and forth have just become a normal part of our lives." It was a fantasy, that life was. And I wanted to hear about it anyway. Wanted to live in the fantasy for one night. "Tell me what it's going to be like this day next year."

"Ah," he said. "Well, first, it's going to be amazing. And incredible, mostly because it'll be hard, but hard things are worth it."

He emphasized the word *hard* by lifting up his hips and rubbing the stiff rod of his erection along the curve of my ass.

"They are," I said with a grin. "But tell me the details."

He paused for a minute, thinking. "We'll fly together to the states that month. I'll be so happy to have you with me, instead of the usual long flights by myself. It's so nice to have you next to me instead. Even when we just fall asleep for the entire flight, it feels less lonely."

I nodded. He was already getting into it, switching into present tense and imagining the moment as if it were happening right now.

"We get into town on the twenty-second and sleep most of the day because of jet lag. And we fuck, because you've been working so hard

I've barely gotten time to see you. Plus, I just like fucking you. So I'm taking advantage of our vacation before we're intruded upon by the kid."

"Good thinking."

He curled his arm tighter around me and started fiddling with the button on my jeans as he spoke, undoing it and pulling down my zipper. "Then the twenty-third, today—a year from today—we go over to Callie's in the morning to pick up Sebastian. She has a long list of orders and instructions. Even after a year of this, she's still overprotective. But she lets us go eventually. Sebastian is bundled up in a snowsuit from head to toe. One of those outfits that are hard to walk in, his hands are covered and we can barely see his face. He's all puffy like a tiny marshmallow man. Because we're going over to Prospect Park. To go sledding."

"Sledding?" My voice hitched as I said the word, Weston's hand slipping in underneath my panties at the same time. "It's been years since I've been sledding."

"It's fun. Though, you might get wet." He slipped a finger down the seams of my pussy, sledding through the wetness down to my hole before dragging two fingers up again to tease my clit in large lazy circles.

"Go on," I urged, meaning both his story and his hand.

"After the sledding, we go back to our apartment, which is not too far from the park, to get dried off. Sebastian takes his nap. We fool around. Obviously." He smirked, dipping his fingers back to my hole, then returning them to my clit to resume his slow torturous pattern.

I let out a soft moan, the pressure already building and tightening inside me. "What next? What's after his nap?"

"Then we go into the city and see the trains at the botanical garden. Sebastian's so excited by that. It's better than meeting Santa Claus. We have dinner next. Somewhere family friendly. When we get home, Sebastian's wiped out. But he's not too tired to examine all the presents under the Christmas tree."

"When did we get presents? And a Christmas tree?" It was hard to talk with Weston's assault on my pussy. Hard to even think, but the fantasy had to be perfect in my head.

"I had the tree put up the month before. The gifts . . ." He thought about it a minute, creating a likely scenario. "We enlisted Callie and Dana for that." He was quiet for a few seconds. "Still can't believe they're lesbians."

I nudged him with my elbow. "Stay focused. Go on."

"Go on like this?" he asked, trailing his fingers back to my hole. This time instead of just teasing me at the rim, he stuck them inside, long and deep, curving them until he hit the spot that made my back arch.

"Yes," I hissed. "And the story."

"We're total pushovers, you and I, as parents."

I managed to glare at him—I didn't particularly picture myself as a pushover for anything.

"Okay, *I'm* a total pushover. So we let Sebastian open one gift. It's a stuffed giraffe that he names Dog Man because I'm raising him right. He loves it so much, we can't get him to let go of it, even to get him changed into his pajamas. He wants to sleep with it. So we let him."

"Ahhh." It was really hard to focus on the story now. Weston's hands were too good, the way they plunged in and out of me, his palm rubbing against my clit.

"He doesn't want to stay in his room now, and like I said—push-over—so we bring him in with us. He likes to snuggle. He cuddles up with his head under your chin. I hold you both to me, sniffing his head and his fresh new scent, and kissing your beautiful pouty lips." He added a third finger then, stretching me, filling me the way his dream story of our future was filling me, warming me with this beautiful lie.

"When we're sure he's knocked out, you and I slip out to the living room. You remember to move the elf on the shelf. Thank God. Because I always forget the damn thing."

I giggled, but it came out as a whimper, my orgasm reaching the threshold.

"And then I curl up with you on the couch, and finger fuck you until you're coming all over my hand like the dirty, sexy girl you are."

My body started to shake, and I closed my eyes, ready to lose myself to the entire fantasy.

"Eyes on me, Lizzie."

I turned my head, opening my eyes, my gaze crashing into his, eyes so blue and unwavering.

He sped up the thrust of his fingers and slid his other hand up under my shirt, pulled down my bra cup, and teased my nipple, the whole time keeping his stare locked on mine.

"Just like that, baby. You're almost there. You're so good and tight on my fingers," he praised. "Fuck, when you make those sounds—I could also come on that alone." He rubbed his erection on my ass again, and my eyelids started to flutter, the intensity of the coming climax bearing down on me.

"Stay with me, Lizzie. Stay here."

My eyes shot open again, and this time I pinned my eyes to his. I didn't want to look away. Wanted to keep looking and looking at what I saw there.

Jesus, he loved me. It was written everywhere in his expression, in his face, in his stare, in his voice and hands.

"I love you," I whispered, knowing he heard me. So much. Like his soul was my own soul. Like his heart was my own heart. "I love you," I cried over and over as my orgasm rocked through me, shaking me, tearing me apart, destroying the vision he'd planted in my head with its vibrancy. The words he'd said were false, a dream we'd never have, but these words, this passion, was raw and honest and surging through me.

This was truth. This moment. This feeling. It was truth and it was fleeting. It couldn't last. It wouldn't.

But for this moment, at least, I could look at him, could love him. Could stay with him before I let him go.

CHAPTER
SIXTEEN

Weston

"OKAY?" ELIZABETH ASKED, her head tilted, studying my features as she waited for my response.

It was one word, a simple question, but difficult to answer. We had already had an eventful morning—opening presents with Sebastian at Callie and Dana's had been even more exciting than getting presents myself. It had been hard not to spoil the kid, but luckily the short amount of time had limited us to five wrapped packages.

Even that number of gifts had turned out to be overwhelming, particularly when my little boy wanted each and every one set up immediately. Thank God for four adults buzzing around to help cater to his every whim. The fresh mimosas that Dana made didn't hurt either. I was really starting to appreciate what she brought to our little family.

Then we'd all loaded into the car. Like the first time I'd taken Elizabeth to my parents' house, I borrowed Donovan's Tesla. It was strange how it seemed like an entirely different vehicle with a booster seat in the back, lodged between two mothers. Less sportscar, more practical. Sebastian napped the entire ride to Larchmont clutching onto his baby doll, still his favorite toy despite all his new loot.

Now the five of us stood on my parents' front step, and after several deep breaths, I still hadn't gotten the nerve to knock.

I'd told them I was coming—that Elizabeth and I were coming—but

I hadn't told them I was bringing anyone else. I still hadn't told them about Sebastian. I thought that was a conversation better had face to face. Now, however, I was nervous about my decision.

And there were so many other things to say today. My shoulders were tight and tired from carrying all the loads that I needed to lay down.

So was I okay? God only knew.

"Don't you have a key?" Dana asked impatiently behind me.

"Yeah." The last time I'd come, I'd used it. That trip, I hadn't wanted to see anyone. Now it seemed more appropriate to be open about my entrance. "I think it might be more polite, though, to knock."

"Well . . . ?" She pushed again.

I looked to Callie, who was rocking her weight from one foot to the other, Sebastian's head resting on her shoulder, not quite awake from his nap. Then I turned to Elizabeth, who merely shrugged.

I paused too long. With a huff, Dana brushed between me and Elizabeth and knocked herself.

"Well, okay then," I muttered under my breath.

Elizabeth again shrugged, but I saw the smile she was trying to hide.

A moment later, the door opened and there was my sister, dressed in black leggings and a red dress, her blond hair pulled behind her into a low ponytail.

She squealed at the sight of me. "Weston!" Before I could even cross the threshold, she flung herself into my arms, wrapping me into a giant little sister embrace. "I can't believe you came! I'm so happy!"

"I'd be happy too, if you'd let us in the house and out of the cold," I said into her neck.

"Oh yeah! Of course. Come in." She let me go and scuttled backward so that we could walk into the foyer, her brow knitting slightly in confusion when it wasn't just two of us that entered, but four adults and one adorable toddler.

"Elizabeth, I'm so glad you came! I've been dying to get to know you better. I've always wanted a sister. It's not fair that Weston's kept you from me." Noelle lunged at my wife as soon as the door was closed, not even letting her take her coat off first.

Teenagers.

Thankfully, I'd married the most amazing woman on the planet. "I've always wanted a sister too. Only child here. Let's make sure to talk all the shit on Weston before I leave today."

"And every day," Noelle said, conspiratorially.

"But let's get in most of it today," Elizabeth insisted. Probably because she knew we were moving soon and that we wouldn't be around much, no matter what happened with my parents at dinner.

God, I loved this lady.

Next, Noelle turned to the women behind me. "And, I'm sorry. Weston didn't say that he was bringing anyone else. At least, Mom didn't tell me?" Her voice lilted up in a question, leaving room for me to introduce the rest of the guests.

Like on the doorstep, I hesitated again. I had no problem introducing Callie and Dana, but I didn't want to tell Noelle who Sebastian was without Mom and Dad.

"These are some friends of mine. Callie, Dana, this is my sister Noelle." I turned to my sibling. "We drove up together, and now they are going to have dinner at a nice little place in town."

Callie took the cue. "We'd better get going if we're going to make our reservation." She began to hand over Sebastian, so I dropped my coat into Noelle's hands and took him from her.

"Here's the diaper bag. He's at the stage where he sticks his fingers into everything," Dana said. "I left a Ziploc bag inside with some outlet protectors. Make sure you put them in around whatever room you're going to be in if you're going to have him on the floor. Here's his booster seat for the dining room table. There are snacks in the bag as well as wipes and diapers. You have our number. You know how to reach us if you need anything. But, please—" she paused, her eyes suddenly taking on a pleading expression. "Don't need anything. I can't tell you how long it's been since someone else has poured our wine."

"Got it. We'll be fine. I promise." I even sort of meant it. With Elizabeth at my side and in my family home surrounded by my parents and sister I was sure that we could handle a two-year-old.

I turned to Callie. "Thank you so much for trusting me."

She gave me a tight smile that made me wonder if she actually did trust me, but she left in the end, taking the keys to Donovan's Tesla (I may not have told him that was part of the bargain when I borrowed it).

Then I turned back to my sister and Elizabeth. Our coats were hung up now, except for Sebastian's. I stood him up on the bench near the door and began unzipping his jacket.

"So . . . you're babysitting?" Noelle asked, her face squinting in confusion. "On Christmas?"

"Uh . . . where's Mom and Dad?"

"In the kitchen. Finishing up with dinner. Seriously. What's with the kid? Practice baby?"

My sister was tenacious.

"Sebastian, this is Noe," I said, introducing my sister with her long-time nickname as I took his baby doll from him and maneuvered his coat off. "Want to say hi to Noe?"

Sebastian's face grew concerned at the meeting of a new stranger while in the midst of a strange house and he sidled up closer to me. "Daddy," he said reaching up for me.

"Is that something he says to all guys?" Noelle asked, "or . . . ? *Weston*. Holy shit. Mom's gonna freak." Then she called louder. "Mom!"

"Hey, hey!" I shushed her. "Let's just go in and do this all together. Okay?" I was about to seriously bribe her to get her to shut her mouth.

But Noelle surprised me. "Fine. If this is what got you to come home for Christmas, then fine. But I definitely want to be in the room when you tell Mom she's old enough to be a grandma."

A wave of nausea rolled through my stomach, and I had the sudden urge to flee, but then there was Elizabeth, slipping her hand through mine. Warm, comforting, reassuring.

"You've got this," she said.

And because of her, I knew that I did.

With my free arm, I hoisted Sebastian up onto my hip, and the three of us trailed after my sister into the kitchen to find my parents.

We saw my mother before she saw us, bent over a platter of ham, artistically garnishing it with parsley and cranberries, humming a Christmas carol off-key.

My throat tightened.

I hadn't realized how much I'd missed my mother until I saw her in her element, cooking for her family, the house spruced up to look like a page out of a Martha Stewart catalog. She was happy, and I knew that a good part of it was because she knew I was coming for dinner. How easy it was to give this woman joy. How much had I hurt her these past years by keeping my distance, whether it was justified or not?

Was the pain she'd caused me worth the pain I gave back?

Noelle, impatient and intent on stirring up shit, cleared her throat, announcing our presence.

Mom looked up. "Weston! Elizabeth—is it Elizabeth?" She turned from the meat to wipe her hands on a dishtowel. "Or do you prefer something else? Liz? Beth?"

"Elizabeth is fine," my wife said after glancing at me. I was glad we were on the same page—Lizzie was a name that belonged to me. And Sebastian.

"I was just finishing up here. You're right on time! Dinner is ready, and as soon as my hands are all clean and I get this off, I can give you both a hug." She tugged at the strings of her apron, then threw it on the counter. "There's a bottle of wine chilling on the sideboard in the dining room, and your father is already loading up the table with dishes so we can . . . oh!" She'd started around the kitchen island to greet us properly, and finally, she'd noticed Sebastian. "Well, who's this little cutie pie?"

"Just wait," Noelle said, saucy and snide as she leaned a hip against the island.

My father chose that moment to enter from the dining room. "I thought I heard you all in here. You shouldn't be in the kitchen. You're the guests! You should be around the table."

His jubilant smile faltered only slightly when he followed my mother's gaze and discovered the little boy in my arms. "It looks like I need to put another table setting out," he said calmly, as though there was nothing out of place with me holding a child.

That helped me to *feel* less out of place holding a child.

"Before you do that, Dad, I was just about to . . . um . . ." I looked from one parent to the other, not sure where to start, as always.

Elizabeth leaned over to whisper in my ear. "Should they be sitting for this?"

"Probably." I seriously didn't know what I'd do without that woman. "Do you guys want to sit down?"

"Why don't you just spill it? I'm sure we can handle it." My father was obviously unconcerned with the gravity of what I had to say.

Alrighty then. "Mom, Dad—this is Sebastian. How's this for a Christmas present? He's your grandson."

MY MOTHER DIDN'T faint, thank God, but she did cry. So much so that it took twenty minutes of hugging her and letting her hug me and Sebastian before we could finally sit down at the table. By then, much of the food was lukewarm, but no one complained.

Most of the meal was spent explaining how Sebastian had come into my life, what little I knew about him and his mother, plus delivering the blow that I was soon moving to France. The last bit of news set off a new round of tears from my mother, but fortunately we had Sebastian at the table with us. His adorable antics made it hard to be upset about anything for long.

I loved watching my parents dote on my kid. My mother had always been attentive, but I'd forgotten my father's ability to be imaginative and playful. Or maybe he'd just matured. Maybe he was different with a grandchild than he had been with me and Noelle. It was hard to say. Either way, it was possible to overlook a whole lot of grievances in order to be in a room with both my parents and my child.

It occurred to me, in a stupid sort of epiphany, one of those kinds of epiphanies that really should not even be an epiphany, but somehow it shatters the earth when it falls into place, that my father was just a man. A man who had tried the best that he could to be a good father. And maybe on a lot of days he got it wrong, but at least he was there, trying. Unlike Elizabeth's father, who hadn't even bothered to show up.

And here I was, about ready to divide my life between a child and a woman, between two continents. The reasoning made sense perfectly inside me, but one day when Sebastian looked back on it, would he resent me for not doing more for him? For not giving more? Was he going to hold me to the same standard of perfection that I had so long held my dad to?

God, I sure hoped not.

Sometimes we fathers needed to be given a break.

After dinner, we all helped clear the table—well, everyone except my mother, who was too busy oohing and awing over her grandson. Then everyone headed to the living room, but halfway there, I stopped my parents.

"Mom and Dad, can I talk to you for a few minutes?"

Elizabeth picked up the hint immediately. "Maggie, let me take Sebastian and see if he needs a diaper change." She somehow got my mother to relinquish the little boy, and then asked Noelle to show her to a place where she could change him.

Alone, my parents and I headed to the library.

It was strange being in my father's favorite room, not because I hadn't been in there a million times before. In fact, the last time I'd been there I'd been with Elizabeth. Right now, how I longed to be alone with her again, longed to pull her into my lap and bury myself inside her, thank her for always being a warm, safe place.

But I had things to say. Things to get off my chest, and that was what was strange about being in there now. I'd never felt like this room was a place where people actually talked. It was meant for studying and reading. Meant for silence. And here I was about ready to say the most important words I'd ever said in this house. Ever said to my parents.

This time I did make sure they were sitting, and I took the armchair next to my father. I leaned forward, my elbows on my thighs, and gathered my thoughts before I began.

"When I first found out about Sebastian, I freaked out," I said. "I couldn't be a dad. I didn't know the first thing about being a father. And the only people who've taught me about parenting—my own parents—were a million miles away from me, in so many ways. I didn't feel like I could even ask you for help."

My mother shifted on the couch, but she didn't say anything.

"Of course, the reason you were a million miles away was because I put you there. And the reasons I put you there were because of mistakes that Dad made in business. Not because you were actually all that bad of a dad."

My father hung his head and studied his hands. It was progress, considering that the last time we'd talked about the corruption at King-Kincaid, he'd wanted only to defend himself and barely let me get a word in edgewise.

I supposed that was a natural response to being accused of being a terrible person by your son. I couldn't imagine hearing the things I'd said to my dad coming at me from Sebastian. Silently, I promised to make sure he'd never have to.

Could my dad promise that I'd never have to say them again to him?

"The thing is, I don't want to spend forever . . ." There were a million ways I could finish that sentence. I didn't want to spend forever hating them, blaming them, defending them. Without them.

"I miss you," my voice cracked. I swallowed. Swallowed again when the ball was still lodged at the back of my throat. "But I'm still really mad at you, too."

"Weston, I—"

My mother put a hand on my father's back. "Nash, let him talk."

"I understand some of it, Dad. I understand that you couldn't just leave the company. If you'd taken the fall, everyone who works for you would have lost their jobs when the company fell apart. Maybe you were actually doing the noble thing by staying in charge and helming the ship through the scandal.

"But I don't understand why you would need to have used such unethical practices in the first place. And I don't understand why you let Daniel be the one who suffered for it. It was wrong, Dad. It was a big mistake."

I straightened, letting my pronouncement fall on the room and settle. "It was a mistake," I repeated, "but I get that you're not perfect, that you are doing the best you can. And I forgive you."

God, that felt good to say.

Like a two-ton boulder had been lifted from my back, and I hadn't even realized I'd been carrying it. I'd had no idea how much I needed to say it.

I'd needed to say it so much, I said it again. "I forgive you, Dad. And you, too, Mom."

A choked sob erupted from the couch, but when I looked at my mother, who was indeed tearing up, I realized the sound had come from the person at her side. From the man I'd never seen shed a tear in my entire life. The King of the financial world, my father, was crying.

My mother wrapped her arms around her husband and held him.

My own eyes stung as I fell to the floor in front of them and placed my hands on his knees. "I forgive you, Dad." Apparently he'd needed to hear it as much as I'd needed to say it.

"Thank you, son," he choked out. "That means a lot."

"But forgiving you doesn't fix everything. It doesn't make amends."

He looked at me, intently focused.

"I've been giving the Clemmons family money every month, trying to help them out, but it's not enough. I'm going to give them my trust fund. It doesn't feel right for me to have all that when they've had to sacrifice everything for me to keep it."

"No," he said. "That's your money. I saved that for you."

"I know you did. And I'm giving it to the Clemmonses. Because they suffered for *you*."

He wiped his eye with the flat of his large palm as he shook his head. "No, please. Don't do that. It's not your job to fix this. It's mine."

The ball thickened in my throat. "This was your money. You wanted me to have it. I figure you suffer by me giving it to them."

"That's very noble of you," he chuckled. "But I'd rather suffer by giving your trust fund to Sebastian, if you refuse to touch it. And I'll donate the same amount that's in your fund to the Clemmonses. It's what I should have done all along. I'm sorry I didn't offer it sooner."

"You did have that settlement drawn up for after Daniel got out of jail," my mother said. "Don't forget that."

"You were planning to give him a settlement?" I was more than a little surprised.

"Maggie insisted," he said, looking at my mother. "As soon as she heard the verdict. She also made me put up an anonymous scholarship at the day school that helps care for the twins."

"I hadn't realized," I said feeling the last bit of tension roll off my shoulders. "I didn't realize you were looking out for them."

"You didn't think your compassionate side came out of nowhere, did you?" my mother asked, teasing.

"Eh, let's be clear—he didn't get it from me."

I laughed. At least my dad was honest.

And maybe a better man than I'd given him credit for.

"I'm sorry, Weston," he said. "For a lot of things, but mostly for disappointing you. You're already a better father than I was because you've learned from my mistakes. And you're a good father because you're willing to build your life around him. I'm proud of you."

"Thank you, Dad." My chest burned. "Thank you both. For raising me. For being there, as much as you were. I wasn't there for two entire years of Sebastian's life, and I can't stand how much time I missed with him. It guts me to think of how much of my life I've kept from you." Jesus, I didn't want to be crying.

My mother leaned forward and wrapped her arms around me. "Please just say you won't let us miss anything else."

"I won't," I promised, hugging her. "I won't."

I made other promises too, silent promises, about being a better son and a good dad. Promises to be a good husband and a better human. Not to be perfect—no one could be perfect—but I promised to keep trying.

Because try was all we could do for sure. We could try, and we could forgive.

If we managed that much, then, yeah, we were going to be okay.

CHAPTER
SEVENTEEN

Elizabeth

I TOOK A deep breath, adjusted my teardrop necklace, then stepped out of the elevator onto the floor of Reach's executive offices. I'd been here a hundred times since that first day almost six months ago. How was it possible to feel so lost when I knew exactly where I was going? So out of place in a setting so familiar?

It was only the day after Christmas, but Weston and I couldn't afford any more time off. We had too much to do. Too much to get caught up on. He'd gone into the office early, and I'd started straightaway into my list of tasks. Movers had headed to his apartment today to pack up and collect my things and prepare them for shipment to France. Then I'd had errands, all in preparation for this afternoon's meeting. Everything had been set in motion, each carefully laid out detail now put in place.

All that was left was this.

And this was going to be the hardest part.

Hard things didn't get easier by dragging feet, I'd learned in my short life. So while I dreaded the upcoming conversation, I still forced myself to head toward Weston's office at a rapid clip, smiling and nodding greetings to his coworkers who acknowledged me on my way.

"Mrs. King! What a pleasure to see you. He knows you are coming?" Roxie stood to greet me and gestured for me to hand her my jacket.

"He doesn't. It's a surprise." And not a very nice surprise. But I didn't mention that.

Roxie frowned. "I'm sure he'd like to see you. He has a four o'clock though. They haven't arrived yet—late. You could probably sneak in a few minutes."

"Actually, I'm the four o'clock," I confessed. "I had my assistant make the appointment so that you wouldn't recognize my voice. To make it a true surprise."

"You have an assistant now! How fancy. I like to see women in power." She hung up my coat in the closet behind her desk and then sat back down.

I just smiled, because I didn't feel very powerful, and though I was sure to have an assistant when I got to Paris, I didn't have one yet. Advisor was his official title. And he'd made the phone call to get the appointment as a favor, not because it was his job duty.

"Can I go in?" I asked, nodding toward the half-closed door.

"Oh. Yes. Should I announce you?" Roxie's hand hovered above the receiver of her phone.

"No. I'm sure he knows who I am."

It took more strength to walk to his doors then I would've thought necessary, and, truthfully, if Roxie hadn't been behind me watching me, I might've turned around and fled. But with her eyes on my back, a sort of unwilling, unwitting cheerleader, I made it past the threshold, and shut the doors behind me.

Weston looked up at the sound of the door click. And the way his face changed when he saw me—it was like finally getting to the Hallelujah chorus of the Messiah with his bright smile and lit eyes. He looked at me like I was royalty. Like I was fit to bow down to. Fit to kneel in front of.

"Elizabeth, what are you doing here?" He was already up and out of his seat and coming to me. But when he leaned in to greet me with a kiss, I turned my face at the last minute, so his lips landed on my cheek.

I could be cruel, I'd learned. Especially where my love was concerned.

I brushed the incident off, talking quickly as if that was why I'd moved my face. "I have an appointment with you."

"An appointment? You're my four o'clock?" If he was hurt or worried about my rejection, he was now distracted by this latest news.

"Yep. Surprise."

His mouth morphed into a mischievous grin. "Why, Mrs. King. Did you book me for office sex? What a terribly kinky and amazing idea. Why didn't I think of it?" He rushed to his desk and hit the button that changed the windows that looked out into the office from clear to opaque.

I stepped forward, eager to clear up his mistake. "No, no." Though, now I was regretting that we'd never gotten to have office sex. "I have some other things to discuss. Business things. Formality things. I thought this was the best setting for them."

His smile dissolved into a concerned frown. "Okay. Sure. What's up?"

"Why don't you have a seat." God, why did I say that? Everything terrible began with *have a seat*.

But he unbuttoned his jacket and sat down, so I smoothed my hands over the thighs of my pantsuit and then sat in the seat facing him.

It was so weird, sitting with something so big and bulky between us. It hadn't been that long since we'd finally shed our last secrets, since he'd torn down his last walls. After being that close to someone, it was hard to go back.

No. Not going back. We were going forward—toward where we were both supposed to be. I needed to remember that.

I looked around the room, letting nostalgia take me over for a moment.

"Your office is a whole lot less intimidating than the first time I was in here," I said, because it was true. It was the words that were intimidating, not the office. Not the man.

Weston leaned back, relaxing a bit. "I don't know why I was intimidating. I kept my hands to myself."

It hadn't stopped me from imagining them on me. "I meant that I was so naïve."

"You were ambitious."

"*Overly* ambitious?"

He considered. I was sure if someone had asked him then, he

would've said yes. Now, he said, "I underestimated you. You've come a long way. You've learned a lot. Your passion alone will take you far, but your knowledge will make you a force to be reckoned with."

"But you were right—I *had* been in over my head. I had no idea what I was talking about when I walked into that meeting with you and Nate and Donovan. It was all show. You had no reason to stand behind a pushy, overzealous poli-sci major. And yet you did."

I caught his eyes across the desk, and they felt penetrating.

Abruptly, he sat up straight and started fiddling with the pen in front of him. "Elizabeth, why exactly are you here today?"

I wasn't ready.

I jumped up and walked over to the bookcases, the ones that opened to reveal the dartboard behind them. When he'd opened them that day and shown me the board, his father's face had been pinned to it.

I chuckled at the face there now. "Donovan?" I wouldn't mind throwing a dart or two at the man myself.

Weston rose and came over to the board with me. Not bothering to remove the staples, he ripped the photo down. "He's the most recent person I've been mad at, I guess. But I'm not really mad at him right now. Not really mad at anyone at the moment."

Not yet.

"Lizzie . . . ?" It was a repeat of the question he'd asked at his desk. Why was I here?

He anchored his hand on my cheek, and I was very aware that he knew something was off, that he wanted to fix it. I could feel his anxiety creeping up like a spider crawling on my pant leg.

"What you did that day—letting me throw darts at my father's face? I don't know that I ever thanked you for that. It was sort of life-changing," I said.

"No, it wasn't."

"It really was. And not just because you told me to throw darts at my father's face, but because you got down on your knee and put a ring on my finger. Not because you loved me, but because you thought I was cool enough to fight the stupid demands of his will. And cool enough to give up your Friday nights to teach me basic business, knowledge that you spent a fortune to learn. All my life, I always thought I wasn't the kind of girl who'd ever find someone who would want to give me that much attention."

His expression was baffled. "Are you kidding me? You were made to be worshipped."

"No one ever treated me like I was until you. Maybe that was my fault, because I hid behind my father, but that's what started to change that day. I started to realize that I didn't have to live in his shadow anymore. *You* did that for me. Pulled me into the sun. And I'm so grateful, Weston."

The words came out slower than I usually spoke. I was choked up saying them. But these were things I really wanted him to know, and what I'd said had only scratched the surface of the universe of gratitude that dwelled within me.

But this was all I knew how to express. It would have to do.

I put my hand over Weston's and twisted my face to kiss his palm before I dropped my arm again.

His eyes sparked as he rubbed his thumb along my cheek. "How come all this feels like something someone says when they're about to die? Are you trying to tell me you're dying, Lizzie?"

Feels like it. "I'm not dying, you jerk. I'm grateful. You changed me. I wanted to be sure you knew."

"Okay. I know." He still seemed hesitant. He wasn't dumb. Then, after thinking a second, he added, "You've changed me too."

"I know," I answered with a smug smile.

"Of course you do. My smart girl. It was your hot brains that I fell in love with, the minute I saw you." He dropped his arm and stuffed both his hands in his pockets. "But this isn't what you came to tell me. And if you didn't come to have sex on my desk, then . . ."

God, it already hurt. And I hadn't even gotten to the part where I slashed us both open yet.

I walked back to my seat and sat down so I could lean over and dig into my purse on the floor. Weston followed, strolling back to his side, then sinking slowly into his chair.

I can do this. I can do this, I told myself.

"I called Darrell today," I said out loud, still bent over. "Finally. I told him that I hadn't known about your child before we got married." When my fingers closed around the paper I'd carefully folded into thirds earlier, I pulled it out, sat up, and set it on the desk between us. "I explained to him that it was a big blow, naturally—"

"Elizabeth," Weston warned, sensing where I was headed. Trying to head it off.

I raised my voice, undeterred. "And that I couldn't continue to be in a relationship, let alone a marriage, with a man who had lied about something so important. Which he understood."

"No. No, no," Weston said quietly, shaking his head.

He continued repeating the same word, over and over, as I went on. "I went to my lawyer's office next, and filed for an annulment. Marriage based on fraud."

There. I'd said it.

This part I'd rehearsed, though, so it was supposed to be the easy part, and it wasn't easy at all. It was the hardest thing I'd ever told a person in my life.

Now I had to stay strong while the man I loved tried to change my mind.

"Here." I pushed the folded paper across the table toward him.

"I said no." He didn't look at it. He didn't have to. I'd just told him what it was—the proof that I'd begun the process to end our marriage. "Did you hear me?"

I let out a breath. "You can't just say no. That's not how annulments work."

"I don't care how annulments work. We're not getting one." He shoved the paper back toward me. "We've discussed this. This was not an option. You can't get one anyway without losing your inheritance," he added with smug relief.

I had an answer for that. "I worried that was true as well. But my lawyer feels that since the dissolution has occurred through no fault of my own, we have a leg to stand on. He's sure there's enough precedent for me to take charge of the company for the time being, and if it goes to court, we'll likely be nearing my twenty-ninth birthday by settlement anyway."

"That's an awful lot of maybes. What happened to doing everything so carefully, being on guard every minute, taking no chances, so there was no way in hell you'd lose your company? There are possible holes in this route, Lizzie."

I didn't want to say it, but he left me no choice. "The holes are unlikely, but if it comes to that, I'll have to remarry. The court battle will buy me time."

He looked as though I'd slapped him. "You won't do that. You won't marry someone you don't love. Not after us."

"I'll do what I have to, Weston. For both of us."

"I don't accept this."

"Don't make this harder than it has to be." My voice was thinner than usual.

"Elizabeth, don't do this." He gave a pleading smile, just enough to show his dimple.

The sight increased the tightness in my chest. Made me feel like clawing at the air in frustration. Made me feel like shouting from the rooftops that I wasn't doing this because I wanted to.

I picked up the damn paper and held it toward him, my hands shaking. "It's already done. See? Look." He didn't move. "Look!" When he didn't take it I threw it back into my purse. "Whether you look at it or not, it doesn't change the fact that I filed it. It's done."

He leaned forward, putting all his weight on his forearms on the desk. "Then we'll get remarried. The first ceremony was for show anyway. This time we'll do it for real. We'll do the first dance, and we'll cut the cake."

Jesus, he was breaking my heart. "Don't," I said. It was all I could manage. "Please, don't."

Showing him my hurt was the wrong move. He clung to my pain. "You want that, don't you? You can't tell me you don't want that. I can see it in your face. Marry me again. I'll even pick out the ring this time. Just marry me."

I couldn't help myself. "I loved this ring," I said softly.

"Then marry me."

I closed my eyes. Shut them tight against the threatening tears and focused on why I was doing this—for *him*. For Sebastian. I couldn't let that out of my sight.

When I opened my eyes again, I felt stronger. "I wouldn't need another wedding, Weston. The one we had was perfect, and I'll cherish it forever. Now it's time to move on." I wasn't sure how I'd gotten through that statement without my voice cracking when my insides were shattered.

He pushed his lips together in a straight line while he processed.

Then he was done processing and back to refuting. His gaze flew around the room, as though looking for another angle to come at me, then zoomed back to land on me when he'd found one.

"What about the company?" he asked, a spiteful glint in his eyes. "You've learned a lot, but you need someone to help advise you. You're not ready to lead."

"Fuck you," I said, despite knowing his words came from a hurt place. "And I've already thought of that. I've asked Clarence to come to France with me. As an advisor—"

"Clarence Sheridan?" His face puffed up and went red.

"Yes, and he agreed. It's a paid position, of course, a really good opportunity—"

"A really good opportunity to get in your pants." He was mad, and I couldn't blame him.

But I couldn't help defending myself, anyway. "That's assuming I can't take care of myself. That I'd let him into my bed. And if I *do* let him into my bed, that won't be your business anymore. We have to be over, Weston. I'm leaving tomorrow. Clarence will meet me later. You need to be here for your son. And I need to put all of my focus into my company."

He slammed his hand on the desk. "Dammit, we can do both!"

"Maybe we could." I was purposefully quieter in comparison. "But odds are that we can't. And we could do a lot of damage to a lot of innocent people while we're trying."

"So you're just going to give up?" He spit the words at me.

"I'm not giving up. I'm giving us both a better chance." I met his eyes and held his stare for long seconds. They were cold and hard like ice, but I could glimpse the sea underneath and it was rocked with turbulent waves.

I was rocking his ocean. I was the storm on his main.

Fuck, I hated this. *Hated* this. Hated hurting him and me. But mostly him.

Storms pass. He's going to have a better life because of this. With his child. Now was his chance to do right by his son, and I couldn't stand in the way.

"You are going to be an amazing father. You already are. And I want you to know that in an alternate world where my dad was still alive and his company wasn't up for grabs, I know I would have found a way to you anyway. And I would have married you and had a hundred of your babies, and we'd be happy together." Yeah, I was definitely crying now. "I know you'd make me happy forever. I know you would. In a timeline where there isn't this other thing pulling at me. This other obligation. This other responsibility. I'm sorry that we can't be in that world, but it helps for me to believe that somewhere it might exist."

"An alternate timeline, Elizabeth? Let's talk about *this* fucking timeline, okay?"

I cowered at his volume.

"In this timeline, we work best when you're my wife, when I'm beside you. You say I'm going to be a good dad? That's only when you're there. You're my home, remember? You're my queen. I don't work without you next to me."

I shook my head. "Now you're not giving yourself enough credit."

"Elizabeth, don't do this." He got up from his chair and came around to me. "You're reacting too quickly. We haven't even tried anything out yet. You don't know what it's going to be like." He crouched down next to me, but I refused to turn toward him, keeping my body angled forward.

"I *do* know what it's going to be like," I said. "You'd try to make it work for everyone. You're going to try to fix things for me and for

Sebastian and you're going to end up sacrificing yourself. Just the same way that you don't want to watch me stay here and give up the things that I want, I can't watch you tear yourself into pieces trying to be everything to everyone."

"I won't. I can do it. I'm stronger than you know."

He tried to swivel me toward him, so I stood up and walked out of the chair the opposite way. "You're strong now. But it will break you down. Give yourself the best shot at fatherhood, Weston. Think about Sebastian. We have to do this for him."

Of course he followed me. "How can I be a good father when I'm a miserable wreck because you've left me?"

He was just a few steps away from me.

I put my hand out to stop him. "I've made up my mind, Weston."

He stopped and stared at me, pleading with his eyes. I could feel his body aching to reach me, just as mine was aching for him.

I couldn't let him get to me. It would undo everything.

It would undo me.

I forced myself to look away, forced myself to go on, finish up. Cut the cord and get out. "I'm not going to pretend this is easy. I'm not going to say that I don't love you. Because of course I do. You know that I do. It's *because* I do that I'm doing this. It's because I love you that I have to let you go."

He took another step toward me, and he was close enough to pull me into his arms.

I took a step back, out of his reach. "Let me go, Weston. If you love me, let me go."

And because I couldn't stand to be there anymore, because I couldn't take the way his eyes felt on me, and the weight of his love pressing, pressing, pressing on me, I rushed over to grab my bag, then hurried out before he could say anything else. Before he could stop me.

Before he could truly see me break down.

CHAPTER
EIGHTEEN

Weston

I WATCHED HER walk out the door.

I stood there, dumbfounded, frozen in place while rage and pain and disbelief swirled through my veins, a wild tempest within me. I heard the muted sound of her voice as she spoke to Roxie, and then it was quiet. Too quiet.

I should have known.

Everything had been too perfect. And she had felt distant. Closed off. And I blamed it on the chaos and the circumstances because I hadn't wanted to believe it was something else. Because I was determined to believe she couldn't be considering this. Never this.

I let the rage and fury have free rein as I swept my arm across the desk, throwing everything on top of it to the floor.

That crash, that explosion breaking through the silence—that was what it felt like was going on inside me. Like noise and thunder and wreckage.

Roxie ran in through the door. "Are you all right?"

I didn't answer her. I just pushed her aside and ran out of the office, hoping I wasn't too late.

I ran down the halls, but when I reached the elevator, the doors were already shutting. I pressed the call button, I pounded on the steel, but she was gone. Unlike that first day I had run after her, this time I didn't catch her.

I turned and leaned against the closed elevator door. I could try to run down the stairs, but that was a long shot. She was gone. I had let her go.

I trod back down the hall, ignoring the looks from the staff, but instead of heading toward my office, I went straight for the lounge. There was a liquor cart there, and I poured myself a drink. I swigged it back in one gulp, then poured another. I snatched my glass and started to leave, had second thoughts and went back for the bottle, taking it with me to my office. If she was gone, I was going to be drunk. There was no way in hell I was going to deal with it sober.

Back in my office, I found Roxie on the floor trying to clean up my mess. "I won't ask what happened, but do you really need to take it out on the office equipment?"

She lifted up the computer monitor and set it on the desk.

"Go home," I growled. And that was an attempt to be friendly.

"I'll finish cleaning this mess up first." Roxie was never afraid of my moods.

She'd never seen this mood though. I shook my head, my whole body moving with the action, and this time I roared. "Go home!"

I'd hired Roxie because she was smart. She proved it when she didn't say another word, just stood up and silently left, shutting the door behind her.

Alone, I sank into my chair and took a big gulp of my drink.

Fuck her.

Not Roxie. Elizabeth.

And not really. I didn't really mean fuck her, I meant fuck her decision. Fuck the idea that she could choose this without me having any say in it.

If she could plan our lives out without my input, then why couldn't I? Why couldn't I choose what happened between us, what our future looked like? I took another swallow, finishing off my glass and then refilled it.

I could. I could choose. Why not?

I could stick with the plan I had before. Move to France. Travel back and forth. What was she going to do if I showed up there anyway? Refuse to see me? If I was living in France three weeks out of the month anyway, would she just refuse to acknowledge my existence?

Not a chance.

I was going, and that's all there was to it.

I marched out of my office toward Roxie's desk. She'd gone now—it was almost closing time anyway, and, like I'd said, she was smart. I was pretty certain she stored unused boxes in the closet behind where she sat.

Turned out, she did.

I grabbed a couple, then returned to my office and began packing things up. I started with my books, the business-related ones. I wanted to have those, especially for Elizabeth, in case she needed to look up some professional information. She could use them in her resource library.

Then I moved on to my desk drawers, cleaning out files and binders. When I'd filled the two boxes, I went and got two more.

I kept packing and drinking until the office was quiet, and I was sure most everyone had gone home. I'd made it to my graphic novels by then, my collectibles. My first edition of The Walking Dead was missing. I tried to remember if I'd loaned it to anyone.

I hadn't. That left one person to blame—Donovan. He was the only one who would mess with my shit.

Speaking of Donovan—I needed to tell him I was leaving.

I tramped out of my office and started toward his, but the dark hallway said he wasn't there. I was desperate to tell him anyway, eager to make it known, so I shouted it out. "I'm moving to France."

"You are?"

I looked to my side and found Nate was still here. I'd missed *his* light on.

"No," I said, sullenly, feeling the loss of my wife all over again. Then I remembered I was going to move to France anyway. "Yes. I mean yes."

Moving to France. It was laughable. *I* was laughable. She didn't want me, and I was chasing after her.

What the fuck was I even doing?

Except she *did* want me. She'd just decided we were better apart.

Lies.

Lies, lies, lies.

I needed to find her. Needed to tell her she was wrong about her decision. Convince her we belonged together.

"I have to go," I said, heading back for my coat.

"To France?" Nate called.

"God, I hope so." I put my coat on as I walked toward the elevator, wondering if I should call for an Uber or if there'd be a cab.

I looked at my phone, meaning to pull up the Uber app, but got distracted when I saw my wallpaper—a picture of Sebastian that I'd taken the day before. "Did I tell you I'm a dad?" I called back to Nate.

I didn't even know if he could hear me anymore; I was almost at the elevator, and I couldn't see him past the dark sections of the hallway.

"That sounds about right," he yelled back.

It did sound right. But it didn't *feel* right without Elizabeth. I had to make her see that, too.

⟃⟄

I USED MY key to get into her apartment, then shut the door and pressed my back against it while I let my eyes adjust to the dark.

It was only a little after eight o'clock. Fuck, was she even here?

I didn't want to turn on the light and announce my presence in case she was. Not yet, anyway.

I started through the foyer into the interior of the apartment and bumped into the end table, knocking into the boxes stacked on top of it. "Shh," I told them as they rattled, afraid they would crash to the floor. "Shh." Fumbling, I managed to steady them just as the light flicked on.

"What are you doing here, Weston?"

Well, at least now I knew she was home.

I ran a hand through my hair and straightened my jacket, which was rumpled from packing, a general day's wear, and my drunken state. I'd lost my tie hours ago, probably left behind at the office.

A quick once-over of my soon-to-be ex said she'd taken a bath. The bottom half of her hair was limp and damp. She was wearing one of those nighties that always drove me crazy in the early days because of how sexy she looked in them.

They still drove me crazy.

Her eyes were swollen and puffy, and maybe should have been a comfort to know that she was also miserable, but if she was really miserable, then why the fuck was she doing this?

I stormed past her into the living room, pulling the string of another lamp. Everything was gone. The walls were empty, her knickknacks missing. All that was left were a few pieces of furniture and some miscellaneous boxes.

"It's bare in here," I declared. "Like my insides. Scraped out. Gutted." I pivoted to see her reaction.

"I know. I'm sorry," she said wrapping her arms around herself.

Sorry? I was empty. I was hollow, and she was just *sorry?*

"I don't know how you manage that—that—that *ice queen* bit of yours, but lucky you. It's sexy as fuck, how you don't have feelings."

"I have feelings. This is killing me." She said it so quietly it was almost a whisper.

It didn't matter what she said. What she'd done erased anything else, so I pretended I didn't hear her. "It will come in handy when you're ruling your empire. Not having to care about anyone else. Your father seemed to have that figured out. You really are daddy's little girl, aren't you?"

"Fuck you." Her hands were fists now at her sides, her entire body trembling with rage. And with pain, probably.

Good.

I needed to see her hurt. I needed to see her devastated. Like I was.

"You did fuck me. You did." I spun around to take another look at the stark surroundings and tripped on the edge of the couch.

"Are you drunk?" she asked behind me, the sentence lilting in that way that said my actions might be forgivable if I were.

I shrugged. "Sobering up." I ran my hand along the arm of the couch, realizing she was likely getting rid of it. That I also had to make my goodbyes with her belongings and the memories they held. I wouldn't even be able to picture her somewhere far away remembering us when she sat on her sofa or curled up in her bed. She was erasing our entire life together.

"What's going to happen to all this stuff?"

"My personal belongings have already been shipped. Everything that's left is going to be sold or donated." She paused, and I had to give her credit—she was being really patient with me, considering. "Is there anything here you want?"

"You." I twisted to see her response. The deep frown and the creases in her expression, signs she was on the edge of tears, was almost worth it.

"Weston, you should go," she was nearly begging. "This is only making us both miserable."

I stepped—stumbled, maybe—toward her. She backed up. I took another step, steadier this time. She backed up again, hitting the wall behind her. I stopped, a foot in front of her, pleased with how she cowered under my size and dominating posture.

"Tell me you don't love me," I demanded, studying her eyes and her lips.

"I told you I wouldn't say that."

"Tell me it won't feel like a hundred razor blades cutting into you every morning to wake up without me next to you."

She tilted her chin up slightly. "Tell me it won't slice away a piece of your heart every day that you don't get to see Sebastian."

She had me there.

"Look me in the eye, Weston, and tell me a handful of stolen moments every month is going to be enough for you with him. With your parents."

I almost lied to her. Because there was a part of me that believed it *could* be enough. That seeing my kid's face a few hours a day for five days before disappearing again would be plenty.

But the reality was I was already struggling to catch up from my two-week honeymoon at my job. Balancing work and cross-country and intercontinental flights seemed exhaustingly hopeless when I tried to picture it. And after only seeing Sebastian on two occasions, I already missed him like he was a piece of myself that I'd left behind. I supposed he *was*.

But so was she.

And I was just as hollow inside at the thought of how much I was going to miss her.

It was madness. Fucking impossible. I wanted it all, and not because I was an ambitious guy—that had never been me—but because I *loved* too much. I'd never imagined that as my destiny. An ironic ending for a player like me.

Maybe it was better to ice it over like Elizabeth, to go numb, but right now I resented her for being able to shut me out. Resented that she could put up barbed fences and stone walls and live safely alone inside her encampment.

I wanted back in.

I inched closer, careful not to touch her. I studied every feature of her face, every tiny freckle, every tiny pore, features I'd already memorized a thousand times over. My eyes traced down the length of her lashes, past the swollen bags under her eyes, along the slope of her nose to the curve of her lips, down her chin and jaw to her neck where I could see her swallow. I lingered at the neckline of her nightgown, silently cursing its presence for obstructing the view of her beautiful, gorgeous form.

"Take it off," I ordered, wanting it gone, wanting there to be no barriers between us, no oceans, no walls, no flimsy silk material.

"Weston . . ." She trailed off. She didn't say no.

"I said, take it off."

Her hands moved up to push the spaghetti-thin straps from first one shoulder, then the other. She had to shimmy to get it to fall past her breasts, but a few seconds later it was pooled at her feet.

Her chest rose and fell more quickly now, her nipples perked up as though reaching for me. As though begging for my tongue to lave along their peaks, to ease their ache.

I wanted to touch her, to cup her breasts, to squeeze them and fill my palms with them, wanted to hear her moan and gasp and give her relief.

But she'd said she wasn't mine anymore.

So I kept my hands at my sides, and trailed my gaze down further past the swell of her abdomen to the band of her silk white panties.

"Take them off," I said nodding to them.

She didn't hesitate this time, pulling her panties down her long, slim legs, then kicking them and the nightie aside before standing up to her full height.

I stared at the V between her thighs, the sacred cave I'd buried myself in so many times. There was a glint of moisture along her folds—she was wet. Just from my eyes. Just from my proximity.

How could she really say she could live without me? Without me with her? *In* her?

I placed my palms on the wall at either side of her head, and her breath hitched.

"Undo my buckle. Undo my pants."

Her eyes were sad and dilated, but her hands began the work immediately, quickly loosening my buckle and unzipping my pants, then pulling down my briefs to expose the rigid steel underneath. See? I *had* sobered up.

I slid my hands down, and grabbed her under her thighs, the touch of her skin searing my palms as I hoisted her up around my waist, trapping my cock between us. Using the wall I pushed her high and tilted my hips so that my crown was pointed right at her entrance, so that I could thrust right in, but I didn't do it.

"Put my cock inside you," I told her.

"What?" Her voice was shaking with need.

"Put my cock inside you, Elizabeth. Put me inside you."

Her small hands came to circle around my dick, she angled me the way she needed, then pushed her hips forward, filling herself entirely.

Bright lights smeared across my vision, warmth shot through my body, and I had to force myself to breathe in order not to come right then. She felt so good, warm and tight like sex but also like home. She felt like the warm, tight security of home.

I hugged her closer to me, kissed her face—her jaw, her lips, her chin. Kissed her mouth as I moved in her, frantically trying to plant myself as deep inside her as possible. So deep that she could never get rid of me.

I took each whimper and moan from her, swallowed them into my own body, absorbed her sounds and scent and taste. And when she came, my cock vice-gripped by her pussy, I continued to plunge in and in and in. She could push me out all she wanted, try and try, and I would come right back. And I would stay.

I would stay.

I was sure I muttered that as I ground out my own orgasm, bucking into her with a fierceness that I'd never before used on her body. Shooting stars of light and pleasure exploded through me, and I was almost certain that I was putting every bit of my soul inside her with my semen as I rode out my climax.

But then it was over, and the adrenaline and the hormones settled. And I realized I was still a little drunk, and we were still just Elizabeth and Weston. I still had my soul inside me. It was dwelling right alongside my broken heart.

I set her down, hoping that this had changed something, afraid that it hadn't.

"Don't go," I said selfishly. Because even I couldn't pretend anymore that I was going to be happy dividing my life between France and New York. "This proves we belong together. That we shouldn't be apart. So don't go."

She sighed as she leaned down to gather her clothes. "The only thing this proves is that I know how to spread my legs."

She really was an ice queen. I'd always known she was royalty.

I stepped backwards in a daze as I put myself away, not quite sure what to do next.

Of course *she* knew.

"This isn't mine," she said taking the engagement ring off her finger. She came to me, turned my hand over, and set it in my palm. "You can keep your wedding band. I don't want it back."

She'd paid for the wedding bands. What was I supposed to do with mine now?

Obviously I was going to keep it forever.

I looked down at the engagement ring in my hand. "This is Donovan's, actually," I said, my head foggy.

"Then give it to Donovan." She pulled her nightie over her head, replacing the barrier between us. "You'll be happy together."

With her panties in her hand she turned on her heel and headed toward her bedroom. Over her shoulder she called, "Turn the lights off when you leave, please."

She went into her bedroom, and for the second time that day, she shut the door between us.

CHAPTER
NINETEEN

Elizabeth

EVEN AFTER WALKING into the lobby, waiting for an elevator, and taking it all the way up to my mother's floor, I still felt as cold as I was when I was outside. It wasn't even a particularly chilly day, but my fingers and toes felt numb. And no matter what I did, I couldn't get warm.

Come to think of it, I hadn't really felt warm since I'd left Weston's office the day before. Even a hot bath and the strange goodbye sex had done very little to ease my chill. Was this just how I was now? Permanently cold? Ice through and through? Dead inside?

I wouldn't mind so much if I were really dead inside. If it didn't feel like my chest was being stretched and pulled like taffy at the same time.

Crying didn't help. Sleeping didn't help—I hadn't slept well as it was. I'd tossed and turned all night, missing Weston's body next to me, feeling alone in a deserted bed much too big for one person. I was sure that flying across an ocean wasn't going to help either, but it was next on the agenda, after saying goodbye to my mother.

It took me a few minutes to find her in her apartment. I'd checked all the usual places before sticking my head into the barely used office.

"What are you doing in *here?*" I asked, as I pushed through the French doors.

She was out of place behind the giant redwood desk. My mother was not the type to do any work that required a flat surface. My mother wasn't the type to do any work period.

She looked up from what she was doing and smiled brightly. "I'm signing checks!"

"You don't have people for that?" I walked deeper into the room, still perplexed by this image of my mother.

She turned the page in her book of checks and went to the next entry, which had already been filled out for her—all except for the signature. "I have people for everything but this. You should always sign your own checks. Oprah says so." She signed another one in a big flourish of cursive handwriting then paused to admire it. "I like doing it. It makes me feel like a celebrity. Signing my autograph over and over again."

I laughed. *My mother.*

She signed a couple more, then shut the book and turned to face me. "How are you feeling today?" she asked, her elbows propped on the desk.

I'd called her, of course, after I'd left Weston's office, and I'd told her everything. And I'd cried, because somehow mothers made it easy to let the tears out. She'd understood and supported me. Was proud of me, in fact. I hadn't told her about his later visit, and I didn't see the need to. It hadn't changed anything, though I was sure she'd understand it too.

I ambled in and sat on the edge of the desk, facing her. "Okay, I guess. Tired." I shrugged in case she wanted more of an answer. I didn't have one to give.

"You can sleep on the plane today. You're still meeting with Darrell tomorrow?"

"Friday."

"Good. It will give you a day to recover. Maybe the swelling in your face will go down by then." She reached up to touch the tender skin underneath my eyes; I batted her hand away.

"Mom," I groaned.

"Wear an ice mask as much as possible. And remind me to give you my cream. It will help." She really was genuinely trying to be helpful.

"Maybe I don't want the help," I said, pouting. "Maybe I like the souvenir." Something to prove to the outside world that my heart was breaking inside.

"Sure. If that's what you'd like." She patted my hand and sat back and looked at me with an inquisitive eye. "Are you really taking Clarence Sheridan with you?"

"You don't think I should?"

"I don't think you need to."

"That's sweet, Mom." It was hard not to laugh. She thought I was Wonder Woman sometimes, that I could do anything. "But even though I know things now, I still don't have any experience. I'm not going to fuck this up by going in green."

"You're trying to be wise. I get it. But Clarence isn't any older than you. Have you looked at his credentials? Does he really know a lot more than you? Is he going as an advisor or a security blanket?"

Hmm. Well.

I hadn't really thought about that. I'd just assumed everybody had more experience than I did. And Clarence had been so eager to do anything I asked.

"If you need an advisor," my mother went on, "hire a *real* advisor. You don't need anyone to help you stand on your own two feet. That's what was stupid about your father and his will in the first place—it showed he didn't value *you*. You all on your own. Don't make the same mistake he did." She pushed her chair back and stood. "Think about it."

"I . . . will." It was a lot to chew on for some reason. Even though she hadn't said very much, it felt like her words had a lot of meat.

"And Elizabeth," she added, "if you are still miserable when you get over there, then turn back around and come be with Weston."

"Mom!"

"What?"

"You're the one who said to let him go!" Who was this woman? Giving me one line of advice one day and steering me in another direction the next. She had me twisting and turning and chasing my tail.

"I want you to be happy!" she said as though that explained everything. "That's all. And if *this* doesn't make you happy, and Weston does, it's okay to change your mind."

I blew out a puff of frustrated air. "You drive me crazy."

"Well, now I'm going to have to drive you crazy on FaceTime." She put her hand up to bop my nose. I grabbed it and held onto it so that when I jumped off the desk I could easily pull her in for a hug.

"I love you," I said into her neck. I held her for a long time, hugging her tighter than I usually did, letting her hold me tighter than I usually did.

For the first time that I could remember, she was the first to let go.

"You've given me a lot to think about, Mom. Thank you."

"You're welcome, and I love you too." She circled around me and started to walk around the desk. I turned around, meaning to follow her, but stopped to run my hand across the redwood surface, remembering all my years that I'd spent doing homework sitting in that very spot. I'd moved out of my mother's apartment years ago, but I'd still been nearby. Leaving the country was the first time I really felt like I was leaving home.

"You want me to have it sent to you?" she asked.

I looked up. "What? The desk?" I hadn't been considering it. But now that she'd mentioned it . . ."It was Daddy's."

"Once upon a time. I think you've used it more over your lifetime than he did over his." She fiddled with her earring while she talked. "When he first moved out, you used to sit there for hours. You were so little. The desk was so big in comparison, it practically swallowed you up. I think you were waiting for him to come back."

Always waiting for him. How much of my life had I spent waiting for him?

"Do you remember that?"

"Sort of." It was vague. I'd been really young when he'd left and all the memories after blended together. "I used to write him letters. A ton of them. And I begged you to send them as soon as I'd finished."

"I did, too. I was very good about that. You told him everything in those notes to him. Don't think I didn't read them before I put them in the mail."

Thank God I started mailing them myself when I got older. Half the things I wrote to him were complaints about her. They'd almost been more of a diary than for him. "He never wrote back. I wonder if he even read them. Probably not. I don't even know why I kept writing them. I guess it made me feel close to him somehow. Made it feel like it wasn't my fault. At least I was making an effort even if he wasn't. You know?"

She gave me a sympathetic frown, one that said *I feel bad because you feel bad.* "I'm sorry he couldn't be the man you wanted him to be, sweetie. He disappointed me a lot too. But he made you! So I've always been fond of him for that."

I guess he had done that. And not just biologically. In so many ways I wouldn't be who I was if it weren't for him—for the person he'd been to me.

"Is it time for you to go yet?" she asked.

I looked up at the clock on the wall, an antique with a cuckoo that ticked audibly. "Almost. I'm just going to make sure I got everything I wanted out of here first."

That was code for I needed a few minutes.

She translated the message perfectly. "Okay. Make sure you leave enough time to give me a proper goodbye. I'll be in the living room with my feet up. Maybe I'll get Marie to fill a bowl with warm sudsy water so I can soak my tired hands. Being a celebrity is so much work." She winked, wiggling her fingers in the air, then she turned and disappeared out the doors and down the hall.

Chuckling, I plopped down in the big chair and rolled up close to the redwood desk. It was majestic and sturdy, very masculine in its design and ornamentation. It was probably worth a fortune. I was a full-grown adult, and I still felt so small sitting behind it. So overwhelmed.

Had my father ever felt that way? Had he ever felt tiny in his place? Had his ambition ever scared him the way mine scared me all the time? The way it scared me now?

There was a lifetime of questions I'd wanted to ask him and never got the chance. An encyclopedia of things I'd never get to tell him. So many words left unsaid.

On a whim, I opened up the top drawer and found my mother still kept a box of stationery there. Just like in the old days. I'd usually picked something simple with a modern design, but the light lavender floral would do. What I was intending to write wasn't getting sent anyway.

I took out a single sheet and picked up the pen my mother had used to sign her checks. Then, without thinking too much about it, I set the tip to the paper and let everything out, the words flowing once I started.

Dear Dad,

There's been a hole inside me since the day you moved away.

Each day we were apart, every year that went by without spending real time with you, that hole grew wider and deeper, leaving a cavernous empty space, so big it left little room for anything else. That was all I was—the shell that you left behind. The little girl you didn't want.

For the longest time, I believed the only way to fill that emptiness would be to get you to notice me. Then, when you died, I thought I could fill it by filling your shoes. By taking your place at the head of your kingdom.

But I've learned I was wrong. I don't need your company to be fixed. I don't need a man at my side or a marriage certificate. The way to fill the hole was learning my worth.

I've learned my worth, Daddy. I've learned my value, something that you couldn't ever quite see. But I can't be mad at you anymore because your ignorance and the way you treated me have forged my path as much as your DNA. You made me who I am, with every missed phone call and forgotten birthday. With every canceled vacation. With every stipulation on my inheritance.

You made me, and I like who I've turned out to be.

Maybe I won't run the company with the same cut-throat ambition and maybe my mistakes will be obvious and irreparable, but I'm going to be okay because I know who I am. I'm a queen. Not because my father was the King of Media—though that too. Not because I married into royalty.

I'm a queen because I decided I would be one.

I love you. I've always loved you.

But I love me now too.

Your daughter, Elizabeth

When I was done, I dropped the pen and laid my palms flat on the desktop for support. I was out of breath, like I'd just finished an advanced ballet class, and it took several seconds before my heart rate had settled.

But then I felt . . . good.

Really good.

Like, I really believed what I'd written. That I was going to be okay.

I mean, I still felt heartbroken and devastated about Weston, but it felt like maybe even that might be okay eventually, somehow. With these words written, the future felt less set in stone. More malleable. And instead of being terrified about that unknown, the vagueness of it made it seem less impossible to figure out how to fit Weston into my happy ending.

Mostly, it felt like the chill in my bones was beginning to thaw, and that the anger and resentment I'd been holding against my father for so long no longer fit inside of me. I could finally let it go, and I wouldn't even notice it wasn't there anymore.

The cuckoo came out of the clock then, chirping one o'clock. Quickly, I folded the letter in half and then wondered where to put it. My purse? My pocket? I didn't want to take it with me, though. That didn't seem quite right.

Finally I tucked it in the bottom of the stationery box and shut the drawer again.

Then I ran out to find my mother so I could tell her goodbye. My cab would be here soon to take me to the airport.

"Oh, and, yes," I told her first, before we got all emotional, and I forgot to mention it. "I do want the desk."

"Good!" she exclaimed. "It suits you."

"I know," I said, because I finally did.

CHAPTER
TWENTY

Weston

"BIRD!" SEBASTIAN SQUEALED, slapping his hands emphatically on the tray of the stroller. The few pigeons scrounging for food in the snow nearby ignored his exclamations, apparently too accustomed to the sounds of city life to be disturbed by an excited toddler.

"He's never going to fall asleep," Callie complained, studying him covertly as she walked next to us.

"Yes he is," Dana insisted. She reached over and flicked the canopy down on the stroller, obstructing his view. "Sebastian," she warned. "Lie down. Close your eyes."

"You're supposed to be ignoring him," Callie said through gritted teeth.

"Does this usually work?" I asked, veering the stroller around a slick piece of ice then centering it again on the sidewalk. It was Wednesday, and rather than sit at my desk and dwell on the fact that my wife—soon-to-be never-was wife—was likely boarding a plane and leaving the country at that very moment, I'd texted Callie and asked if I could crash her day.

Dana's office was still closed for the holiday, so she also had the day off. We'd planned to take Sebastian to the park to play in the snow, but he was supposed to have napped and been up by the time I got there. Instead, I'd arrived to find two mothers stressed and frenzied from dealing with an overtired two-year-old who refused to nap.

At her wit's end, Callie had suggested we take him for a walk, bundling him up in his snowsuit and a quilt on top of that.

"The motion usually knocks him out," she said now. "If he's not too distracted."

I wasn't the one distracting him. I'd hoped he'd be the one distracting me. Pushing the stroller, we couldn't even see each other. But there were plenty of other things in the park for him to be interested in—the birds, a bunch of older children building an emaciated snowman, the *squeak squeak* of the stroller tire as it went round and round over the uneven ground.

Actually, that last one was rather mesmerizing. If someone were pushing me in a giant-sized stroller, maybe it would even help *me* fall asleep. I hadn't slept well the night before without Elizabeth, tossing and turning, missing her warmth, my mind replaying every word she'd said, wondering if letting her walk away was the right thing to do. Scared that I was failing a test. Knowing I didn't have any better answers, even if I was failing.

Except I hadn't failed anything. I hadn't given up yet. I was just on hold for the moment. Until I figured out my next move.

"Are you looking for apartments yet?" Dana asked, interrupting me from my broody thoughts. "There's some amazing units in Park Slope over on Union."

I hadn't yet told the women about me and Elizabeth, mostly because once I said it, said that we were over, it meant that I believed it was true. So right now they thought I still needed a place closer to them for my travels back and forth across the pond. I didn't want to lie, but I didn't want to tell the truth either.

So I hesitated.

"Are those two bedrooms over there?" Callie asked while I tried to figure out how to answer.

"I think so. Maybe not available right now. But Claire and Karen are over there and they have the twins so they can't all be one bedroom."

"That's the building with the amazing playroom, isn't it? And oh my God that roof terrace!"

"I'd give my left tit for that terrace."

Turned out if I just paused, I didn't have to say much at all with Callie and Dana around.

A notification from a phone went off, and Callie reached inside her coat pocket to pull hers out. She unlocked her screen and after a few seconds of staring at her phone, she groaned.

"Is it him again?" Dana asked.

"It's not even from him. It's his secretary," Callie answered, stuffing her phone back in her coat pocket.

I slowed the stroller to prevent it from jumping over a bump, then hurried to catch up. "What's going on?" I asked, because I was nosy. And because I'd rather talk about whatever the unwanted notification was than why I wasn't looking for an apartment in Brooklyn.

Callie let out a deep breath, her air forming a cloud as she exhaled. "My father's been picked for the president's Cabinet." She bent down to peer inside the stroller. "He's asleep by the way."

Dana gave a silent golf clap with her gloved hands.

"Congratulations! On both your father and Sebastian. Do we need to head back now?" I could turn around if we needed to, but I was enjoying the crisp air, enjoying being somewhere other than stuffed inside where my thoughts were stifling.

"No, we need to keep going for at least thirty minutes to make sure it sticks," Callie said.

"And no congrats on her dad," Dana added. "When we heard he was being considered, we were happy at first—it would get him out of the state, and we wouldn't have to see him as much."

The two exchanged a glance over the stroller that I didn't have to see to understand. Though I'd recently reconciled with my parents, it had definitely been tough to rebuild that bridge.

"It's always a strain when we have to do family events, you know?" Callie offered. "Dana always comes with me, and she's so, so gracious, even though he ignores her the entire time. Or worse, says things about gays being the abomination of the Earth."

"That doesn't just affect me," Dana pointed out.

"I know." Callie looked away, and even from behind her, I could sense she felt guilty and torn. "I don't care so much when it affects me. It bothers me that he says it about *you*. And eventually Sebastian is going to get older and hear all this about both of us. It's messy. But I don't want to officially divorce myself from the family, and you don't tell my father how to act or what to say. That's not how he rolls."

"No," Dana agreed.

I thought about that, thought about Sebastian learning how to treat women, how to treat his mother from this terrible role model. It bothered me. My skin pricked, as though I had feathers and they were ruffling, and I debated whether I needed to stomp my foot and make some demands about how much time he spent with his grandfather. Was that even something I could do?

I wasn't sure. It was definitely something we were going to have to talk about more.

"Anyway," Callie said, deciding for me that we were discussing it now, "the president's office is asking for a ton of publicity with this Cabinet position. From the entire family. They want me and Sebastian to go to New Year's parties and campaign events and fundraisers. It's not even my political party. Like, I voted independent." She whispered *independent*, as though some secret government official would hear her and take away her membership to her family. "And since New York is so close to DC, a lot of these events are in town, so we aren't really getting away from him at all."

"It's ridiculous what they expect of you," Dana complained.

"I know. I'm going to have to start telling them no—except that's just going to break my mother's heart and cause a whole scene. I don't know how to avoid upsetting people either way."

Dana turned to face me. "I'm not very helpful. I can't go to any of these. The media thinks Callie is an unwed mother. Be careful, now some of them think *you* are in the picture, thanks to that article. They may start trying to grab you for these."

Callie laughed. "Good thing you have Elizabeth. Tell them *you're* married to someone else, and they won't try to hook us up." She laughed again, and this time Dana joined her.

I definitely didn't laugh. Though, maybe I should have. To someone else, it could be quite a funny situation.

"What's wrong, Weston? You don't find the idea of arranged marriages amusing?" Dana's eyes sparkled.

God, if she only knew.

I cleared my throat, unable to let the truth remain burrowed inside any longer. "Quite amusing, actually. Except, Elizabeth filed for an annulment."

There were exactly four seconds of silence before both of them started speaking at once.

"Oh my God!"

"What? When?"

"You two are ridiculous around each other! So obviously in love! You can't be breaking up!"

"I think I got knocked up just from being in the same room with you together."

Their shock made me feel both better and worse. It validated that Elizabeth and I belonged together, and also made me feel truly shitty for not fighting harder for her.

And now they were both looking at me for an explanation, an explanation that I felt hard-pressed to give when I barely knew how to explain it to myself.

"It's complicated," I said defensively.

But that was a lie. "Okay, it's not. She has her company in France, as you know. I want to be here for Sebastian, and I'm sure you both realized how terrible the idea of going back and forth is—though I was willing to make it work. I really was. She thought it would be too much pressure on our relationship. And on both of you. And on him."

The silence that followed said that as much as the mothers of my child believed in my marriage, they also understood why Elizabeth did what she did.

For several long moments, the only sound was the fall of our steps on the sidewalk, the hypnotizing squeak of the wheel, and the imagined voice in my head yelling for everything to just stop.

Dana eventually broke the silence. "So why don't we all move to France?"

"Don't joke about that. Please." I was too depressed to even imagine the scenario anymore.

"I'm serious," she said. "Give me a job there, and I'm on board."

"Um!" Her wife exclaimed.

Um! I echoed silently, though I was much more excited about the prospect than Callie sounded. "What do you do exactly? You work for the State Department?"

"I do. I'm in public relations."

She was in fucking PR?

I'd assumed she was a bureaucrat—*but PR?* I owned an advertising firm. "I can totally get you a job! A really good job."

On the other side of me, I could feel Callie nervously fidgeting. "Dana! Shouldn't we *talk* about this?"

"We're talking about it right now. You don't want to move to France?" she asked as though everyone wanted to move to France, which was totally not the way I'd looked at it when I'd first heard the idea.

"I don't know," Callie said, with a tone that said she'd never really thought about it.

"It would get you off the hook with your parents. Get me out of this job—which we both hate. They legalized same-sex marriage there years before the U.S. did."

Callie's head bobbed back and forth, considering. "Universal health-care," she said dreamily.

"No school shootings." Dana spoke the words as though they were candy.

To be honest, that sounded enticing to me, too.

"I don't think the education system is that good, I'm sure I read that somewhere." Callie pulled her phone out of her pocket, and I assumed she was looking this fact up.

"We'll do private school. *Everyone* does private school in Europe.

It's all the rage."

"Are you speaking out of your ass or do you know this?" Callie glared at her spouse.

"Does it matter?"

Callie turned to face me. "It's all good, Weston. The education will be fine. Dana's right. We'll do private school."

I shrugged. Education was the last thing on my mind. The kid was two. "I'm still so new to this parenting thing, I barely have time to realize I should be worrying about something before you guys are telling me it's okay."

"This one *is* okay. I'm generally always in a state of worry," Callie told me.

"Noted." I paused for a fraction of a second. "Can we go back to talking about moving to France? Because you guys can't just yank my chain on this one. I was seriously going to ask if you'd consider it before, but when I realized you were together, and that you had a job, Dana, I didn't think it would even be an option." I was getting excited. Too excited for something that we were just bouncing around.

"You should always ask, Weston," Dana said seriously. "For no other reason than because I love shooting people down. Especially Callie's ex-lovers."

Callie stifled a giggle.

I was not laughing about this. "Are you shooting me down right now?" I asked, staring Dana straight in the eyes.

She stared across the stroller. "Callie?"

They were taking it seriously. I could feel the brevity of the moment, the weight of this decision pressing down on me, knowing that if they just said *yes*, every bit of pressure that had been piled onto my shoulders would immediately evaporate.

"I'd pay for all moving expenses," I said, desperate. "And help you find a place to live. You could stay with me and Elizabeth until you found your own apartment. I haven't seen ours yet, but she says it's humongous, and I'm guessing it's probably quite nice. Used to be her father's. I'm sure there's more than enough room for everyone."

Callie made a humming noise like she couldn't believe she was even thinking about this. "This isn't something we should be deciding on a whim."

Dana's eyes were bright, excited, the way I felt inside, bubbling like a lava lamp. "No, we probably shouldn't. But isn't it awesome that we have the means to be impulsive? If we want to be?"

I stopped the stroller, unable to move until this tension was unraveled.

"I don't know when we'd have the chance to be this impulsive again," Callie said, coming to that conclusion slowly.

Dana nodded. "We should do it. Raise our kid in France and open ourselves up to new experiences and adventures. We should totally do it."

She and I both looked to Callie, waiting with bated breath.

Slowly, Callie's indecisive expression eased into a smile. "You only live once," she said.

I suppose that meant yes, because then Dana and Callie were hugging each other and kissing, and it was probably pretty hot, but all I could think about was turning the stroller around, getting back to my apartment, packing up, and getting on a plane so I could get to my wife as soon as humanly possible.

When the two of them finally broke apart, they held hands and looked at me. "What do we do next?" Callie asked.

I didn't hesitate for a second. "We go to France and get my wife back."

⌣⌒⌐

I CAUGHT A cab and headed back to the city, but instead of going to my house to pack a bag and make arrangements, I went to the office first. There was someone I had to deal with, someone I should have dealt with a while ago.

It was still early in the afternoon, so fortunately Donovan was in his office. I could see him through the clear glass, and he wasn't on the phone, so I strode right by his secretary, walked in, and shut the door behind me.

"I'm in love with Elizabeth. I married her for real, and we're going to stay together." I probably could have called, but I wanted to see the look on his face when I told him this.

Except he just leaned back in his chair, crossed one leg over the other, ankle resting on the opposite knee, and said, "I know."

"What do you mean you know?" How could he possibly know? Even Elizabeth didn't know as of right now.

"You went off-script at the wedding. Said your own vows. That had to mean something. Had to mean you'd fallen for her. And doesn't every woman fall for you?" He cocked his head, smugly.

"Every woman doesn't . . . no." *Did they?* I wondered. *Didn't matter. Elizabeth did.* "Yes. She's in love with me too." It irritated me that he had this figured out already. But not enough to dim my mood. "Invoice me for your ring. I'm keeping it." I'd debated getting her a new one, but there was sentimental attachment to this. It was the one I'd already proposed to her with, and she'd told me she loved it. It was part of our history, and I was eager to put it back on her finger and didn't have time to get another one.

"Sure thing." He raised a brow. "Anything else?"

"And I have a kid." He *definitely* didn't know about that.

"I know."

Fuck him.

"How? I haven't told anyone?" I mean, I told some people. Nate— did Nate tell him?

"I read an article about it online," he explained matter-of-factly.

"But that was . . . How did you . . . That was a gossip site! Why would you even think that was real? How did you even see it?" Jesus, did this man know *everything*?

"I've had Google alerts set for both you and Elizabeth since you got engaged. I've told you that. I wanted to get ahead of any bad press or rumors if need be. When that came up, I remembered you telling me about hooking up with that senator's daughter. Plus, a player like you was bound to knock a girl up eventually."

Fuck him again.

"Okay. Fair." I definitely had something that would throw him a curveball though. "And we're moving to France. I'm taking over the new company there." No way he could have guessed that one.

"I know," he said, again. And before I could ask how, he added, "Of course you are. You were always going to move to France. Elizabeth's company is there. Why did you think I wanted this merger to take place so badly?"

"Oh, don't pretend you thought we were going to get together the whole time. That you were arranging the whole situation so I could have something to do in a foreign country." He might be a puppetmaster, but surely that was taking it too far.

He only shrugged. "Sabrina will be better at your job here. She knows more about your accounts than you do at this point."

I tilted my head, unsure whether I wanted to punch him or give the guy a hug.

I settled for a smile. "This thing you do? This big brother thing, where you fix everything in my life, save the day every time?" I let him think about it for a minute. "You don't have to do it anymore. I've got it together now. I can take care of things from here on out."

"You sure about that?"

He was a righteous little asshole, but deep down I was sure he knew I was saying thank you.

"Yeah, I'm sure."

"You're welcome."

I turned to leave, then remembered. "Hey, I want my Walking Dead comic back."

His eyes narrowed. "Did you watch the security tape?"

I shook my head, baffled. "I don't need to watch the security tape. I know you're the only one who takes my shit. Hand it over."

He paused, reluctant. Then he tugged open a drawer and pulled out my revered issue and handed it over.

"Thank you. For everything." I backed out of the room, still looking at him. "Oh, and Donovan, one more thing."

"Yes?"

"Can I borrow your plane?"

CHAPTER
TWENTY-ONE

Elizabeth

MY FATHER'S HOUSE was ridiculous. A private mansion with a sprawling landscape and wooded garden. The twenty thousand square-foot residence included an indoor swimming pool, extensive wine cellars, roof terrace, and staff apartments. There was even an actual petrol pump on the grounds.

As a child it had felt large and overwhelming and hollow, even with its fully decked out playroom and million-and-one places to hide. I'd only ever wanted to just crawl up in the library. And that was the one room I'd always been kicked out of, not because I was too young or because my father forbade children from touching his books, but simply because there were always so many other adults ambling over and through the rooms and offices that my presence in the library was always a nuisance.

Even with the bustle of his fully staffed house, it had felt like a lonely place. So when I landed in Paris at 7:00 a.m. on Thursday, I chose not to drive the twenty minutes to Neuilly to change and settle into the house, which was kept up by two live-in staff members, and instead made my way to his much smaller, six thousand square-foot apartment in the heart of the city.

My apartment now.

The five-bedroom penthouse apartment overlooking the Eiffel Tower was also too quiet, even with the live-in maid who greeted me when I arrived. My feet echoed on the wood floors, and while I had the entire library to myself, I'd never wanted to be anywhere less.

How was I ever going to make a home here?

Those weren't thoughts for dwelling on when I was jet-lagged and miserable from missing Weston. And this was only day one without him. I had the rest of my life to get used to my new reality.

I had a feeling I'd need that long to adjust.

"MR. HUBER ISN'T quite back from lunch yet. I do apologize he's not here to greet you." Darrell's secretary was overly kind and penitent, speaking so quickly I almost missed some of her words in her accent. I was glad, though, that she chose to speak English since my French was rusty.

I looked at the time on my phone. It was a little before one and my meeting was set for half past.

"I'm early. It's my fault." I tried to put the woman at ease.

"I am sincerely sorry, Ms. Dyson. He really wanted to make a good impression. Can I get you some tea? Coffee? Pastries? Something else to drink or snack on?"

I'd been attended to my entire life and still had never had anyone fall over me as she was doing.

"Nothing, please. Though, I could use a place to make a phone call. International."

"Please. Use Mr. Huber's office." She was already up and headed toward Darrell's door with her key before I could stop her.

"I don't want to intrude on his personal space," I attempted anyway.

"It's no trouble. He would want this. It will be your office soon anyway," she said, smiling over her shoulder as she pushed the door open.

I had to take a deep breath then to steady myself, my legs all of a sudden feeling wobbly on my heels. It hadn't occurred to me that I would be taking over Darrell's spaces, places he belonged and worked in. Lived in. I wondered what his staff—what *my* staff—thought about that.

I didn't linger on the thought too long, because the door was open now, and I could see into the office that had once been my father's, a place I'd visited often as a child when I'd made trips to France. It had always seemed like a secret cavern. Like the holiest of holies, a place in which I'd never been fit to truly dwell. I'd always been excited and thrilled and honored when I'd gotten to visit my father there, even if it was only for a few minutes to kiss him on the cheek before being bustled away to a nanny.

I stepped into the room reverently, shutting the door behind me so I could make my call in private. While I hadn't meant to arrive early, and I certainly hadn't meant to overtake my father's former office on my own, I was glad now that I got this chance. There was an emotional element to being in the Dyson Media headquarters that I hadn't quite counted on. Sentimental nostalgia and the first true sense of grief at the loss of my father that I'd had since his death. I took another deep breath and let the emotions settle in me as I took in the room.

It was large, spacious. Not much had changed since the last time I had been there. The couch and chairs that surrounded the fireplace and bookshelves were still exactly the same. My father's oversized executive desk still sat ominously near the windows where he could look out at the park while he thought. A second, more modern desk sat perpendicular to it now. This was the one that was stacked with files and papers and Post-it notes with memos jotted down in illegible handwriting. I assumed that was where Darrell worked, and I made my way over to my father's leather wing chair—his throne—preparing to make my call.

It was only 8:00 a.m. in New York. Early still, but business people were already at their offices. As I dialed the United States country code, I tried not to think about Weston or wonder what he was doing. This conversation wasn't about him. It was about me, and it was short and brief. My mother had been right—I had hired an advisor as a crutch. It was much easier to tell Clarence I didn't need him in France, it turned out, then it had been to tell my husband.

My soon-to-be former husband.

Of course, that was because I *did* need Weston in France. When I'd told him I didn't, it was a lie.

I felt the loneliness and sorrow of missing him prick at my eyes, and

I tried to distract myself, running my hands along the top of the desk, focusing on how different the feel of this oak was to my palm from the one in my mother's apartment, the one that would soon be shipped to me.

"Teach me how you did it, Daddy," I said quietly to the desk, to the office, to his ghost. "Teach me how you learned to cut your ties."

I was answered with silence.

I hadn't remembered wishing I could talk to my father like this in a long time. And I'd wished so many times.

With Darrell still gone, I searched for something to occupy my mind. I opened one of the desk drawers, looking to see if it still contained my father's items inside.

The first drawer had miscellaneous desk supplies and didn't give me any true hint as to whether they were of a personal nature or not. The second seemed to hold frequently used files. Many were missing and I assumed Darrell had pulled them out as he needed them. The top drawer on the left-hand side was a different story. As soon as I opened it, a single piece of paper fell to the floor. Which was sure to happen, because the drawer was crammed full of folded papers, not at all organized like the other drawers had been.

When I bent to pick up the dropped note, my heart skipped.

I recognized the paper stationery.

With shaky fingers, I picked it up and unfolded the item, scanning through the carefully written words to be sure, but only took one glance to recognize it as mine. I pulled more from the drawer, unfolding each of them, checking them one by one. All of them were from me. My letters—the ones I'd mailed him throughout my life, stuffed here in his left-hand drawer, the one at the very top, overflowing, some of the papers so worn they'd obviously been read many times.

Maybe letting go of attachments wasn't a lesson my father could teach me after all.

If there wasn't a sudden ball at the back of my throat, I might've muttered a thank you to the air. An *I love you*. An *I forgive you*. But, if he was out there somewhere, I had a feeling he already knew what I was trying to say better than I did.

"That was the only drawer I didn't go through," a deep voice said, pulling my attention.

Darrell had walked in without my noticing.

"We cleaned out most of his other stuff, but I thought you'd want to do that when you got here, personally."

I nodded. Swallowed hard, then thanked him.

Awkward silence fell between us. I sat in my father's chair and Darrell stood there looming in the doorway of his office—my office?—my *father's* office, unmoving. He was a tall man, and I'd always felt small in his presence.

But today, even in my sitting position, he didn't feel so overwhelming.

Perhaps it was the power of Daddy's throne.

We both seemed to realize that one of us needed to talk at the same time. "I'll just sit—" he began gesturing to the seat nearby while I simultaneously said "I could move over to your desk—" since there weren't other chairs around my father's.

We both smiled.

"Shall we sit on the sofas?" I asked.

"After you." He held his hand out toward the seating area, but we fell in step together walking toward the arrangement of couches and chairs as though we were equals.

It was only twenty feet to our destination, but while we crossed I had a sudden flashback to the first meeting I'd had with the men at Reach, when I'd gone in with false bravado, determined to run the show, intent on proving that I had "balls."

I planned on leading today as well. Strangely, these six months later, I felt more aware of all the things I didn't know—about business, about life—but the confidence I wore was genuine. After everything that had happened, it was validation to recognize I'd grown. If it was the only thing I walked away with, it wasn't nothing.

"Your marriage—" Darrell began as soon as we were seated, quick to get to the heart of things.

I interrupted him. "—Is being annulled, but should not stand as a barrier to my inheritance, according to my lawyer. If you wish to contest,

I will fight its validity considering the circumstances surrounding the ending of my marriage. You should also know that I'm not above staying married in name only if it's how I hold on to the reins of my company."

He opened his mouth to speak, but I lifted my hand to silence him. "I'm happy to discuss that matter further and at length, though, before I do, I have a question for you. You may find that the subject of my marriage or my inheritance isn't as entertaining once we've talked."

His forehead wrinkled in a single spot, a section of muscle that was due for more Botox. Then he settled back into the couch, his mouth in a straight line. "Go on, then."

I hadn't needed his permission, but it was a relief not to battle. Hopefully we could stay on friendly terms. "I've been watching you since you've taken over the company," I began. "Many of your decisions have seemed in line with my father's vision at first glance, but on further inspection, it appears you may have different intentions for Dyson Media. What is your overall agenda as CEO?"

"Well." His lip quirked up in a snide smile. "You may not enjoy hearing this, Elizabeth, but your father, good businessman that he was, was not exactly a saint in terms of his human relations, and he was not quite on the cutting edge of the new era of technology. Knowing that this company would only be in my hands for a short time, but that I would still hold shares after Dyson's inexperienced, overzealous daughter took over, I've been trying to make changes that will have long-term impact for good. I've changed the hiring policies to bring on more diverse employees, cut off dead weight, and invested in contracted relationships with partner companies that will bring beneficial change to how media is viewed in Europe and possibly worldwide."

He was smug and boastful in his delivery, as though he thought this might be his last chance to passionately speak his mind about the business he cared for deeply.

I could see it from his side, actually. Darrell had twenty years on me. He'd spent his life on his career, and a twenty-five-year-old rich bitch had shown up to pull the rug out from under everything he'd worked so hard to earn.

I imagined I'd be sour about it as well. Though, I doubted I'd be so nasty.

Temperament aside, his answer had been the one I'd been hoping for. "I appreciate your candor, Darrell. And I'm in full agreement about your assessment of my father's outdated business vision. Which is why I'd like to ask you to continue on as the CEO of the company. I do hope you'll say yes."

He blinked several times, his eyes wide. "I thought . . . It seemed that . . . You aren't planning on taking the job for yourself?"

It was awfully delightful to see Darrell Huber at a loss for words.

"I'll retain my executive position, and I do expect to be very involved."

"Sure, sure."

"I won't be here full-time, though. I plan to be traveling back and forth between here and New York every month."

The crease in his forehead returned. "What's in New York?"

"My husband." I grinned so hard my cheeks hurt. I hadn't let myself get my hopes up so this was the first time I was admitting my plan to anyone. It hadn't made sense for Weston to be gone so long from his son, and it wouldn't have worked if Darrell had turned out to have ill intentions for the company. I would have put Dyson first because I was responsible for all the employees and the legacy and the entire billion-dollar corporation.

But Darrell shared my vision, and I was desperately relieved, because in the wretched endless few days without Weston I'd realized I couldn't live without my kingdom *or* my king. With my cousin at the helm, my kingdom could wait. I couldn't wait for my king.

"I'm confused . . . You said you were getting an annulment."

I waved Darrell's comment away with my hand. "A minor technicality. I know I'm not making any sense. Just . . ." God, how did I explain this?

"No worries. I understand. You love him." This time my cousin's expression was warm and empathetic.

"Yeah. I do." My eyes burned with threatening tears. I blinked them back. "I understand that an annulment puts my inheritance in a grey area.

I'm hoping that with our arrangement, working side by side, you'll find the idea of years in court just as tiring and wasteful as I do?"

"I can certainly think of better ways to spend my time," he said with a chuckle, and I finally was able to take a full breath, sure that things between he and I were going to work out fine.

"Thank you, Darrell. I value your years of experience, and I want to learn and apprentice at your side so that when you're ready to retire, perhaps, then, I can take over."

"Right. Okay. That won't be for another ten to fifteen years, though."

"Perfect! I want to make sure I have time to enjoy my family. Weston's son has become quite dear to me." Just the thought made me eager to get back on a plane and cross the ocean to see Sebastian and Weston again as soon as possible, despite being as jet-lagged as I was.

I owed them both a thousand apologies.

Darrell and I spoke a few minutes longer, most of the conversation focused on the explicit agreement that he wouldn't contest my inheritance and that I'd leave him at the head of Dyson Media where he'd teach me the ropes. We decided the details of our arrangement would be settled after the holidays, and I said a hurried goodbye, anxiously excited, already planning what I'd say to Weston when I arrived back in New York. Man, I was looking forward to that surprise.

Except, when I walked out of the office, I was the one who was surprised.

Weston was waiting there. And he wasn't alone. Sebastian was in his arms and Callie and Dana were standing behind him.

"What . . . ? What's going on?" I asked, my heart pounding at the sight of him. "Why are you here? How did you find me?"

"Your mother said you had a meeting with your cousin today. This nice lady," he nodded at Darrell's secretary, "said we could wait out here. As for why . . . well . . ." He looked at the women behind him. "We're moving here. All of us."

"What." I was too flabbergasted for it to even be a question. "You are?" I couldn't breathe, fearing it was all a dream.

Callie and Dana nodded, both wearing ridiculous grins.

"Dana's going to work for me," Weston explained. "She's in PR."

"Public Relations! Oh my God!" I'd thought she was a bureaucrat with the State.

"I know, right?" Weston's dimple appeared. "And they really want to move here. It was their idea actually. We haven't packed or arranged the actual moving part, but we all wanted to be together when we told you. So we sort of borrowed a plane and here we are."

"Here you are." I was breathing now, but tears were rolling down my cheeks. *Here he was.* Five feet away, which was still too far, but so much closer than he'd been. "I can't believe you're here." I took a step toward him, needing his arms around me.

"Hold on," he said, suddenly.

I stopped mid-step as he whispered something in Sebastian's ear. Then he knelt to set his child down on the ground, put something in his hand, and gently pushed Sebastian in my direction.

"Give Izzie!" Sebastian toddled excitedly over to me, waving his hand.

I bent to take what was in his tightly clenched fist. He didn't want to let it go at first, and it took a bit of encouragement, but when I pried his fingers open, there was my engagement ring.

I looked back at Weston and found him on one knee. "Elizabeth Dyson King, you're already my wife, whatever the law says. But I'll do it again to make it legal. I'll do it a thousand times over if that's what it takes to make you mine for real. Lizzie, my love. My home. Will you marry . . ." He looked around at everyone he'd brought with him. "Us?"

I wrapped an arm around Sebastian and lifted him as I stood up, then we crossed over to my husband and the two of us fell into his embrace.

"Yes, Weston, my king," I said between salty kisses. "I will marry all of you."

Weston took the ring from my hand and slipped it on my finger. "I love you," he said softly. "I can't live without you. You're a silly fool for thinking I could even try."

"I know. I was wrong. Thank you for showing me I need you too." We kissed, longer and slower, forgetting for a moment we had an audience until I heard one of the women sniffling behind us.

I pulled away, my cheeks heating, and beamed at Dana and Callie, who was sniffling and red-eyed. "Thank you," I told them. "I'm so grateful. You can't even know."

"What's family for?" Dana asked with a shrug.

I looked back at Weston, a face I could never get tired of looking at. "You better be paying her well."

One eye narrowed. "We haven't really discussed that. This was kind of impromptu."

"Uh . . ." I bit my lip, trying not to laugh.

"Oh, he'll pay me well," Dana winked.

"He will. I know he will." He was the most generous man I'd ever met, after all.

And it didn't matter that I'd already worked out another plan to get us back together. This one was better. There'd be no flying back and forth, no frequent separations. We'd all be together. Reach would take over Dyson's advertising subsidiary and Weston would manage it. I'd still work less, train with Darrell. Maybe not renew my birth control.

The sound of a phone ringing reminded me we were still in an office. "We should get out of here. Have you checked in to a hotel anywhere? There's more than enough room at my place for all of us."

"We came straight here," Callie said. "Our luggage is downstairs at security."

I laughed. "Let's take care of that."

We stood up together, Weston moving Sebastian to his hip. He looked good as a dad. Grown-up. Sexy.

With his free hand, he took mine and tugged me close so he could whisper in my ear. "Those are dirty thoughts in your eyes, Lizzie. Are you going to share them or keep them all to yourself?"

"I was just wondering how you'd look with a little girl in your arms," I said coyly.

"Not as good as you'd look." He seemed to remember himself. Remembered my former plan to wait. "We'll find out in ten years," he said, a slight hint of disappointment in his tone. "When you're ready to take a break from being the leader of Europe's media empire."

"About that . . ." Maybe that surprise could wait until we were alone.

"Elligator!" Sebastian said as we squeezed into the small Europe-an-style elevator. Weston helped his tiny finger push the button for the ground floor, and my chest blossomed with warmth that exploded and reached throughout my limbs. We were together. All of us. My new family. I'd been a girl who could never want for anything and this ending was beyond any I could have ever imagined for myself.

"Where should we go?" I asked the group. "The apartment or the house in Neuilly?"

Weston peered over at Callie and Dana, who shrugged. "Which do you like better?" he asked me.

"It doesn't matter." I looked around at all of them and settled on Weston. "You're here," I said. "Wherever we go, we'll be home."

EPILOGUE

Weston

ELIZABETH PEERED OVER the top of the stroller at Sebastian's pajama-clad body. "Is he asleep?" she whispered tentatively. I hadn't taken my eyes off him the entire last seventeen trips down the long hallway. His breathing was steady, his cheeks flushed rosy red. His grip on his baby doll had loosened and the toy had slipped from against his face and was now wedged between his torso and the carriage.

"Yeah," I answered just as silently. "I'm pretty sure he's been out for at least ten minutes. Let's hurry and get him to his room before we jinx it."

It was a Saturday evening in early April. The dark, cold months were over, and all of us had settled into France the way spring was settling into the countryside. Dana had given only three weeks' notice at her government job in New York and, as part of her compensation package from Reach, she, Callie, and Sebastian had moved into Elizabeth's Paris apartment before February was over. *Our* Paris apartment—I was still getting used to the whole *what's hers is mine* bit.

Elizabeth had been right in assuming that establishing the merger and the official new Reach firm in France would be more work than I'd estimated. I spent more hours at the office than I would have liked, more hours than would have been possible were I traveling back and forth to the States. Donovan was a good boy and left me alone, mostly. Dana turned out to be a great right-hand man, though, and Dylan Locke came over from the London office almost bi-weekly to help out. It wasn't a routine I meant to keep up, but it was doable for the short-term.

Elizabeth and I had chosen to live in the Neuilly house. It was definitely too big for either of our liking, but we'd already begun renovations to turn part of the mansion into offices. While neither of us intended to work full-time forever, we did intend to have careers. We also wanted to focus on Sebastian.

And Elizabeth was past due for her next birth control shot. On purpose. Which meant we were officially "trying."

Tonight, though, was for a different kind of trying—it was the first time we had Sebastian for an entire weekend without Callie and Dana. Like any new parents, we were nervous.

And excited.

Nervously excited.

The day had gone well, for the most part. Sebastian had refused to eat the first two meals we'd put in front of him so he ended up having a lunch of animal crackers and chocolate milk, and dinner was corndog bites, but we considered anything in his tummy a win. We'd both played with him all day and packed his nursery with enough toys to entertain him for hours.

Bedtime had been the first real challenge, when he'd refused to fall asleep. After two hours of trying everything we could think of, I'd dragged the stroller in from the garage. We'd buckled him in and used the spacious estate to walk the kid to sleep.

Finally, it had worked.

Elizabeth wheeled the stroller into his room and put the brake into place with her foot. Then she walked around to stand next to me so we could admire our achievement.

"Damn," she said, snuggling into my arms. "That was a pretty great trick, King. Where did you learn this wizardry?"

"The moms."

We stood quietly for another long moment, gazing down on him.

"Now what do we do? Do we try to move him to his bed?"

Last time I'd done this with Callie and Dana, it had been for a nap.

And we'd decided to start packing for Paris right after. "Uh . . . I'm not sure." If we moved him, he'd definitely wake up. "I think we can leave him?"

"Okay." She didn't seem so sure, but she tucked his blanket around him and said it again. "Okay."

I turned on his nightlight and made sure the monitor was on while she pulled the string for the lamp to turn it off. Then I grabbed her hand and tugged her out of the room and shut the door silently behind us.

"Phew," she sighed. "That was . . ."

"A turn-on," I finished for her. Seriously, she was hot doing the whole mom thing. I couldn't wait to put a baby in her tummy. I especially couldn't wait for all the "trying."

"I was going to say stressful and exhausting," she said, but she was staring at my lips.

So I kissed her.

Her mouth opened easily, her tongue darting out to greet mine as I wrapped my arms around her body.

"Not *too* stressful or exhausting, I hope?" I tested, my lips hovering above hers.

"Definitely not. But we need to go to bed now."

"I'm not going to argue, Mrs. King."

Lacing my hand through hers, I led her to our bedroom, my finger stroking against the ring that said she was mine forever. We hadn't needed to repeat our ceremony, it had turned out. Because of the holidays, the annulment paperwork still had yet to be processed. A simple phone call to her lawyer had been enough to end that near-disaster.

Or, not disaster. I would have married her again. And again. As many times as she'd let me. In fact, we were talking about having a repeat ceremony for our anniversary, just so we could do all the things we'd missed the first time. So we could declare in front of everyone how much we loved each other for real.

Right now, though, the only one I wanted to declare my Elizabeth love to was Elizabeth.

And we needed to be naked for what I had in mind.

In our bedroom, I made sure the baby monitor was turned on, then immediately got to the business of undressing. I was down to my underwear when I realized she was still fully clothed, her attention on a white Priority Mail bubble envelope and its contents.

I came up behind her and moved her red hair to one side so I could kiss the delicate white skin of her collarbone. "Elizabeth, whatever you are doing, that was not what I thought you meant when you said let's go to bed."

"I know, I know," she said, half moaning as I traced my tongue up her neck. "Just . . . Donovan sent this, and I'd forgotten about it until now."

"Donovan?" God, what a boner killer. "What is it?"

"I don't know. A disc. And a note that says 'To set the record straight.'"

I reached around her and took the note from her hands. There was nothing else written on it. "He sent this to both of us?"

She looked at the envelope. "It was addressed to only you, I guess."

I shook my head, chuckling. Good thing I had no secrets from the woman. She had zero boundaries. "We can watch it tomorrow."

"Come on. Aren't you curious?" she pleaded, her lips turning down into an irresistible pout.

"Not really." I mean, yeah, but Donovan was a mood killer. Whatever he'd sent was certainly not going to lead to getting laid.

Apparently my opinion didn't matter because she was already dragging out her laptop and settling in on the bed.

Fine. But if we were watching it, she was going to have her clothes off while we did.

I climbed up on the mattress beside her and wrestled her shirt over her head while she popped in the disc and opened the only file on the directory. My hand was tucked into her bra cup, massaging her nipple into a tight bud when the screen began playing a silent black and white movie.

No, not a movie.

Security footage. Of my old office.

Starring Donovan and Sabrina.

"What the heck?" Elizabeth asked, straightening her legs to balance the computer on her lap.

Fuck if I knew.

My fingers slowed their assault as I watched the two onscreen, trying to figure out what was going on and, more importantly, what it was Donovan wanted me to see. My gut said it wasn't good.

It became obvious as soon as Sabrina removed her panties and handed them to D who promptly sniffed them before putting them in his suit pocket.

"Oh, no," I said, reaching for the laptop.

Elizabeth bent away from me, taking the computer with her. "No, I want to see! Oh my God, he's going to fuck her in your office!"

"Oh, hell no!" I grabbed again for the computer, outraged both that Donovan would send me this and that he would make it in the first place.

Again, my wife maneuvered the computer away, "Weston, wait, let's watch!"

"You want to watch my best friend—" I reconsidered. "*Ex* best friend, considering the circumstances, fuck my *ex-lover* on *my* desk?"

"Yeah. I do. It's hot." She was turned with her back to me now, her feet hanging off the bed, but I could hear the excitement in her tone. Could hear the rapid rise and fall of her breathing, now that I paid attention.

I crawled up beside her so I could watch her, not the computer, and saw her eyes were dark and dilated as they remained pinned on the screen.

"Mmm," she hummed, biting her lip. "He just spanked her. That's . . . whoa . . ."

I peeked at the footage. Sabrina was bent over the desk now, her skirt gathered around her waist. From the camera angle, only the side of her bare ass was visible, but the one cheek was clearly red as Donovan rubbed it. Then he spanked her again.

"You like the spanking? Or the watching? Or . . ." *I* liked watching Elizabeth this turned on. I was quickly getting hard from her reactions.

"All of it. I like all of it." She was breathy and flushed and God, I was going to fuck her so hard.

I pulled her bra strap down her shoulder. "Is this what it's like watching porn with someone?"

"Yes! Isn't it awesome?" She glanced at me, her lips quirked in a naughty smile. "Donovan's so thoughtful. Making us homemade porn."

I laughed. "I don't think that's why he sent it."

I pulled the cup of her bra down and palmed her tit. She leaned into my hand, moaning. She was so fucking turned on. I had to have more of her. Had to have my mouth on her.

I bent forward intending to bring her nipple into my mouth, and she gasped.

Which was cool, except the gasp came before I'd done anything.

"Wow, Donovan is hung," she exclaimed. "Not King hung, but no wonder he's so confident."

I turned my attention back to the screen late enough to miss his dick (thank God) but in time to watch him thrust into Sabrina who seemed to cry out in pleasure.

It *was* kind of hot, actually. If I didn't look at Donovan. And if I stopped thinking about how weird it was.

"It's really not fair that they got to have sex in your office, and we didn't, though. Oh, shit. Donovan sent this to you so that you'd know that Sabrina was *his*, didn't he?"

That *was* what he was doing. How fucking annoying. "All he had to do was say he was interested. Was I supposed to read his mind?" Oh. That was why he'd stolen my Walking Dead issue. He'd hoped I'd watch this.

Clever. Sort of.

Elizabeth shook her head. "He's such an asshole. But that's kind of hot too. Claiming her like that. Lucky Sabrina."

"Okay, okay, that's enough." I grabbed the laptop and shut the lid before setting it on the nightstand. Then I wrestled Elizabeth's body around so she was underneath me, her hands pinned above her head.

"So I guess Donovan and Sabrina had their happy ending," she said, giggling.

"We're about to have ours too, if you'll cooperate."

"Do we? Have a happy ending?" She was serious all of a sudden, and I could tell she wasn't talking about the same kind of happy ending my cock was aching to pursue.

"Do you really want an ending?" I asked. "That sounds so boring. And over. How about a happy beginning instead?" I rocked my pelvis against hers, though, so she wouldn't forget about the hard steel between us in all this flowery romantic talk.

"I like that. A happy beginning." Then, she was grinning again. "Let's play a game!"

I groaned. I didn't want to play around anymore. I just wanted to be inside her.

"This is a good game," she promised. "You'll like it. You be Donovan, and I'll be Sabrina, and you can spank me for being such a dick-tease." Somehow she managed to roll out from under me before I could agree.

But I was totally going to agree.

Dirty, sexy roleplay with my gorgeous wife? That was the kind of game I'd always say yes to playing.

ACKNOWLEDGEMENTS
&
AUTHOR'S NOTE

SOMETIMES A BOOK journey surprises you.

Dirty Sexy Player and Dirty Sexy Games were supposed to be my easy books. The previous duet, Dirty Filthy Rich Men and Dirty Filthy Rich Love, were edgier and darker and the journey to get those out was not that smooth. So I was looking forward to writing Weston and Elizabeth, thinking their story was more straight forward and therefore easier to write.

Then I got to the actual writing and realized something - I'd set up both characters to have father issues. And I have father issues. And thus this "simple" story turned into an exploration through memories of my own past. I had to face things with my parents that I hadn't yet faced. It was tough and therapeutic and I shed a lot of tears. So much of myself is written in Elizabeth and her relationship with her father. So many of her memories are variations on my own wounds. Her grandmother and that house in Utah is directly captured from my own Mormon family that I love very much. In the end, it was a very important story for me to write, and I hope you found as much value in the telling as I did in the writing.

Much thanks is required for books like these, but I'll make it quick.

Rose Hilliard who had enough faith in my concept to offer to publish these in audio first.

Rebecca Friedman who makes every publishing deal a reality.

Candi Kane and Melissa Gaston who run the entire show.

Kayti McGee who knows what I'm trying to say better than I do.

Nancy and Erica and Michele for making sure the words were the right words.

Christine Borgford for making sure the words looked pretty.

My LARCs who give me more support than I deserve.

The Sky Launchers who make my day more than they know.

My readers everywhere who continue to let me write my silly stories and give me a job that I look forward to every day.

My besties in the biz who guide me through every decision I have to make - Melanie Harlow, Kayti McGee, Sierra Simone, CD Reiss, and Lauren Blakely.

My mother, husband, and daughters who show up in more of my books than I should admit.

My God who sticks by me, even when I invite the trauma in.

ALSO BY
LAURELIN PAIGE

Visit my website for a more detailed reading order.

THE DIRTY UNIVERSE
Dirty Filthy Rich Boys
Dirty Duet: *Dirty Filthy Rich Men* | *Dirty Filthy Rich Love*
Dirty Games Duet: *Dirty Sexy Player* | *Dirty Sexy Games*
Dirty Sweet Duet: *Sweet Liar* | *Sweet Fate* (early 2019)
Dirty Filthy Fix (a spinoff novella)

THE FIXED UNIVERSE
Fixed Series:
Fixed on You | *Found in You* | *Forever with You* | *Hudson* | *Fixed Forever*
Found Duet: *Free Me* | *Find Me*
Chandler (a spinoff novel)
Falling Under You (a spinoff novella)
Dirty Filthy Fix (a spinoff novella)
Slay Trilogy: *Slay One* | *Slay Two* (fall 2019) | *Slay Three* (winter 2019)

FIRST AND LAST
First Touch | *Last Kiss*

SPARK - short, steamy sparks of romance
One More Time
Ryder Brothers: Close
Want by Kayti McGee | *More* by JD Hawkins

HOLLYWOOD HEAT
Sex Symbol | *Star Struck*

Written with SIERRA SIMONE
Porn Star | *Hot Cop*

Written with Kayti McGee under the name LAURELIN MCGEE
Miss Match | *Love Struck* | *MisTaken* | *Holiday for Hire*

ABOUT LAURELIN PAIGE

WITH OVER 1 million books sold, Laurelin Paige is the *NY Times*, *Wall Street Journal*, and *USA Today* Bestselling Author of the Fixed Trilogy. She's a sucker for a good romance and gets giddy anytime there's kissing, much to the embarrassment of her three daughters. Her husband doesn't seem to complain, however. When she isn't reading or writing sexy stories, she's probably singing, watching *Game of Thrones* and *the Walking Dead*, or dreaming of Michael Fassbender. She's also a proud member of Mensa International though she doesn't do anything with the organization except use it as material for her bio.

www.laurelinpaige.com
laurelinpaigeauthor@gmail.com

Let's keep in touch!
Join my reader group, *The Sky Launch*.
Follow me on *Bookbub*.
Like my *author page*.

Sign up for *my newsletter* where you'll receive a free book every month from bestselling authors, only available to my subscribers, as well as up-to-date information on my latest releases and a free story from me sent a chapter a time starting May 2018!